Assignment 1989
Daughter of Time Travel

WAL OZELLO

Second Edition

Copyright © 2015 Wal Ozello

ISBN: 0-615-85865-1
ISBN-13: 978-0615858654

This book is a work of fiction. Names, characters, places, and incidents are products of the author's imagination or are used fictitiously. Any resemblance to actual events, locales, or persons, living or dead, is entirely coincidental.

August 2013

DEDICATION

This book is dedicated to my goddaughter, my nieces, my cousins and all young women everywhere. You have the strength within you to overcome anything and be what you want to be.

"The only reason for time is so that everything doesn't happen at once."
-Albert Einstein

PROLOGUE

Standing on the corner of Central Park West and 72nd Street, James Eviston did not look like a 1980's New York Policeman. Every New York Cop from that era was a burly Italian or Irishman who walked around with the attitude that they were a member of the best law enforcement in the country. They believed they were a model of strength, intelligence, and athletic prowess, even though the average officer was at least 30 pounds overweight. And while James was full-blooded Irish, he was in his late 50's. Way too old for your average street cop. His age, along with his thick white hair and unkempt uniform, made him look like an old Professor in a Halloween costume, which is exactly what he was.

And he was nervous, very nervous, as would be anyone else in his shoes because going back in time to stop John Lennon from being murdered was not easy work. Even though he and his graduate students planned out every detail of this moment for months, there were still things James couldn't predict that he'd have to instantly react to. They had read every article they could about John Lennon, Mark David Chapman, and the Dakota. They had poured through every word in the *Rolling Stone* magazine that gave a detailed account of the murder. They watched every John Lennon documentary they could get their hands on over and over again. The team had created a robust accurate timeline of the murder, detailed to the second. They knew all the players, the doorman, the cops that came to the scene of the crime, the limo driver, and the photographer who took the picture of Chapman and Lennon. They even had a diorama of the Dakota and 72nd street, made to scale, thanks to the Architecture Department.

Then he and his graduate students came up with the plan to keep John Lennon from getting murdered that Monday evening, December 8th, 1980. It was all part of their experiment to disprove the Butterfly Effect. James theorized that time moved forward, and we were all pulled towards a thing he called "temporal gravity". It's kind of like magnetic

North. He once lectured that "it doesn't matter how you influence a mass, in the grand scheme of things, that mass will move in a specific direction – towards temporal gravitation." The academic community laughed this off as "Predestination" and pointed towards earlier research that eminent scholar David Peterson conducted proving if a butterfly beat his wings differently everything in history would change. Peterson theorized that one small change in the past can have a domino effect on everything after it. For example, if your dad got a flat tire on the way to his first date with your mom, then they would never meet. If they never met, then you'd never be born. And if you were never born, consider all the interactions you'd never have. This example could go on forever.

James and his students knew this was outrageous. To think one small incident could change time forever was just egotistical. Man's scientific fallacy is the assumption that everything revolves around himself. Instead, what if time works in a directional nature? So your dad gets a flat tire on the way to meet your mom and misses the first date. What if there was another way they meet? A follow up date? If temporal gravity wanted them to be together, it would somehow pull them together.

So James and his students set out to prove the Butterfly Effect wrong. Just like Galileo proved the sun didn't revolve around the earth, they would prove that there was a great magnetic-like power that influenced human destiny. And now that Professor Eviston and the team had invented a way to travel through time, they would disprove Peterson's work.

So they combed through history to find the best moment to change. They considered Lincoln's assassination, Kennedy's assassination, Pearl Harbor, 9/11, Watergate, and a dozen others. But one of James' graduate students was a huge music fan – Steve Manring insisted that saving John Lennon's life would not only change the music scene for decades, but change the world forever. Lennon's death had ended musician's commentary and influence over politics and humanity.

That's why James Eviston is standing on 72nd street, across from the Dakota at 10:30 pm decades before he was even born. He was pacing back and forth, trying to avoid the policeman patrolling the opposite side of the street next to Central Park. They would know he was not a New York Cop. They would arrest him and take him away. Not only would that keep James from preventing Lennon's murder, but they'd certainly find The *Rolling Stone* magazine from 2055 that included a feature article commemorating the 75th anniversary of Lennon's murder. They'd also find his sonic stun gun which wasn't invented until 2022.

James could see Mark David Chapman from across the street, moving away from the crowd of fans and into the shadows of the archway at the entrance of the Dakota courtyard. This was James' cue to step into action. He crossed the street, halting traffic as he walked. Lennon's limo turned onto 72nd street and made its way to the entrance.

James' plan was a two pronged approach. First, get the limo off the street and into the courtyard. This would get Lennon and Yoko away from the fans and Chapman. The second move was to take out Chapman with the sonic stun gun. He'd never know what hit him.

As the limo pulled up, James waved him through to the inside courtyard. The limo driver stopped the vehicle and rolled down the window.

"Get off the street!" James yelled in a fake New York accent. "Keep on moving."

"Do you know who this is?" the driver yelled back. "This is John Lennon."

This argument was not part of the plan. James was to flag the driver into the Dakota and the assumption was he'd listen. Instead, the limo driver's response gave John Lennon and Yoko Ono just enough time to slip out of the limo and start greeting the fans. Yoko went first and headed into the courtyard. Lennon was a few steps behind her. Chapman was stepping out of the shadows and getting into a military stance.

James had to improvise before it was too late. He leaped

over the hood of the limo, quickly pushed fans aside and ended up knocking John Lennon down to the ground. James now stood between Lennon and Chapman, who had one knee to the ground and was pointing his gun right at James, trying to take aim on Lennon. Sweat poured down James' forehead. He and his graduate students had never even consider that James would turn into a target himself. James was here to do research, not to be caught in a gunfight. Lennon was starting to get up behind him.

"What the devil is going on?" he heard in a thick accent.

"Mr. Lennon," Chapman yelled. But he couldn't get his sights on Lennon. James was still in the way.

James pulled out his sonic stun gun and hoped he was in range. He aimed and fired. A deafening sonic boom filled the air as powerful sound waves emitted from James' gun straight towards Chapman. He was suddenly knocked out of his military stance and thrown backwards against the stone of the Dakota archway. James knew he was successful in saving Lennon, now he had to save himself.

The crowd started screaming and running in all directions. The Limo driver got out of the car and rushed to Lennon's aid. One doorman went to Chapman to hold him down. The other, only steps away, went straight towards James. He saw the doorman out of the corner of his eye, and as he leaped to tackle him, James broke out in a run through the panicked crowd. He was a human pinball bouncing off the bodies running in all directions.

He was out of the doorman's reach and took off towards Central Park, passing by the patrol cops that were now heading towards the Dakota. He crossed through the traffic on Central Park West and he headed deep inside the section of the park that's known as Strawberry Fields in current time. He ducked behind some large trees and looked around. No one had followed him and there wasn't anyone in sight. James pulled out his nightstick and unscrewed the wooden cap on one end, exposing a red button. He held the stick above his head like an umbrella and pushed the button. Instantly, metal spokes made of Osmium sprang forth from the stick forming a sphere around James. The spokes then expanded to create a solid globe of Osmium, one of the strongest metals ever created.

Inside the globe was a set of controls and displays. One display, marked RETURN, currently showed December 28th, 2060. James strapped himself onto a leather bench which had dropped down from the walls of the globe and then pressed the red button next to the display.

White light exploded everywhere as James shot through time and space and temporal gravity returned him to his initial state in time. Almost instantly, he was back in 2060 as if he never left. He unstrapped himself and the globe retracted. He was back in his lab deep underground Wright-Patterson Air Force base.

His graduate students cheered him as he stepped out of the Particle Accelerator that sent him back in time. They were all smiling.

"You did it, Professor," announced one of his students, "Check this out." He handed him a copy of the *Rolling Stone* 75th Lennon Anniversary issue. It had been sealed in a special envelope and kept away from any time travel activity. If time had changed, it would be reflected in this magazine when compared to the original one James time traveled with. James' was printed before he time traveled and it would reflect true history.

James placed the two copies side by side. The front covers were identical. Each commemorative issue reprinted the Anne Liebowitz picture of John and Yoko, and had the headline "75 Years After the Murder" and the subhead, "How Lennon's Death Changed the Music Scene Forever."

As James theorized, Lennon was still murdered that night. James turned to the featured article inside each of the magazines and found the discrepancies. In the original *Rolling Stone* there was a picture of Mark David Chapman sitting on the sidewalk of 72nd reading *A Catcher In The Rye*.

In the new *Rolling Stone* was the same feature article, but in this version James recognized a different person sitting on the sidewalk. It was the limo driver that he yelled at to keep on moving into the courtyard. The article went on to outline how the limo driver was insane, but still pleaded guilty to the murder charges just like Chapman originally did. A side bar article featured all the conspiracy theories that stated it was really the government that planned to murder Lennon. People claimed the CIA had programmed the limo driver to kill him as well as back-ups in case the limo driver couldn't come through.

"This proves our theory of Temporal Gravitation Pull," exclaims James. "Lennon would have been shot and killed that night no matter what would have happened. The Butterfly Effect is invalid."

James' research that night changed the field of time travel forever.

ONE

Ever since I left the movie theatre someone has been following me. There's been a distinct repetitive shuffling, clip-clopping, pause and then wait of Doc Martens several feet behind me for the past five blocks. I can't turn around and look, because he'll spot me. So I casually keep walking and hope that I can catch his reflection in a store front window. A car drives by and its headlights provide a momentary flash of short, thin alternative type. It's definitely the guy I saw as I was leaving the Cineplex.

The movie? *Halloween 5: The Revenge of Michael Myers*, and yes, it's terrible. As the credits rolled, I got up out of my chair and walked down the theatre aisle. Half way down, there was this strange guy with long black hair trying to look inconspicuous. He was wearing the typical 1989 fashion: acid wash jeans, aviator jacket, and a collared shirt with a collar on the outside of the jacket. He was playing the part well, too much if you ask me. He's gotta be someone from the future, but I didn't recognize him.

I'm not worried about what he'll do when he catches up to me. It's how I'll react is what I'm concerned about. My first instinct is to immediately go on the offensive and take him out, but that means I'll need to be close to an alleyway of some sort to dispose of his unconscious body. It will take a while to clean up any mess and it would be a long and convoluted process. Someone could see me. I can't be caught by the police in 1989 because they don't know I exist here.

1989 isn't when I'm at, it's where I'm at.

There's nothing I did wrong nor did I give him any reason to follow me, but none the less, he's on my trail for a reason. I can't afford to mess this up or worse, yet, get myself hurt. I got a lot at stake right now and if the Department of Homeland Security gets pissed at me then I certainly won't get my way this time. As a Time Inspector for the U.S. Government, I should have been smarter than this. People expect me to do everything perfectly.

I've waited too long and decide to call it in. I put my

Walkman on and press the play button.

"Central Command," I whisper into the bottom of the case. "Is anyone there?" My Walkman broadcasts my message through time, all the way back to 2085.

"Hey, Alex. It's Alissa, what's up?" Awesome. Alissa is the Dispatcher this evening. She was my best friend in high school. We ran Cross Country together.

"I think someone's following me," I state calmly.

"You always think someone's following you," she grumbles out.

"Well if you were me, you'd be paranoid, too," I argue.

Alissa lets out a heavy sigh and says, "Oh, all right, what's the person look like?"

"He's got that Asia-Pacific alternative thing going on," I explain, "But isn't quite nailing the part."

"Hold on, I'm checking the International Inspector Database to see if there are any new arrivals," she says. "It's going to take a few moments. The Department of Homeland security just updated this thing. We're tracking more than just the Time Inspectors from the major countries, we're tracking the smaller ones as well. Even Palau has an Inspector now."

"Wow," I say shockingly, "Looks like every one's getting into the Time Traveling Espionage game these days."

"I wouldn't call it time *traveling*. That makes it sound like a vacation," Alissa jests. "No, it's inspecting. It's your job – 'vigilantly looking for aberrations in 1989 to see if anyone is trying to take advantage of the good ol' U.S.A.' How many years you been there?"

"Five," I state.

"God," she groans, "I'd shoot myself."

It has been a long time. Strange thing is, I'm hoping and praying for another tour of duty.

"Yep, I think I got your suspect," Alissa finally chimes back in. "Chances are he's is Taufik Khan, a new Time Inspector from Malaysia. We're currently at war with Malaysia over fungi."

"You mean mushrooms?" I ask.

"You got it," responds Alissa, "Apparently there's a strain native to forests in East Malaysia that cures skin cancer. Malaysia wants to manufacture it and charge a huge premium for it."

"That's ridiculous," I say.

"Listen, I don't make the news, I just report it," says Alissa, "Besides, if I could make a billion dollars off of some mushrooms in my back yard, I'd do the same."

"Fair enough," I agree.

"Hey, kiddo," Alissa adds in, "Watch your back. The database says Taufik is a top notch Inspector. If he can kidnap you and bring you back to 2085 in Malaysia, then you'd be a great bargaining chip for them."

"Understood," I respond.

"I got to go," She says. "The 1945 inspector is calling in on the other line with another emergency. Probably needs a recommendation for a restaurant in London again. I've been trying to explain to him that the food sucks there but he can't get it through his head."

Radio silence.

I have a feeling Taufik's still a half a block behind me but I don't want to glance over my shoulder and give him a sign I know what's up. Instead, I reach into my jean jacket and place my hand on my 1989 standard issue pistol, a Colt Double Eagle, just in case I need it.

Killing Taufik is a bad idea on so many levels. First, we're not really at life or death war so it's not really allowed right now. Also, it will fuel the rage of Malaysia and heighten our countries' little argument to a full scale altercation. And then, like I said, it will cause a huge complication here in 1989 because the cops here will find his body. While they'll register him as a John Doe, there could be some inquisitive minds that dig a little deeper. If that's the case, I may have to face the U.N. Temporal Board, again.

Instead, I stop in the corner drugstore to see if I can throw off the guy a bit. After nodding to the cashier, I step back to the refrigerated coolers and pretend I'm looking at the flavored wine coolers. The doorbell to the store's front entrance chimes and footsteps approach. It's a small store but the aisles are tall so I can't see who came in. I gingerly step to the left side of the store and peek down the aisle. It's empty except for the endless supply of toothpaste, shaving cream, razors, mouthwash, and other essentials. As I quietly walk up towards the front of the store, I can hear a step of footsteps in the aisle next to me going the other way. I make it to the door and open it without being noticed. Stepping through the entrance way signals doorbell and my position is revealed.

I can't get caught.

I sprint out of the store and discover an alley around the corner. Assessing my opportunities, I find a fire escape that would take me several stories above, a garbage can to hide behind, a doorway that probably leads back into the drugstore, and an exit at the far end of the alley to an avenue on the other side of the block. My instincts say run, but my gut says hide. So I tuck myself behind the garbage can, grip my gun, and wait it out. From my vantage point, I'm able to peer around the corner and still hide in the shadow so I can't be seen.

After a few moments, my pursuer reveals himself. It's the guy from the movie theatre but I can't quite see his face to tell if it's Taufik or not. He cautiously steps through the alley way as if he doesn't want to be here and I decide I can help him with that.

"This is the end of journey tonight, Taufik," I say, stepping from the shadows and taking aim at him, "You're going to head home and we're both going to pretend this didn't happen."

"Don't shoot," a woman's voice shouts and she spins around, raising her hands defensively. She's frightened and I don't recognize her. Great... now I've engaged with a local citizen. In my defense, she does look Malaysian and has that androgynous 80s look going on, like an Asian-pacific version of Robert Smith from the Cure.

I lower my gun.

"I'm Jojie Natividad, an inspector from the Philippines,"

she admits. "I followed you because my tour of duty is ending and I need a picture with you."

"Need a picture?" I say, "You sat through a lousy movie and stalked me several blocks for a picture? Why do you need a picture with me?"

"I told all my friends back home that I was working with you here in 1989," she confesses, "They won't believe me unless I show them a picture. Please?"

A fan. I've been worried about a fan.

"Sure," I give in. I hate this stuff but I accommodate.

Excitedly, she pulls out her Walkman and places it sideways on the lid of a garbage can. I turn towards it and she steps in beside me, placing her arm on my shoulder casually.

"Keep the gun out," she instructs. "It will make it look more impressive."

She fixes her hair, strikes a pose, and says, "Take picture."

The Walkman flashes. "Picture complete," it announces.

Jojie steps over to the Walkman, opens up the cassette part, and checks the screen inside.

"Perfect," she exclaims. "My friends didn't believe me at first, but now I got evidence that I spent my tour of duty with the one and only Alex Eviston."

"Happy to obliged," I mumble out unenthusiastically.

"Everyone's going to be jealous that I met the most famous woman in Time Travel. I can't believe how lucky I am," she gushes. "Tell me, how was it growing up as the daughter of the man who invented time travel? I bet he was amazing."

"It was thrilling," I lie.

TWO

As I walk back to my apartment, I can't get Jojie's question out of my head. It's the expectation that life should have been wonderful growing up with my Dad. Reality is that his off-the-chart IQ didn't make him a great father, it only made him a brilliant scientist. How smart is he? For Dad, genius came easy. While everyone else was trying to figure out how to harness more energy from the sun, Dad cracked the code on how to travel back in time.

Back then, Time Travel was all hypothetical based on Albert Einstein's theory of relativity. Scientists thought that if you could move faster than the speed of light, while the world around you moves at its regular speed, then you could in essence move faster than the rest of the world. Relativity speaking, your time wouldn't change, but the world could.

It sounded plausible because Einstein seemed like a really smart guy. But the problem was no one was able to ever travel at the speed of light to prove his theory right or wrong. So everyone accepted his hypothesis as theory.

Everyone but my dad.

My dad thought Einstein was an ignorant and self-centered. Einstein saw man as the center of the universe. He never once looked at the universe as a whole and to understand man's part it in. To physics, man is just another mass. Physics doesn't care if we're clay, dust in the wind, or flesh. While biology cares if we're alive, physics just doesn't give a damn.

My dad made disproving Einstein his life's work, and when my dad does something, he's all in. While studying at M.I.T., Dad theorized that time has a gravitational direction and any mass that exists within time is pulled in that direction. Ever think your life has a destiny? That you've been selected to go somewhere and be something? That God has a plan for you? Turns out you were right, but it's just merely gravity. All you needed to Time Travel was a vast amount of energy, like the Big Bang, to knock you out of your gravitational temporal pull.

At first, people thought Dad was crazy and the university

almost kicked him out in embarrassment. Thing is, he had the mathematical model to prove his temporal gravity theory. Even the best mathematicians (who were all at M.I.T.) couldn't discount him. So they quietly let him finish his undergraduate work knowing they'd be done with him in three years.

My dad graduated M.I.T., without honors, and was rejected from just about every major university that had a respectable math, physics, or engineering department. All but one. Dad was accepted into The Ohio State University. But unfortunately, OSU wasn't that respected in Dad's field. They were better known for their hybrid regenerative grass on their football field than their Engineering or Physics departments.

Needless to say, Dad wasn't that thrilled about being accepted into a second tier research school - until he got there. Turns out the Buckeye State was the best place to perfect his time travel theory. The Ohio State University was partnering with NASA Glenn Research Center to build the world's largest Particle Accelerator deep underneath Wright-Patterson Air Force base in Dayton. The great state of Ohio was first in flight and now wanted to be first in time travel. And they needed my dad to put his theories to the test.

Eventually Dad discovered you didn't need a vast amount of energy like The Big Bang to knock mass from its gravitational temporal pull. The amount from a High Energy Particle Accelerator would be just fine. The extremely intelligent engineers at NASA found a metal that could withstand the force from the energy without breaking apart: Osmium, one of the hardest metals known. On July 11th, 2029, they were able to send the first object backwards in time. It was a miniature DeLorean, the size of a matchbox car, made of pure Osmium.

Over ten years my dad led a team of military, government, and university scientists to perfect time travel. They were able to not only send objects back in time, but bring them back through a reverse process using the same temporal gravitational pull that kept them there in the first place.

Dad went from being a crazy research scientist from M.I.T.

to the most famous and revered scientist that ever lived. All that time he spent in the lab researching, calculating, experimenting, thinking, and publishing had finally paid off.

Since he spent all his time with his work, he had practically no time for me. If I wanted to play soccer in the backyard, I'd have to kick the ball against the garage door and then pretend it was someone from the other team coming after me. When my bike chain got all caught up in the back wheel, I had to untangle and repair it myself. Navigating boys was difficult to say the least. I couldn't even have an awkward conversation with my dad about the birds and the bees so instead I totally gave up on having a boyfriend in high school.

Dad was rarely there for me but there was always the expectation that I succeed as he did. Good grades were unacceptable; they had to be excellent marks. My extra circular activities needed to be things like Academic Challenge Team, Robot Club, or Chess. Once I expressed interest in writing for the school newspaper and I was told no because it was beneath my capabilities.

Even in graduate school, when I was working on something in my dad's field of research, he wasn't there for me. I was finishing my studies at The Ohio State University's Temporal Engineering School and the Division's Captain Training Center. When school was over, I'd immediately join the ranks of leaders in the Temporal Investigative Division where we'd strategize how the enemy would manipulate time for their benefit and what we'd do to counter their moves. As my final thesis, I was trying to prove how a person can travel back in time and create an event that causes future events to happen quicker than expected, or slower than expected. Intrinsically, I knew this was true. But I had no data or scientific research to prove this.

So I did what any researcher would do. I created my own data. I traveled back in time to 1.7 million BC before Homo erectus and introduced fire to man. Well, technically not man, I gave it to women because they are typically more resourceful and would know what to do with it.

This was about 200,000 years before Homo erectus discovered fire. When I traveled back to current time I learned that I messed up everything all the way to Roman Civilization. Jesus Christ showed up as early as 1100 BC. Which completely messed up the calculation of time since BC stands for Before Christ and technically AD starts at his birth.

The United Nations was furious with me. At that time there were strict international laws governing time travel and I had broken exactly sixteen of them. They had to send an International Peace Keeping unit back in time to undo what I did. They wanted to kick me out of grad school and the Temporal Investigative Division, but I pleaded with them that was I did was in the name of science and asked them to forgive me. My dad never came to my defense and was nowhere to found. The one person that had enough pull to save me was probably off using my research to prove some theory of his own.

The United Nations task force took pity on my and instead of suspending me from the Temporal Investigation Division, they assigned me to the worst year possible. It's where they send all their rejects - the year 1989.

They originally had me do a three year tour of duty, but the year grew on me. I became comfortable with the routine and besides the occasional fan like Jojie, people left me alone because the average citizen had no idea who I was. The anonymity was something I never was able to experience and I enjoyed it, so I signed on for an additional two years. It's been five years now and I've requested more. Tomorrow is the day I find out if they've granted my extension.

My duties for the night are over and I head towards my apartment. I'm housed at the luxurious Watergate Apartments. Not for the comfort but for the accessibility to all I need in Washington D.C. In case anyone has forgotten, they placed a historical marker out front that explains the significance of the hotel during the Nixon Administration and what's commonly known as the Watergate Scandal. It's several hundred feet from the main entrance as not to be an eye sore but I can't help but pass it every day during my morning jog. Rounding the corner, I'm a little shocked to find it missing. I stop for a moment and look around to see if I'm standing in the right spot. Confident that I am, I walk over to the exact place that it should be and find no remnants of a pole or anything.

Odd. It was there this morning.

Guessing it's out for repair, I continue on my journey home, step through the main entrance, take the elevator to my floor, and let myself in my apartment.

Crunch.

In between my foot and the floor is a now shattered copy of Cher's *Heart of Stone* cassette tape.

"Damn it," I say out loud.

It always happens this time of year, if there's one thing I can count on cycle-to-cycle is that my Cher cassette breaks the night of November 1st. Of all the music I am required to listen to, Heart of Stone is my favorite. It's the one with the song "If I Could Turn Back Time." I have to giggle to myself every time I hear it because I know it's scientific fact that you can.

I pick up the shattered tape from the floor and toss it on my desk. I'll have to wait until next year to listen to it again.

After changing into my pajamas and brushing my teeth, I take one last look at the Washington Monument. I count the flags around its base to make sure there are still fifty and then close the blinds. I lay in bed hoping that tomorrow I find out that my tour of duty is going to be extended again. I'm 99.5% sure that it will. No one really wants to come to 1989 and they try to avoid sending anyone to this miserable year. The only one that really has the power to pull me back to the future is my dad. Chances are, he's too preoccupied with a new research project to worry about me.

THREE

Every day I wake up at 6am to music on my clock radio. Some days it's good, some days it's really bad. Today it's the latter. It's Bette Midler's "Wind Beneath My Wings". I wish I'd never have to listen to that song again. Ever. But for now I have to memorize it note for note, because if there's something different, I must report it to Central Command.

After listening for a few moments, I discover it's the same old pathetic piano part and annoyingly airy vocals that it always is. I sit up in bed and stretch away the stiffness of a crummy mattress. My apartment is pretty plain. There's no fancy furniture and no special decorations. Inspectors are told not to assimilate your apartment too close to the current year. It can become disorienting and over time you can believe you're part of the year rather than just observing it. Which is fine with me, I don't want to hang up any posters of New Kids On The Block.

I swing my legs over the side of the bed, force myself to stand and saunter into the shower. Everyone has something that wakes them up: music, coffee, breakfast... mine is a warm shower. This morning I need a hot one.

Afterwards, I towel myself off, wipe on some Soft & Dri deodorant, stare at myself in the mirror and grimace at my hair. When I was a younger girl I had wavy deep auburn hair. I got it from my mom. Dad always said I looked like her. It was so long that it looked like a comet trail whenever I went running in the park. As I got older, it curled even more. The sides circled my face to accentuate the freckles on my nose and ocean blue eyes. My hair was one of those defining features that helped distract from my small stature and less than female defining body. My mom made me keep my hair long all through middle school, in part because it looked cute, but mostly so people didn't mistake me for a boy.

But when I got into college, the little girl cuteness needed to go away. If I was going to be taken seriously in the research world, my hair had to look proper. So I painstakingly got it chemically straightened every month. I still kept the length, so I wouldn't be mistaken as a boy, but pulled it back into a ponytail. I planned for this to be my look for the rest of my professional life.

But when inspectors go back in time, they frequently have to change themselves to fit the era that they are in. The "Historical Costume Department" wanted me to look like a more modern 1980s woman. They decided against the woman with big hair standing about a foot above her head, thick red lips, skintight cut-up blue jeans, mesh shirts, and snakeskin boots. They also decided against the alternative girl – half shaven head, earrings galore, acid wash jeans, a long collared jacket, and Doc Martins.

Instead, they showed me pictures of Julia Roberts in *Pretty Woman* and my heart sank. It was basically the same hair cut I had when I was a child. The one I left behind to be an adult.

I argued that the film was from 1990, and that style wasn't yet in vogue. Then they showed me pictures of other women from 1989. Same haircuts. I was told to grow out my hair and come back.

So I stopped straightening my hair and the waves and curls all came back. I went back a month later and the hairstylist didn't have to do a single thing. Her only comment was: grow it longer. Now my hair looks bigger than my body. I'm this petite little thing with a huge frizzy mop on my head.

Now that I'm here in 1989, I've been trying to figure out a way to control it. But every morning, I wake up and look in the mirror and BAM – there's my hair. I throw some mousse in it and it looks tamer. But I'm still not happy with it.

I make one more grimace and decide to start my day. I put on a little make-up, slide on my jeans, throw on a baggy white shirt (with the mandatory shoulder pads), grab my jean jacket and head out the door. Time to start my day. First stop is to meet up with my Canadian counterpart, Frank, at our favorite coffee shop.

Frank's my strongest ally. He's the first person I should turn to in the event of a catastrophe and I can't get a hold of

Command Central. We meet for brunch every morning at M. E. Swing Coffee House on 17th and G Street. They roast one of the best damn cups of coffee I've ever had.

The aroma of freshly roasted coffee fills my senses as I walk into M.E. Swings. Frank's doing his usual thing, standing at the pick-up counter and flirting with a barista. Today, it's a blonde who's twirling her hair around in her fingers and laughing at something funny he's just said.

Girls come easy to Frank. In fact, he's one of those people magnets. Girls, guys, whoever, it doesn't matter. He's likable. The fact that he's six foot two, broad shouldered with a warm welcoming smile helps a lot, too. Out of the corner of his eye, Frank sees me and his attention immediately turns away from the cute barista to me.

"Alex," he smiles at me and pulls two coffee cups from the counter. "Good morning, here's your cup of Joe."

The blonde barista shoots me a dirty look and goes back to cleaning the counter.

Frank is the only person I can permissibly hang out with in 1989. He's my Canadian counterpart and member of the Royal Canadian Temporal Police Force. Frank's family is practically royalty in Canada and comes from a long line of prestigious military that he can trace all the way back to the French Revolution. They were generals, leaders, ministers of defense, secretaries of states, and presidents, all holding some high ranking office. Frank was destined to follow in their footsteps.

"Alex Eviston, you are always late," Frank said with his warm smile.

"Well maybe I need to get a time machine." This was Frank's and my little routine. It was funny at first. Now it's comfortable. When you're out of time and everything is different, you have to create a new sense of comfort. This was our normalcy.

"I got you a Costa Rican – Columbian blend, Spanish roast."

Frank's been ordering my coffee for several years now. I used to get those frou-frou white chocolate mocha cappuccino espresso drinks until he put a stop to it. He now has me hooked on straight black coffee.

"Thanks for the coffee," I say with a smile. "Let's sit down. I have to tell you about my evening."

"Did you have a date?" he slyly asks and motions for me to go to the table first.

"No," I sigh, "I ran into a fan."

"Ugh," he says, pulling my chair out for me to sit in. "Everyone wants to meet the famous Alex Eviston. You're Miss Popular."

Frank is one of those super cool smooth guys. In high school, he was captain of the hockey team and led them to second place in the state championship. In college, he ended up as a starting forward all four years for the University of New Brunswick. Every guy wants to be around him, and every girl wants to be with him.

When he sits down his runs his hands through his wavy, sandy brown hair which shows off his heroic face. Along with this friendly smile, he's got a square jaw and a dimple in the middle of his chin. These were all traits that made me fall madly in love with Frank when I first met him. But I tragically discovered that he was out of my league. I knew I couldn't woo him with my less than girlish looks, so I'd have to impress him with my vast knowledge of historical culture. Unfortunately, we'd never relate on that level. You see, what Frank has in the leadership bucket, he lacks in intelligence. At the Royal Canadian Temporal Academy, he got a "C" in Significant Historical Events and barely passed Introduction to Temporal Physics. It's not that Frank didn't apply himself. It's that his brain just doesn't function that way. Put a hockey stick in his hand and he is in his element, but a text book? Never.

Because of his less than stellar academics, Frank wouldn't get a chance to lead a unit for the RCTP. On the other hand, there's no way they could kick Frank out. His father was the Prime Minister of Canada. Instead, they played on his strengths and sent him back to keep track of Wayne Gretzky, the greatest hockey player that ever lived. He's been banished with me to 1989. And for that, I'm very thankful.

"So it's November 2nd," Frank says anxiously. "Today's the big day, right?" Frank knows I'm supposed to hear from Central Command today on the status of my extension request. He wants me to stay as much as I do.

"They haven't pinged me, yet," I shrug. "You know the U.S. Government. They'll tell me when they are good and ready."

"If only you could travel to the future, I mean past 2085, and find out what they are going to tell you," chuckles Frank.

"You're fully aware that dozens of scientists have already tried that, including my Dad," I respond. "You know what they say about the future."

"Um," Frank stutters, "Let's pretend I fell asleep during that lecture at school."

I sigh, "Famed Temporal Scientist, Tosha Peters theorized that the future doesn't exist, yet. That temporal gravity hasn't pulled any mass together so time and space hasn't been made. So you'd be time traveling to something that isn't there, kind of like traveling to some black hole."

"Yeah, yeah, I remember that," fakes Frank. "Any way, all I know is that I'm stuck here for some time now, maybe forever, and I don't want you traveling to the past or the future. I want you here with me. "

"I'm not leaving here," I add. "I like the routine. And I really don't want to go back to 2085. I haven't been there for five years and I'm really not interested in dealing with all those people in the research division, especially my dad."

"You know, we should take a vacation next cycle!" exclaims Frank. "Go see the Exxon Valdez spill to clean some birds or go protest in Tiananmen Square and lay in front of army tanks."

"Vacation means going to a beach."

"Perfect! We'll schedule time in the Caribbean next cycle during late September and watch Hurricane Hugo come in."

"Frank, the sun is a requirement for visiting the beach on vacation."

"You know, The Kings are coming into town in a few weeks," he grins.

"The Kinks?" I say with a smirk.

"The Los Angeles Kings! Wayne Gretzky!" shouts Frank.

I know exactly what Frank is talking about. He's been trying to get me to go a hockey game for the past three cycles to see the greatest hockey player of all time. I used to think that Frank had a crush on me and it was his way of asking me out. Then I realized he just hates going anywhere alone, which is kind of a shame because he's got these deep chocolate eyes that I find myself getting lost in every now and then. But, unfortunately, Frank and I got trapped in the "friend zone" a long time ago. At least he's a loyal friend.

"Do you want to go this year? The Great One is awesome to see live." I have to admit, Frank is pretty tenacious. One year I may join him, but not this year.

"I can't," I say as Frank saddens. "I unfortunately have to watch *Say Anything...* again."

"Wait a minute, that's a great movie," he counters. "Classic John Cusack."

"It was a great movie the first fifty times I saw it. But as the Chief U.S. Movie Analyst for 1989, I've seen it over 100 times. And seriously, Diane Court is not a great catch. She may be smart but she totally lacks any personality or attractive features beyond her smarts."

"Sounds like someone I know," Frank teases.

I kick him under the table. Hard.

"Hey!" he responds.

"I am not Diane Court," I argue.

"Gee... You are super sensitive," Frank smiles. He knows my looks are a sore point for me.

There's an awkward pause for a moment, just like there always is when he jokes about my looks. I think Frank has spent too much time in locker rooms hanging out with the guys, and not enough with girls. Even after five years with him, we have these awkward moments when he doesn't know what to say. I always have to speak up.

"So it's a crazy week here in the U.S.," I break the tension. "It's election season."

"That's right," agrees Frank. "You elect your first African-American mayor of New York City this week."

"And governor. Glad you know your U.S. History," I say.

"Oh, come on, Alex. You're fully aware I'm terrible at U.S. History. Sports? I can give you the play-by-play of the last 3 minutes of the Super Bowl and explain exactly how the 49ers beat the Bengals. U.S. History? I'm lucky to know the president's name," responds Frank.

"Well then how'd you find out about our historical events?" I have to admit. I am pretty surprised he knows what's going on in the U.S. this week.

"Mojmir," he blurts out.

"Mojmir?" I almost spit out my coffee. "Mojmir Ivanov?"

"Yep," he quietly admits.

Mojmir is our Russian counterpart. His mind is a photographic library of information which he can access in a split second. If he saw it, not only can he tell you every minute detail of the event, but he can tell you when he saw it, where he was, and other ancillary memories like what he was wearing and doing at the time.

He is by far one of the best inspectors that ever lived. Because not only can he see things that others can't, he understands the motivation and manipulation behind it. But Mojmir really doesn't like to follow rules or commands from his superiors. Legend has it he was working in the section of Germany that was annexed from Poland. He was following a lead and instead of reporting it back to his superiors, he decided to get himself captured and sent to Auschwitz. The Soviet Committee for Temporal Security couldn't find him for over three years and considered him dead. But he came out alive.

Apparently, Mojmir altered the past and freed many of the Jews destined for the Gas Chamber. The United Nations was furious with Mojmir for manipulating time. While saving the mass killing of Jews may seem like the right thing to do, it could soften hatred towards Nazis and never allow Jerusalem to be returned to the Jews. The Soviets were embarrassed and they sent Mojmir here to 1989 so he couldn't do any more harm. He's now on a long term assignment and a few years from retirement. Mojmir's checked out and hasn't been the same man since.

That's the one thing we all have in common here in 1989. We've all messed up somewhere along the way and were sent here as some type of punishment, like a dog that chewed up the couch and then put outside in the pouring rain. We're kind of like the land of misfit toys, banished to a year that history finds bland, boring, and pretentious.

I haven't met Mojmir, yet. As a member of the Temporal Investigative Division, I really shouldn't cavort with inspectors from other countries that aren't our official allies. But I'm kind of a celebrity around here since my dad invented Time Travel. Unfortunately, Frank likes showing me off – like I'm a trophy wife or something. I'm sure Frank will try to introduce me to him one day.

"So, you've ran into Mojmir?" I ask.

"We've been talking since last September," Frank admits.

"September this cycle? Or last cycle?" It's so hard to make a time reference. You have to be completely precise in how you communicate "when" or people will totally misunderstand you.

"This cycle. Two months ago. He thought he discovered some aberrations in Madonna's "Express Yourself" video and wanted to check with you for accuracy. So he tracked me down."

"And you're okay with this?"

"Mojmir is harmless. And Canada doesn't have the Soviets on our official "don't talk to" list. We're neutral with them, remember?"

Who's the enemy and who's an ally is a complicated thing. Time Travel uncovered that the world was ruled by several distinct governing units. The rumors of the Illuminate weren't really rumors. Throughout time there are six clear superpowers: U.S., Chinese, Soviets, Germans, Romans, and the Egyptians. Either you are them, or you're friends with them. Except for the Swiss. Their destiny is to be forever neutral.

In Frank's case, he's Canadian and clearly we're allied with him. But Mojmir is Soviet. The jury is still out between the good ol' U.S.A and the Soviets. There are times when they were our ally, like World War II, and times we couldn't trust them, like the Cold War. So we're always on a little bit of alert with the Russians.

Now if he was German, there's no question I couldn't trust him. I mean, how many innocent people did the Nazis kill over the centuries? Plus, the Nazi Party's resurgence since 2025 has really concerned us, as well as the United Nations. Nobody ever trusts a Nazi. There are strict rules with our Temporal Division and I could be sent to Leavenworth for just talking to my German counterpart. But there's a little leeway with the Soviets and Frank is fully aware of that.

"Mojmir and I have become kind of acquaintances. He's been explaining some observances to me in past several months. I didn't want to tell you about it because I knew you'd have issues with it."

"Mojmir's back in the business?" I'm shocked. "I thought he was just riding the wave until he officially retires. Pre-close mode."

"Mojmir is like one of those kids at a restaurant that can't sit still very long," smiles Frank. "He's still sitting back and watching the world go by, but every now and then he calls me with something. This one's the Madonna video that he wants you to see."

"I'm not the music expert," I claim. "That's Mojmir."

"That's the interesting thing. Lyrics, dance moves, clothes, cast, were all spot on. It's the art direction that was slightly off."

"That video was inspired by Fritz Lang's *Metropolis*, right?

David Fincher directed it."

"Exactly. But Mojmir claims the buildings weren't Art Deco. They were something called 'Severe' Deco."

That's why Mojmir's sending it to me. He knows I have expertise in historical architecture. "It's a common term for the style the Nazi's used," I explain. "I took this class in grad school with Professor Janiak. We would travel to all these places in time to check out how things were built. He kept on talking about how the Nazis did Art Deco the right way, incorporating more Roman Neoclassical artwork instead. Hitler saw the Romans as an early Aryan Empire."

"Hitler was crazy," comments Frank.

"So did you see much difference?" I ask. Frank knows nothing about architecture. If he can see an aberration, than it's a huge one.

"I can't tell. It all looks the same to me."

"Okay. Give me the VHS."

Frank gives me that boyish grin of his. I now realize this was his plan all along. He knew that if he would have just handed me the tape and said it was from a Russian I would have turned him down in an instant. But he had piqued my interest and now I have to see it.

"I'll take a look at it," I say. "But I don't have that great of a track record with Central Command. I'm not sure my opinion really counts anymore."

"You're better than you think you are," argues Frank. "One day you'll make a bigger contribution to science than your father."

"Whatever."

"It's not just me that thinks that. Others think it, too."

"Who? Mojmir? Give me a break."

"You know he wants to meet you. He wants to meet the daughter of the Father of Time Travel. See the woman who gave man fire and changed history forever." Frank added a big dramatic wave.

"I'm not a circus act." I get so pissed at Frank when he does this. I'm not some friend to be put on display for the world to see. I'm not a celebrity. I'm just a woman trying to do my job. It may a bit routine, but I'm trying to do my best. He did the same thing with the inspector from Egypt. I think he got a steak dinner out of it.

"Don't worry about it, Alex," he says. "I told him you were off limits. Can't have the Russians and the Americans talking, you know."

"God forbid."

"Alright. It's Noon. I got to go," Frank declares and gets up from his chair. "I have to do my patrol of the Smithsonian Arts and Industries Museum and double check all the exhibits. Let me know what you think of the whole Severe Deco thing. I'll see you tomorrow morning." He pats me on my shoulder as he walks away.

I head out to do my patrols as well. I walk by the Whitehouse, across The Grotto by the Capital Building, stroll down the National Lawn, count the flags at the Washington Monument to make sure we still have 50 states, walk along the reflection pool, get a hot dog, chips and Coke from a street vendor, and then sit on the steps of the Lincoln Memorial to have my lunch. Most of the time I watch the people go by in their Day-Glo shirts, animal print jackets with shoulder pads, and Z. Cavaricci jeans.

Not all that exciting, but it's my job. More importantly, it's my duty. After graduating from Temporal Engineering School you have two choices: enter the field of research, or serve your country in the Department of Homeland Security. Everyone expected I'd join my father and follow in his footsteps. I had made some major discoveries during Grad School and even wrote some ground-breaking papers in my Undergrad. It was only logical for me to be a Research Scientist. As I got closer to graduation, universities across the globe were harassing me day and night to come and teach for them.

But I had other plans. I wanted to be something bigger. I wanted to make more than a discovery; I wanted to make a difference. I had a sense of duty to my country.

But all that changed the day I gave woman fire. My plans got sidetracked and I got sent here. I've learned that as you get older your dreams don't fade away, but instead you get a strong dose of reality. Things aren't the way you wished them to be and you learn how to deal with what you're given. I've been given 1989 and have become comfortable with that.

My average morning routine is pretty cool to me. Every week I'm reminded how great our country is. While our government might be imperfect, it's certainly the best there is.

I finish my lunch and head up inside the memorial. I have a little thing I do every day, not so much because it's my job but because I enjoy it. To me, it's an awesome reminder of why I do what I do. Once I'm inside, I give a little nod to President Lincoln and then walk into the South chamber. There, carved in the wall, is the Gettysburg Address. I read it word for word. There are days that I even whisper it aloud. It never fails, the last sentence always gives me goose bumps.

> "…that we here highly resolve that these dead shall not have died in vain—that this nation, under God, shall have a new birth of freedom— and that government of the people, by the people, for the people, shall not perish from the earth."

I take pride in knowing that part of my job is to ensure my beautiful government shall not perish from the earth.

I head out from the memorial and stroll along the Reflection Pool. It was built all the way back in 1922 and it's about a third of a mile long. Being a time traveler, I'm always amazed about how things last so long. This pool is still as majestic in 2085 as it is in 1989, and as majestic as it was back in 1922. It was built to honor this great country of ours, and it was built to last.

As an inspector, you're taught to constantly observe things because you'll never know when you'll see something that doesn't make sense. I stop for a moment and pretend that I'm admiring the Washington Monument in the pool. But what I'm really doing is checking out the guy that's been following me for the past half hour. He's Niklas Krause, my German counterpart, and he's the most arrogant creep I've ever met. The guy thinks he knows everything. He's trying to disguise himself, but I can see his white blond hair peeking out from under his Michigan Wolverines hat and his cornflower blue eyes darting back and forth. He's so German that if you look up Aryan on the Internet, you get a picture of Niklas. This is the third time I've noticed him in the past several months and I have no idea why he's following me. He hasn't approached me yet, and I'm not going to talk to him either. I'll need to mention it to Central Command the next time I call in. I don't trust Germans, ever. The Secretary of Homeland Security doesn't trust them either. On the list of enemies of the United States, the Germans are in the Top Five.

I start walking away from the reflection pool back towards the Lincoln Memorial. I'm going to make some quick maneuvers along the trees and bushes and try to lose Niklas. I figure it's best that he doesn't know what I'm up to, even if I'm up to nothing. I step behind a tree, then around a shrub, then back around another tree, but I know it's not enough. I peak through some branches to see what he's doing and find that he hasn't moved. He didn't follow.

Instead he keeps checking his watch and looking up and down along the edge of the reflection pool. Niklas isn't stalking me; he's waiting for someone else. I decide to stay and find out exactly who he's scheduled to meet, but I know that my current hiding place will never do. If he didn't notice me beside the reflection pool, he'll eventually catch me popping my head out from behind this tree. I'll look more like a spy hiding in the branches then a tourist. I head up to the Lincoln Memorial steps knowing my best vantage point is up there. I can see the whole National Mall and be far enough away from Niklas that he won't spot me.

About halfway up the stairs is a landing on both sides. I take a left and walk along the landing. Niklas is now heading towards the far end of the reflection pool, closest to the

Washington Monument. I look around to find if there is anyone following in the same direction he is and discover no one. At the end of the pool he sits down on an empty iron wrought park bench, pulls out a bag and starts tossing seeds on the ground for the birds.

"He's out feeding pigeons," I murmur to myself. "There's nothing fishy going on here." I get ready to walk away when someone sits down next to him. He's wearing a fleece gray hoodie and an orange poofy nylon vest over it – classic fashion trend from the 80s. This guy is trying too hard to fit in. He definitely isn't from 1989; he has to be an inspector. Unfortunately, I can't get any closer to see who he is without revealing myself. The two seem to be talking, but are facing forward so that no one can really tell they know each other.

My concentration is suddenly broken by a parent screaming at their kid right next to me.

"MARY!" the mom yells. "GET HERE THIS INSTANT!"

"But mom," she meekly begs, "Can I have 25 cents to look through the big binoculars? I want to see the Capital Building." Mary is standing on one of those large metal binoculars that tourists use to see things far away.

"You can see the Capital Building later. We have to go now. Your brother wants to see the Space Museum."

"But mom,' the nine-year old says, "They make laws in the Capital Building. It's an important place."

"We don't have any money for the binoculars, and besides it's time to go." The mother comes over, grabs the girl's hand and drags her away.

For Pete's Sake, lady, your daughter was interested in the government and how it works. You should feed that stuff. Isn't that the reason you're on vacation here? It's only a quarter to see the Capital Building.

That's when it hits me. If I can see the Capital Building through those things, I can definitely see who's with Niklas. I reach into my pockets, find a quarter, and insert it into the machine. The lenses on the machine open up and I begin to focus in on Niklas. Up close I instantly recognize his companion as Lionel Zarr, head Swiss inspector for 1989. Lionel and I are cordial with each other, as every Swiss inspector is expected to be with an American, but our friendship stops there. Lionel is a chauvinist and doesn't think women should be doing my job. I don't care what he thinks, and that pisses him off even more.

Niklas continues chatting with Lionel as he's feeding the birds. After a moment, Lionel reaches into his nylon vest, pulls out an envelope, and passes it to Niklas. He opens it up and it's full of cash. When he runs his thumb over it and fans through it, I recognize it as German Marks. That's a lot of cash in his hands. Is Niklas going over to Germany for a major vacation? Why is Lionel making this transaction out here in the open instead of at the Swiss Bank where all Temporal Inspectors do their banking? I start looking for more clues. That's when the time limit for the binoculars expires and they shut off. I reach into my pocket for another quarter and find only a couple dimes and a nickel. The binoculars only take quarters. I give up spying for the afternoon. I could try to get closer and follow one of the guys, but I have more important things to do. I can file an official report with Central Command later.

For now, there's an itch I have to scratch. I head back to my apartment, turn on the TV, and pop the Madonna video into my VCR. Once all the electronics warmed up (I so hate 80s technology), I hit play on my remote and started watching.

"Express Yourself" is a catchy little tune. Madonna was in her prime as a songsmith and it shows. The song is rather empowering in a weird kind of way, and I've always respected that as a woman. I quickly review all the elements that should be there. The soundtrack starts with the same synthesized cowbell. Check. The video has the same shirtless muscled men. Check. Madonna's still wearing the olive green dress with the black cat. Check. And there's the bald guy with the monocle. Check.

Wait a minute. I pause the VCR and rewind it. Those lines on the architecture are different. Definitely Nazi Architecture influence. I play through the rest of the video and find it's everywhere. It's a small aberration, but an obvious one.

I begin to have the inner argument I always have when I find a minor aberration. Should I call Central Command or not? Normally, I would. In the past, I wouldn't care if I was overreaching and caused a false alarm. They'd just chalk it up as oversensitive Alex and let me be.

But today, I want something from them. I want to stay in 1989. If I call them and something goes wrong, will they deny my request to extend my duty? Plus, this was brought to my attention by a Russian, which would definitely add fuel to the fire if I was wrong.

Any other inspector would just call and report it. But I have a history of missteps and a reputation to uphold since I'm the daughter of time travel. Maybe someone else will find a similar aberration and call it in. A time traveler from another country perhaps?

After several minutes of debate I decide to call Central Command. Not because I think it's the right thing to do, it's because I won't be able to sleep tonight if I don't tell them. Also, maybe I can get some details on whether I'm staying or should be packing my bags to go home.

I pull out my Walkman that acts as my communicator. All time travelers get communicators that fit the prevailing technology of any society and made to be as compact as possible. The Inspectors of 2010 get iPhones. 1960 has their communicators embedded in peace sign medallions. We get Sony Walkmans.

As I adjust my Communicator setting to Central Command I start to wonder who's working Dispatch tonight. I've pissed off some Captains in my time by making them chase down aberrations that led to no particular issues. Mostly just teenagers joy riding and wanting to catch a particular Guns N' Roses show. But this time I have a different issue.

"1989 to Central Command. Inspector Eviston calling."

"Hey, Alex," responds Alissa. "What's going on tonight? Another annoying fan?"

Awesome. It's Alissa running Dispatch again.

"I got an aberration. Who's working tonight?"

"You sure, cause Captain Blindeyes, I mean Captain Highrise, is on duty."

Karl Highrise is an ass. Worse yet, he couldn't see a full scale international temporal war if it crawled up and smacked him in the face. You've heard of the phrase, "See the problem from 50,000 feet?" Karl can't get pass foot two. Dispatch has nicknamed him Blindeyes cause he can only see what's in front of him. This is going to be an uphill battle for me.

"EVISTON. WHAT DO YOU GOT? HAVE YOU SET YOUR WATCH TO THE RIGHT TIME?"

I think he's deaf, too, because he's always yelling.

"Karl. You know, I'm wearing headphones. I can hear you fine. You don't have to yell."

"EVISTON JUST GIVE ME THE REPORT."

"I have an aberration in a music video."

"SONG LYRIC? MUSIC TRACK? WRONG BAND?"

"Art direction."

"ART DIRECTION? ARE YOU KIDDING ME? YOU'RE WASTING MY TIME FOR THIS?"

The yelling is really annoying. The only way I can deal with it is by yelling back.

"YES, KARL," I shout. "MADONNA'S 'EXPRESS YOURSELF' THE ART DECO BUILDINGS HAVE BEEN REPLACED WITH ROMAN NEOCLASSICAL. IT'S A POSITIVE FOR NAZI ARCHITECTURE."

"EVISTON, YOU DON'T HAVE TO YELL. I'M IN 2085, WE HAVE GREAT SPEAKERS HERE."

"Karl, you have to declare a level two alert," I plead. "There's something strange here. The video was based on Fritz Lang's *Metropolis*. A German film from 1927."

There's a huge pause. I'm waiting for Karl to respond. I'm sure he's doubting whether or not he should act considering this information is coming from me. I've made mistakes before and he doesn't want any part of my failures. The last guy from Central Command that listened to me is now in charge of a unit monitoring the prehistoric evolution of penguins. Finally,

Karl chimes in.

"WELL SOUNDS LIKE THIS IS 1927'S PROBLEM AND NOT YOURS. ALISSA, WHO DO WE HAVE ON 1927?"

"We have Inspector Tanner," sighs Alissa.

Great. Tanner is a drunk, he's probably passed out in some gutter and couldn't tell Art Deco from Sustainable. Karl trusts a drunk more than me.

"Karl, you have to contact the Sergeant on Duty and tell him this is a level two." A level two is not a full scale inspection, but kind of a deep dive. You send a team of 8-10 inspectors directly to the year for an immediate analysis of all cultural data points. I'd recommend one for both 1989 and 1927 but I'd settle for just 1927.

"NOT GONNA DO IT, EVISTON. THIS IS PROBABLY JUST ANOTHER JOYRIDE. I'LL CONTACT TANNER. IT'S HIS PROBLEM NOW."

"No, Karl. You have to…"

"WE GOT THIS AGENT EVISTON. ANYTHING ELSE?"

I think about signing off, but the curiosity is killing me.

"Yes. Any word on the extension of my tour of duty?"

"YEAH. RUMOR HAS IT THE MAIN OFFICE MADE A DECISION TO BRING YOU BACK. YOU'RE TOO VALUABLE TO BE STUCK IN 1989 FOREVER. BUT FINAL APPROVAL HAS BEEN HELD UP ON YOUR DAD'S DESK FOR THE PAST WEEK. MAYBE I'LL HAVE SOMETHING TONIGHT. OVER."

The radio went silent.

Dad's holding up my assignment? I know Dad has power and has been influencing the Secretary of Homeland Security ever since I joined the Temporal Inspectors, but why wouldn't he want me back home to help him with his work? And why would he wait a week? He's typically a "get it done now" kind of guy.

I can't worry about Dad right now. I have to get back to fixing the job at hand. Now, what to do about this Madonna video? I could contact Tanner directly if I knew his communication ID but I don't. I could reach out to Mojmir and see if he discovered other issues I wasn't aware of. Then again, *When Harry Met Sally* takes place in New York City. If there are any more architectural aberrations, that movie would be full of them. Should I spend the afternoon watching that movie?

But maybe Karl's right. Maybe this isn't a big problem. It's just the background of a music video. If it was big thing, you'd hear changes to lyrics, see different dance moves, or even a different artist singing the song. Maybe I'm blowing this out of proportion. But if my analysis is right about this, Tanner will figure it out eventually and maybe I'll get some credit for it.

I go about the rest of my daily routine and even do some more people watching. But I can't shake the sensation that I am right and things are shifting. Maybe it's my imagination but the Day-Glo colors everyone is wearing suddenly seems a little muted. That happy-go-lucky feeling that everyone shares like it was one big Broadway musical is a little less happy and lucky. I'm also seeing less and less shoulder pad jackets.

By evening, I decide to call Frank and see if he notices anything as well. I owe him my analysis of the Madonna video and want to touch base with him about my assignment being held up by my father. The phone rings forever. No answer. How did these people ever survive without call waiting?

So I call into dispatch again to see if Tanner found anything.

"Alissa, it's me again. Any report from Inspector Tanner?"

"Karl hasn't been able to reach Tanner, yet."

"Tanner hasn't responded?"

"Nothing unusual. One time it took us a week and a half to find him. He traveled to London and toured every pub he could find. He was hammered when we finally found him. The Sergeant on Duty wasn't very happy."

"Alright, Alissa, promise me you'll contact me with a report. Okay?"

"Will do," she responds. "One more thing. Your

assignment just came in. Looks like your tour of duty has been extended for at least a year. It's 1989 again for you. Congratulations!"

"Thanks," I say almost shouting for joy. "That's the best news I've gotten in a while."

"I think you're crazy for staying there," she admits, "But I'm glad you're happy."

"Thanks," I hang up and smile. It was a long day and I am beat. Normally I'd crash, but something is still eating me. I pop in the VHS tape to take a look at it one more time.

Everything is fine. Lyrics are on cue, dance moves flawless, and Madonna looks as elegant as ever in the banana yellow dress.

So I change into my pajamas, brush my teeth, and take in my great view of D.C. before going to bed. If there's one thing that's cool about being an Inspector is that your apartment has to have an excellent view of the city. My building boasts one of the best in D.C., From my window at the Watergate Apartments, I can see just about everything, The White House, The National Mall, The Washington Monument, and the Lincoln Memorial. My view is amazing.

"Good Night D.C. See you in the morning." I go to bed comforted that I'll be in 1989 for another full year. The routine I enjoy will still be here and I'll wake up tomorrow once again living my familiar way of life.

FOUR

When I wake up, I know something is wrong. In my dreams the video kept on playing over and over. Madonna's dress had changed from an olive green to banana yellow, to robin's egg blue, to blood red. I'm all ready to jump out of bed and watch the video again until my alarm clock goes off, stopping me dead in my tracks.

The radio clicks on and starts playing the Scorpion's "Still Loving You" except Klaus Meine is singing, "Zeit, es braucht Zeit." The clouded mind that I frequently wake up with dissipates almost immediately. I know that it is perfectly plausible a German band could be singing one of their songs in German, but on an American radio station in Washington, D.C.?

Odd. Very odd.

Sitting up in bed, I look out my window. That's when I see the most shocking thing I've ever seen.

They prepare you for a lot during Inspector Training. They run all these physiological tests to see if you can withstand any traumatic stress or changes in temporal space. They prepare you with situational simulations – tell you your parents are dead. Kids have been murdered. Nuclear War has destroyed your hometown.

Nothing had prepared me for looking out my bedroom window and seeing the Nazi flag hanging from the top of the Washington Monument with an elongated swastika mirrored in the Reflection Pool.

My heart nearly stopped. Is America gone? Has the land of the free and home of the brave been invaded by Nazis? This is not the 1989 I planned to wake up to. It's clear now that the video was a sign of a temporal shift, one in which the Nazis are in some type of control.

I hate the Nazis. They recently regained control of the German government and since then their country has regressed into their egotistical, chauvinistic, and racists ways. Once again they are claiming superiority over the rest of the world, trying to say they discovered time travel long before my father did. Worse, yet, they degraded my mother. She was a world renown Behavioral Psychologist and head of the Psychology Department at The Ohio State University. She was my role model and helped fill the void that my father created.

I once joined her during a seminar at Oxford where she lectured about the similarities in primate and human child rearing. Nazi "scientists" interrupted her lecture shouting that since she was a woman, she should be home raising the children instead of playing with monkeys. I'll never forget the look of embarrassment and anger on her face. To this day, I have more disdain for the Nazis than anything else on this planet.

I take a deep breath and bury my personal feelings for the Nazis. Negative emotions like hatred, fear, and anger can cause confusion in your own mind during what's called a "Temporal Shift". When the mind gets confused, you begin to question what true reality is. This can lead towards assimilation into the new temporal shift, and before you know it, you mentally exist within that time instead of observing it.

That's why they developed a specific protocol all Inspectors must follow when time is altered and they find themselves in a temporal shift. The first step is to not panic. This is something I'm actually very good at. Remember – I've time traveled to caveman days and got back safely.

The next step is to assess the situation. While your position in temporal space is the same, the masses around you have shifted. You are in the same point in time, but objects, events, and people around you may or may have not changed. Also, their perception of time passage may have changed, as well, so you might be in a totally different year by their calculations. What might be 1989 to you could be 1945 to them.

So, you first assess what year it is and then you assess the events and activities around it. I decide to tackle both at the same time by checking out what's on TV. It may be a huge culture shock to my system, but I'd rather freak out here in my apartment than have a reaction in public.

I go to turn on the TV and find that there's no cable box, just a set of rabbit ears. Bad sign. I flip the switch on and look for a remote. No remote. I change the channels and find static on each one. After flipping through channel 13 it circles back around and I get a signal on channel 2. It's a morning show in English with a male and female newscaster in ultra-conservative clothing.

"Good morning, Peter."

"Good morning, Elizabeth."

"I am very pleased to have the sun shining on this cold day." The female newscaster has a slight German accent.

"Yes. It is a bit chilly outside." Peter has a slight accent as well.

"Did you catch the football match this weekend? My husband highly enjoyed it."

Football, thank goodness. Maybe it isn't as bad as I thought it was.

"Yes. Very exciting," monotoned the male newscaster. "Ludwig scored three goals against the New Luxembourg Sentinels and won the game."

Oh. Soccer. Not a good sign.

"Looks like the New Berlin Generals will be the 1989 Champions," responded the female.

"Go Generals!" commanded the male with absolutely no enthusiasm at all.

I turn the TV off and look out the window again. People are heading out for work in uniform straight lines wearing drab gray clothing. They march like ants from their homes to their cars. There is no typical jaywalking. No Day-Glo electric colors. No MC Hammer parachute pants. No t-shirts declaring "RELAX." Basically take 1943 Germany, lift it up, and place it over Washington, D.C. This is a total complete change with an assimilation of another time and another country's culture.

I am looking at what we call a Level Five Temporal Shift. There's no six. I should have never left this up to Tanner last night. I have to call Central Command and figure out a way to fix this and bring things back to normal. After finding my

Walkman, I pick it up and switch it on.

"1989 to Central Command. Agent Eviston calling."

Nothing.

"1989 to Central Command. This is Agent Eviston."

Static.

"Dispatch this is Agent Alex Eviston... DO YOU READ ME?"

The static goes away and there's a click.

"Fräulein," commands a man with a thick German accent. "You are safe now. Stay where you are." The line goes dead.

Holy crap. The Nazis are in control of the future as well. This temporal shift isn't just in 1989 - it lasts all the way to 2085! They must think I'm still in a state of confusion and are trying to get me to assimilate to the new time by telling me to stay put.

Their mind suggestion is the simplest form of control. If you're deep into a Level Five Shift, you can easily become disoriented, confused and, eventually, insane. That guy that you once met on a bus that thought he was Santa Claus? Probably an Inspector that got caught in a Level Five Temporal Shift. In the academy they train you for this – they place more emphasis on mental strength than they do physical strength.

There are three stages of mental awareness: confusion, recognition, and realization. Most people get caught up in recognition. They fail to see that the world around them is wrong and instead they begin to accept it for what it is. Once they doubt their inner beliefs, then it all begins to fall to pieces.

That's what the Nazis at Central Command want me to believe. Naturally, my psyche wants to be safe. So they tell me that. Then they give me a command to stay where I am. All they need is 20, maybe 10 minutes for me to doubt myself before they send their police to come and capture me. They are also betting any Inspector monitoring 1989 is subpar.

What they didn't realize is my father drilled one thing in my head over and over and over since I could ever remember, "Never trust a German." My dad is kind of a bigot and I was rather embarrassed by it when I was growing up, but as I climb out my window onto the fire escape to get away from the knocking and pounding on my apartment door, I'm now thankful for his narrow-mindedness.

Just for the record, my thought process was: Why am I hearing a German voice (confusion)? I hate Germans (recognition). Get the hell out of your apartment before you get killed (realization).

Out on the fire escape, I see what's really going on. There are several black vans parked outside my apartment with two dozen men dressed in black and swastika red armbands, all getting ready to swarm into my apartment and capture me. Classic Nazis. On American soil. Disgusting.

Heading down on the fire escape would take me straight into the lion's den. The best way is up, so I slip on some shoes and start climbing. When I get to the top I'm lucky because all the apartment buildings are about the same height, and butt up against each other. I can safely jump from roof to roof. After about four apartment buildings I'm at the end of the block and far enough away from the black van brigade that's hunting me down. I quietly race down a fire escape, leap into a nearby tree and make my way down the trunk.

This is when I realize my current dilemma. I have a secret liking for bunnies. Don't know why, but I like them. About a week ago, I found these cute pajamas with pictures of bunnies wearing Ray-Ban sunglasses. I picked up a pair and have been wearing them every night – including last night. I'm now standing in broad daylight, in whatever Nazi dream world, wearing tennis shoes and pink pajamas dotted with super cool bunnies, not to mention my big red frizzy hair. Needless to say, I stick out like a green grasshopper among all the gray suited drab marching ants.

I have got to find some new clothes to change into, and then meet Frank at the coffee shop – if the coffee shop is even there. Maybe he's been able to contact Canadian Central Command. He's got to be able to help me fix this.

As I look around, I notice things have changed, but slightly stayed the same. Where there used to be a nightclub, there's a pub. Where there used to be a convenient store, there's a general store. And grocery stores look less like a branded national chain, and more like a mom and pop produce store. Chances are the dry cleaner around the corner is still there, and if I'm lucky they've got something I can acquire.

I take a chance and step out into the sidewalk, into the line of marching humans heading to work. They look at me oddly in my pajamas, but I ignore them. I'll only be in their Nazi conga line for a few moments. I head around the block to find my dry cleaners is now a 24-hour Laundromat. I duck in and have a look around. There's a plain older woman in the back dumping gray clothes into washing machine. She looks up as I walk in and is a bit shocked. Obviously, she wasn't expecting anyone in Pink Bunny Pajamas to walk into the Laundromat. But I do recognize her, I've seen her before. The dry cleaners have mixed up her clothes with mine once or twice. She's the same build and size as me.

She returns to doing her laundry as I walk around the store checking dryers and washing machines for clothes that somebody left behind. Besides one black sock, I find nothing. I head to the back and check the bathroom. Nothing.

My options are pretty limited at this point. Besides going into the Laundromat and probably wrestling the woman for clothes, there's nothing I can do but hang out in this bathroom forever. I mentally gear myself up to knock out this poor woman and steal her clothes. It's the only thing I can do to survive.

So I open the door and race out to find there's no one in the Laundromat. She stepped outside to smoke a cigarette. Not only did she leave her clothes behind, but a cup of quarters as well. So I do what anyone would do when they are trapped in a Nazi Temporal Shift. I grab the quarters, reach into her dryer, snag a pair of pants and a shirt, and run like hell out the back door.

Once I make it down the alley a bit, I step behind a garbage container and tear off my Bunny Pajamas. I don a pair of loose brown khaki's and a plain gray oxford shirt. I pull my hair back in a ponytail and take a look at how much money I have.

The quarters no longer bear an image of George Washington. This coin has an eagle holding a swastika in his claws. Nazi currency in 1989. I need to find Frank and figure out what is going on.

I head towards G Street to M.E. Swing's to meet him for my morning cup of joe. Except when I get there it's no longer a coffee shop. It's a restaurant – Brandeburg's Diner. Looks like it's sausages for breakfast. I'm not happy about all these changes. Not one bit. I hope Frank is inside so we can figure out how to turn this back to the simple life of 1989.

I step into the diner and sit down at the counter. Frank is nowhere to be found. I pull out a menu and browse through it. Sausage. Bread. Sausage. Bread. Sausage. Bread. These Germans are really creative with their food. The waitress fills my coffee cup and I order the Number 3 – bread, bread, and sausages.

As I wait for Frank, I grab the newspaper sitting on the stool next to me – *America Today*. It's also stamped with the swastika. The headline is bold and written in English, "Fuehrer Herrmann Vacations in Yellowstone." The article goes on to explain how much our country's leader loves to vacation in his American colony and enjoy our natural resources like Yellowstone Park and the Rocky Mountains.

All right, that confirms it. Nazi flag on Washington monument. German voice at Central Command. Nazi coins. Fuehrer visiting America. Somehow the Germans manipulated time so the Nazis won World War II and gained control of the United States.

They have the technology to time travel and now they know I exist in 1989. Somehow I've got to find Frank and figure out what to do next. I pull out a few Nazi coins, place them on the counter and go to get up and leave. That's when I notice two Nazi police have entered. They are sitting at the front door and have looked in my direction several times. Do the Nazis already have an all-points bulletin out for me? Has my picture been sent to every police officer with orders to shoot first, ask questions later? No – I would have been approached by now. I just probably look a little suspicious – especially with my wild and crazy red hair. Time to look like I have to hit the rest room.

I get up and head towards the back of the restaurant. I walk down a hallway to the bathrooms, but instead take a right into the kitchen. The line cook looks a little shocked as I walk right by him and through another door marked EXIT. Not everything is written in German here.

I walk outside into an alley, take a few steps and break out in a run. That's when I feel a sharp pain against the back of my skull. Things get a little blurry. My legs give out and I start to fall down uncontrollably. Everything goes black.

FIVE

If you've ever been knocked out, for any length of time, you're fully aware that coming out of it completely sucks. For me, it's not the grogginess or complete disorientation. It's the lack of awareness of what time it is. Imagine falling asleep for days and then randomly waking up. You don't know what time of day it is, nor do you know how many days it's been since you went to sleep. You know how when you visit a friend's house or stay in a hotel, then wake up the next morning and at first you forget where you are? Take that and multiple the confusion by twenty.

The first thought that goes through my mind as I come back to consciousness is: how long have I been out? I review my past steps. It was 1989. I mean, real 1989. Historic 1989. I was evaluating the Madonna video. There were aberrations. I went to sleep and woke up… in Nazi America.

Now I'm remembering what happened. I went to a diner to meet Frank, got ambushed, captured, and now I'm here.

So where am I now?

I look around the room and realize I'm tied to a chair with bed sheets. My hands are stuck behind my back. It's someone's apartment. There's a bed, dresser, and a nightstand. Simple design, muted colors. There's not much on the wall except for a poster of the "Great One," Wayne Gretzky, holding up the Stanley Cup in his Edmonton uniform.

No Nazi would have a poster of Wayne Gretzky. In fact, in this temporal shift, I'm not sure Wayne Gretzky even exists. Or the Edmonton Oilers. There's only one guy I know that worships the greatest hockey player of all time, and that's Frank.

Frank and I argue all the time about whether Gretzky was a Canadian hockey player or an American hockey player. I constantly remind him he played more years for an American team than a Canadian team. He reminds me that he won his four Stanley Cup trophies with the Oilers. It's really the extent of my knowledge of sports, but the argument has given us enough fodder for the past five years and something to talk about other than the weather.

But what am I doing here in Frank's apartment? Could the Nazis have captured me and taken me here as bait for Frank? Where is Frank? I decide I'm not going to wait to have these questions answered. I'm going to break free. I start to wiggle out of the bed sheets, but the knots are tied really tight. They are also bound really well around my chest, and well, I'm a woman so there's a certain part of my anatomy that's preventing me from slipping out. As I continue to struggle (because I'm a woman and we never give up), the door knob starts to turn.

I quickly lower my chin and pretend to be passed out, closing my eyes but squinting enough to see the floor.

The door opens completely and I hear footsteps. They walk across the room and toss some keys on the dresser. I can see the floor in front of me, but not much else. The person comes my way and their feet come into view. He is wearing the same gray drab clothing as me, but with brown Dockers and no socks – definitely Historic 1989 fashion. I can tell it's a guy because I can see his hairy legs.

I can feel him close to me now. He's inspecting me to see if I'm still out or not. This is my chance to make an impression. I head butt him.

I look up and see Frank holding his nose as its gushing blood everywhere.

"Oh my god, Frank. I'm so sorry. I didn't know it was you."

"I knew it. I knew it." He responds coldly.

"Knew what? Frank, let me out of here before the Nazis show up."

"Nazis show up? YOU are the Nazis."

"Frank what are you talking about? Let me out of here."

"Look at you in your Nazi clothes," he jeers with an accusatory tone. "Running around the alleys of New Berlin looking for Canadian rebels. I should have killed you back in that alley. I should have killed you!"

Frank probably hasn't transitioned through the temporal shift well. He doesn't know what's real and what's not because of the time shift. Because he's a little paranoid, he's beginning to believe all Americans are Nazis, including me. Reality is now blurred in his head and I'm a victim of it.

"Frank, call Canadian Central Command," I explain. "They'll tell you I'm not a Nazi."

"THERE IS NO CANADIAN CENTRAL COMMAND," Frank yells from across the room, popping veins in his forehead. He's pissed, confused, and scared.

At first, I'm taken aback. But after a moment, it makes perfect sense that there's no Canadian Central Command as well. Canada's access to time travel is through the U.S. and Frank used the same High Energy Particle Accelerator to get here that I did. The only reason the Canadians know how to time travel is because the U.S. showed them. I have to help Frank realize there has been a temporal shift, or I'll lose him forever. I start by helping him understand I'm not the enemy.

"Frank. It's me. Alex Eviston. I'm your friend."

"You're a Nazi," he snarls.

"Frank. We have coffee every morning together. M.E. Swings. Remember?"

"You are a spy for the Nazi American Army," he convinces himself. "This place is crawling with evil people just like you. I AM TRAPPED. They are hunting down Canadians one by one and I'm next."

When you go through a Level Five Temporal Shift, the first 24 hours are critical. If you don't survive them, you're hosed. Your sense of reality is what keeps you sane, the longer you experience the new different world, the more you think that's reality. This is even worse for an Inspector since the time you are monitoring is foreign to you. But the longer you inspect it, the more you become acclimated and the harder it is to navigate through a temporal shift. They tried to correct for this in the past by having you inspect sequential years, but then inspectors began to believe they were living a new, completely different, life.

Typically when someone comes back from a Tour of Duty there's a team of psychologists that help him or her back to reality, but sometimes people never really adjust. A Level Five Temporal Shift is the most difficult to mentally navigate through, it messes up even the most resolute inspectors. Obviously, Frank is not doing well. And the longer he goes on like this, the less his chances are of ever coming out of it.

"You are my safety net," he says to me coyly. "When they come for me, I'll tell them I have their precious prize. If they want you alive, they'll need to give me passage to my homeland."

"Frank. I'm Alex. I'm your friend."

"Nazi," he responds.

"Remember yesterday, you gave me the VHS of the Madonna video."

Pause. Confusion. Regress. "LIAR."

I had him for a moment, but obviously this approach isn't working. I need to help him remember the past, who he is, who I am, and help him understand what is reality and what is the time shift. I'm the only familiarity he has right now. And he's the only thing I have that's normal. If I can't get him to think clearly, then all is lost for the both of us. The Nazis will find us eventually. He'll turn me over to them; then we'll both be captured. My hope is that our typical argument will shift him out of this confusion and bring him back to reality. I can fix this, but it's going to be hard.

"Frank. Who's that in the poster?"

Frank stops and looks at the poster of Wayne Gretzky. His demeanor changes slightly. "The Great One," he says.

"Greatest Canadian hockey player, ever," I whisper.

"Greatest ALL-TIME hockey player, ever," he argues.

"Yes. Greatest all-time hockey player." I could see a small change in him. His brain is starting to process this. I know I can take him further.

"How many Stanley Cups did he win?"

"84. 85. 87. 88. Edmonton Oilers."

"What happened in 1989, Frank?"

Pause. He's processing. I can tell he's working it out in his brain and I won't let him go back.

"Why didn't he win one again in 1989?"

"He was traded."

"To who?"

"The Kings."

"What city do the Kings play in?"

Pause. Processing. This is my moment.

"Frank. The Great One got traded for the 88-89 season. Where did he play?"

"Los Angeles. Los Angeles Kings."

"Where else did he play after that?"

"St. Louis. New York Rangers."

"How many years did he play for an American team?"

"WAYNE GRETZKY IS CANADIAN!"

"That's right, Frank. What year did he retire?"

"1999."

"How could he have retired in 1999, and played for so many American teams over 11 years when it's 1989 today?"

Frank stops. His confused anger begins to subside. He sits on the edge of his bed, holding his bloody nose, and stares at the picture of The Great One for several moments. I can see the wheels turning in his head. His eyebrows fold in when he's deep in thought. He looks into my eyes, then back at the greatest hockey player of all time. He turns back to me. The tension on his face relaxes. He gets a little red from embarrassment, but that fades, too. He smiles and chuckles.

"He was Canadian. I don't care how many years he played for the Kings or the Rangers. He was Canadian."

"Don't forget about the St. Louis Blues," I add.

"They are not a real hockey team."

We sit there for a few moments as I let Frank soak it all in.

"I almost lost it, didn't I?" he says.

"It's a Level Five. You were stranded, Frank. No Canadian Central Command. I don't blame you."

"You didn't freak," he retorts.

"I knew it was coming. I saw the Madonna video. There

were aberrations. Can you untie me out now so we can figure out our next steps?"

"I think you broke my nose."

"I'll smack you upside the head, too, if you don't let me out."

Frank laughs. "I'm not sure I want to let you go if you're going to act like that." He starts to untie my hands. "Thanks."

"I had to save you," I confess. "I don't know what I'd do without you. It's just you and me now."

Frank pauses, "We need to go check on Mojmir." He's comes to the realization there are more people we need to worry about than us.

"The Russian? No way. We don't know if we can trust him."

"The Soviets fought on our side during World War II, remember?"

"Sure but…"

"Plus, we owe it to him," argues Frank. "If he didn't bring the tape to me, I would have never given it to you. You wouldn't have known the aberrations. Without fair warning, we both probably would have freaked. We've got to go see him. We need to make sure he pulls out of this okay, too."

I stood there frozen. I'm one of those Americans that believe there was no Post-Cold War. The only reason that the Cold War is over is the Soviets just ran out of money. Even a century and a half after World War II, I'm convinced they still hate us. There might not be a nuke pointed at my head, but if they could aim one at us without us knowing, they would.

BOOM! BOOM! BOOM!

"Someone's banging on the front door," Frank whispers, "We have to go NOW."

Frank has untied me and I head toward the fire escape. I look out the window and find three guards heading up the fire escape.

"Crap. Nazis. They got a little smarter this time," I scoff. "We can't go this way."

"Follow me," motions Frank. We go into his bathroom and

close the door. He opens a little small vanity closet above the toilet and clears away the towels. He begins to climb inside. There is no way he's going to fit in there, let alone the both of us, but Frank manages to pull his whole body inside and disappears.

"FRAULEIN. YOU CAN NOT ESCAPE US THIS TIME." We hear above the sound of axes busting through the wooden entrance door to Frank's apartment.

Frank pops his head out of the vanity closet.

"God bless it, Alex. Come on!" He grabs my hand and pulls me in. What seems like a magic trick ends up being a false back into a small room. Frank closes the vanity door, pushes some towels back, and closes the false backing.

"When I was a kid, I was always scared of monsters in my closet or under my bed or behind the door. My parents thought I was paranoid. As I grew older, I realized that my parents were 100% right. I definitely am paranoid. When I moved in here, I knew that one day I'd need a safe room. So I shrunk my bed room, moved my bathroom, and built this safe room behind it. I've never had to use it until now. But I think it's worth it."

My respect for Frank just went up a few notches, but at the same time, he's kind of creeping me out.

"So what do we do now?" I ask. "I mean, we can't stay in here forever."

"We need to get to Mojmir to make sure he's okay," Frank instantly responds. "He doesn't deserve to be hunted like we are."

"We can't wait it out here," I argue. "Even when the Nazi brigade leaves, they'll post guards outside that we can't get past."

"When I built this safe room I figured I needed a way out, too. I thought of an escape hatch. Many apartment complexes have small shafts which house all the plumbing that goes from floor to floor. I built this room right next to that and added a door that only opens from the inside out."

Frank steps over to a small cubby and opens a door. There

are solid iron pipes running from the ceiling to the basement.

"Want to know what it's like to be a fireman?" With that, Frank dives through the door, grabs the pole, and shoots down the shaft.

There's no going back, now. So I follow Frank and fly down the plumbing and land on concrete. Hard. A trash bag breaks my fall as I stumble backwards.

We're now in a small waste closet, somewhere on the first floor I guess. Frank is peeking through the door.

"It's safe," he explains. "The back door of the apartment building is right across the hall. We can make a break for it right now and head out the alleyway. Ready?"

"Wait a second," I say. "Where are we going?"

"I told you, we need to save Mojmir," argues Frank.

"I can't trust him," I counter.

"Well, you're going to have to trust me," grins Frank. "And I'm going to make sure Mojmir's safe."

Frank shoots out of the trash room, across the hall, and out the back door. The paranoid time shifter has faded away and the charming, heroic, flyboy has returned. I have no choice but to follow him. Time to see the Russian.

SIX

Mojmir lives in the next neighborhood over on the lower level of a brownstone. His exterior door is conveniently underneath the stairs to the second floor that hides us from the street view. Frank and I huddle in the doorway, trying hard not to be seen. It's getting easier for us to hide in the shadows since it's late afternoon. Frank knocks.

"Who is it?" a raspy voice whispers from inside.

Frank looks at me oddly and responds, "I'm the one they call Dr. Feelgood."

"Do you have a car, as big as a whale?" a voice with a Russian accent asks from inside. "Is it heading down to the Love Shack?" 80s songs. This must be a little code Frank's worked out with Mojmir.

Frank cringes as he says, "Did I ever tell you, you're my hero? You are the wind beneath my wings."

The door flies open. On the other side is a half-naked skinny Russian with curly black hair half way down his chest, a full sleeve tattoo and a hoop earring hanging from his left nostril.

"WELCOME TO THE JUNGLE! WE GOT FUN AND GAMES!" yells Mojmir. Mojmir extends his arms and gives Frank a manly bear hug. He looks over his shoulder and notices me. A huge look of awe comes over his face.

"Wow. I am in the presence of royalty. Please enter my humble house, dear Princess of Time." Mojmir gestures grandly and bows deeply.

I blush a little bit. Here I am ready to trade insults with this Commie, and instead he welcomes me into his house.

"Thanks, Mojmir."

As I look around, I realize that Mojmir's sense of paranoia makes Frank's look like he throws caution to the wind. We step inside and Mojmir locks three separate deadbolts with keys that hang from his neck. He turns a lever in the center of the door that extends two iron bolts solidly into metal braces soldered to the sides of the door frame. He pulls down an aluminum gate over the whole door and bolts it to the concrete on the floor. When he's all done, he pushes into place a large freezer chest in front of the aluminum gate. I look around the room and the walls are covered in iron panels from the floor to the ceiling. The floor is concrete and poured around the base of the iron wall. The ceiling is large steel sheets, welded to the iron wall panels. This place could withstand several nuclear blasts. Nothing is going to get in here.

"I love your decorating style. It feels so homey and relaxing," I joke.

"You don't know fear until you've lived in Auschwitz," explains Mojmir. "Every morning I'd wake up wondering if that was the day they were going to kill me. Every time they led us somewhere, I dreaded it was a walk to the gas chamber. When I saw a Nazi with a gun, I was terrified he was going to shoot me down. And EVERY Nazi had a gun."

Mojmir sticks out his forearm at me and points to a tattoo of a red dragon. Buried in his tattoo are the numbers 136703. "Luckily, I got out." He stared at the numbers himself. "There's no way those bastard Nazis are going to get me this time."

My enemy's enemy is my friend. And right now, every American Nazi soldier within a 90 mile radius is after me. The only Russian I know just invited me into his fortress of steel. I'll take my chances with the Commie.

Mojmir finally looks away from the numbers. His dark memory seems to fade away and he flashes me a smile. "The Madonna video," he brags. "I was right, wasn't I?"

"Definitely 'Severe' Deco," I agree. "It was obvious."

"I don't get it," says Frank. "How did we see small aberrations in the Madonna video one day, and then a Level Five temporal shift the next day?"

"You are such a young pup." Mojmir explains. "I'm sure the Daughter of Time Travel has it all figured out."

I just realized Mojmir looks like one of those old rock musicians that keep on partying well beyond his prime. His face is weathered and has definitely seen some better days, but he certainly acts younger than he appears. He's like the Russian version of Keith Richards.

"It all has to do with *Metropolis*," I explain.

"You mean Superman?" asks Frank. "Man of steel?"

"The Madonna video was based on Fritz Lang's movie *Metropolis*. Its art direction was influenced by what was going on in 1927," clarifies Mojmir. "And if there was a temporal shift in 1927, the video would change. And whatever ripple effect we'd see from the temporal shift would hit the Madonna video before it would hit 1989."

Mojmir's right. Changes in history certainly can have an effect on current cultural influence. But this is a Level Five Temporal Shift.

"1927 to 1989? That's a super long time for a Level Five Temporal Shift," explains Frank. "We haven't had that length of shift…"

"Since the Daughter of Time Travel gave woman fire," finished Mojmir. "And as a result international time travel laws were established. Of which I think the Nazis just violated a shitload."

"Guys, this doesn't end in 1989. It continues on way past this. Remember, there is no American Central Command."

Mojmir turns white. "What?"

"I tried to contact Central Command this morning. I got the Nazis."

"This goes all the way to 2085 – over a full century." Frank sits down in shock. "How are we going to get out?"

"What about you, Mojmir? Can you reach your Central Command?" I ask.

"My radio has been jammed since last night," Mojmir states disappointedly, "I can't get anyone."

"So the mighty Soviet Bear is immobilized, too," I counter.

"We've all been hoodwinked by the Germans," concludes Frank. How true.

"I need to think," declares Mojmir. "And I think better with Vodka." He heads into the kitchen, pulls a bottle off the counter and takes a swig. He passes it to Frank who's staring off into space.

"Frank. Drink." Mojmir places it into his hand. Frank snaps out of it and takes the bottle.

"So the Germans have somehow figured out a way to manipulate time through several decades, maybe centuries, and avoid historic course corrections." Mojmir seems to be an external thinker. "If they keep it going, they can change time forever."

"Now we're really stuck in 1989," I add sadly.

"Well the good news is this place is more than an apartment," adds Mojmir, "It's a bomb shelter."

"Ain't that the truth," says Frank, "Steel enforced drywall? Really Mojmir, what were you expecting? The Americans to come after you?"

"No. I'm not scared of the Americans." Mojmir winked at me, "I've seen every historic tactical nuclear target maps the Soviets ever made. I know what weapons are aimed at D.C. in 1989 and this apartment is in the blast zone for at least 12 P-36Ms. So I planned for something much worse – the Russians launching World War III right where I'm living. I built a place to survive a massive nuclear attack. Follow me."

Mojmir leads us to a back bedroom that is littered with piles of *Rolling Stone* and *Parade* magazines, as well as albums, tapes, and CDs of every heavy metal band you can imagine. A poster of the *Slippery When Wet* album hangs on the wall.

"Bon Jovi fan?" I ask.

"Bon Jovi, Crüe, Cinderella, Tesla, sure. Throw in a little Warrant and Whitesnake and you have the typical Mojmir mixtape." Mojmir looks back at me and smiles, "I love American hairband music. That's why I asked for 1989 as my last tour of duty."

"You picked this year?" I questioned. "You didn't get banished here like the rest of us?"

"You didn't choose to be here?" Mojmir was truly confused. "I just assumed the Daughter of the Time Travel could choose to go anywhere." Mojmir opened the closet door and pushed aside some snakeskin boots. He reached down, pulled open a latch and revealed a trap door.

"This way." And with that, the Russian crawled down below the floor.

I paused and looked at Frank. "Do you think this is safe?"

"We have nowhere else to go," Frank responds. "Plus, I think hanging with Mojmir is much safer than being out there among the Nazis. Don't worry. I'll watch your back." And with that, Frank followed Mojmir down the hole. I had no choice but to join them.

Down below, about 500 feet below, is a vast cavern of living space. Mojmir had tapped into an abandoned subway space and rebuilt it, sealed it, and made it self-sustaining.

"Welcome to Mojmiristan!" the Russian announced, "A complete underground city. It includes farmland. Textile and blacksmith capabilities. Living quarters for 20 people. Plus, enough geo-thermo electric to power the whole place forever."

I looked around and saw a field of corn, lettuce, and tomatoes. A goat bayed and looked up at me for a moment, then went back to eating grass. Hanging from the ceiling were dozen of "sun lights", lamp fixtures that simulate the rays of the sun and makes you feel like you're truly outside.

"Advanced Russian technology," smiles Mojmir. "It's set on a timer to assimilate the correct amount of daily sunlight depending on the time of the year. It makes the plants grow and gives off the same UVB Ultraviolet rays as the sun which the body converts to Vitamin D. On rainy weeks, sometimes I come down here and hang out."

Upon closer inspection, I find the walls and the floors are completely sealed in lead panels, but oddly the place doesn't feel claustrophobic.

"We got everything down here," exclaims Mojmir proudly. "I have a filtration system that cleans the water on an hourly basis, sustaining power that will last as long as the magma in the earth does, and as long as we keep on reusing the seeds and manage the livestock properly, we have food forever."

"So we're stuck here?" I asked. "Forever?"

"I don't know what else we can do," laments Frank. "Every

Nazi within 100 miles is looking for all of us. They'll probably shoot on sight. This is the safest place we can be right now."

"But there's no U.S. or Canadian Central Command, and who knows about the Soviets," I counter. "Someone needs to fix this."

"Alex, my youthful rosebud," smiles Mojmir, "If there is one thing I've learned in my decades with the Committee for Temporal Security is that there is *always* someone else. I'm sure right now there is a crack team of Russian Analysts figuring out exactly how to stop the Nazis. I, for one, am not going worry about it. I have 16 months left before I retire and I'm not going to risk anything to jeopardize that."

"Listen, the way I look at it Alex, it could be worse," says Frank. "We could be in a Nazi jail or running for our lives in the countryside. Here we have food, clean water, and energy. I say we stay here. I'm not going to embarrass my country by running around trying to do whatever to stop the Nazis. As long as you and I are safe here, I'm fine with waiting this out."

Maybe they are right. I can be a little anxious to fix things at times. This could be a good place to hang out while things right themselves.

"Great," I say. "This is truly how I planned to spend eternity – trapped in gigantic iron lung with a Canadian Hockey player and the world's number one Bon Jovi fan. Where's one of those living quarters you talked about? It's been a long day and I need some sleep."

SEVEN

Being the daughter of the man who invented time travel, you'd think I know everything there was about him and how he invented it. Truth be told, I didn't have much interaction with Dad as I was growing up and even less once I started pursuing this field. Dad was numbers driven. He wanted to know how things work. How complex puzzles were put together.

My mom once sent him down the block for milk. An hour later he hadn't returned so mom called in a missing persons report to the police. They found Dad in our driveway still in his car. Apparently, he was trying to develop a better way to start your car. All drivers can now thank my father for the "key fob wand ignition" method that's now standard on all cars.

As much as everyone I ever met wanted me to be like my dad, I never was. I am much more like my mom. Mom was head of Research Psychology at Ohio State. She was just as analytical as my father was, but one plus one never equaled two in her world.

"People are not that simple," she'd explain to me. "Motivation and capability are a strange mix. One can have huge potential, but lack desire or self-confidence, so they never achieve their full capabilities. Conversely, where there's a will, there's a way. People without knowledge or talent sometimes find themselves achieving their wildest dreams."

Mom and I would often go to the park or the local zoo and sit and watch people. We'd make up stories about where they were going and where they wanted to be. Once my mom turned the tables on me, "Where are you going? Where do you want to be?"

I knew an easy answer like Disney World wouldn't suffice. She wanted to know what I wanted to be in life, "I want to do something big."

"Big? Define big."

"I want to change the world," I said definitively.

"Your father changed the world." She said half-heartedly, "Are you going that route?"

"Dad didn't change the world." I quickly argued, "Dad changed human's *capabilities*. He didn't improve their motivation. Just because we have time travel doesn't mean the world is better off for it. I want to leave this world better off than how it was given to me."

She smiled at me. "Good choice."

Those were some of the last words she said to me. I didn't know it at the time, but Mom was slowly dying from a rare autoimmune disorder. No time machine could heal her. She died early that spring, didn't even get to see me off to my prom or graduate from high school. I had to come of age on my own.

The following year I entered the Temporal Engineering School at Ohio State. I had been accepted to the School of Psychology as well, but decided against following in my mom's footsteps. It's as if the memory of Mom hurt too much at that point in my life. So, I did what was predictable of me – time school.

I almost flunked out my freshman year. There are two courses every first-year student takes – Plane Analytic Geometry and Introduction to Temporal Mechanics. They are "weeder" courses, designed to "weed out" the students who shouldn't be in engineering school. I got an A in Plane Analytic Geometry, but a D in Intro to Temporal Mechanics, mainly because my professor trashed my final paper, *Effects of Momentum on Temporal Gravitational Pull*.

During that Christmas break Dad asked me to come visit him at his lab below Wright-Patterson Air Force base to discuss my grades. It wasn't to celebrate the holidays, or even to check in on me to see if I was dealing well with mom's death. When he made time for me, it was always something serious – especially if it was at his lab. I knew this was about my grades.

Needless to say, Dad's lab was a huge facility. It takes about five football fields to hold a High Energy Particle Accelerator, and that's only half Dad's lab. I kind of like visiting there because everyone treats me like royalty, well, everyone besides Dad. I get full access, answers to any question, and don't even need government clearance.

But when I came to visit, it was a few days before Christmas and practically no one was there other than old man Craig. He's the security guy that sits at the front door and checks people in. He's known me since I was three.

"Merry Chrissssmasss, Alessss," Craig lost a few teeth a couple years back. Now he has a slight whistle went he talks.

"Merry Christmas, Mr. Roberts," I respond and give him a peck on the cheek.

"Oh, you better ssstop that. The missssessss is gonna get jealoussss," he blushes, "and how many timesss have a told you that you can ssstart calling me Craig."

"Lots of times, Mr. Roberts." I have too much respect for old man Craig to not call him by his proper name.

Dad's office is on the sub-tenth floor, the basement floor of the lab, and I have to take the elevator there. When I reach his door, it's obvious he's not there so I head down to the analytic room where I find him pouring over schematics with a slide ruler and calipers. He doesn't even look up as I walk in.

"Prof. Fatica called me the other day," he bellows.

"How'd you know it was me?" I ask.

"I know your walking pattern." He responds. "Heel, toe, heel, toe, shuffle, shuffle, heel, toe, repeat."

I stand next to him for a while, waiting as he continues to analyze.

"I said Prof. Fatica called me."

"Is that a question or a statement?" Dad taught me long ago to only answer questions.

"Good girl," He looks up and smiles at me. "He said he should have failed you."

"Dad, he trashed my paper on Momentum."

"Was it any good?"

"Good? Of course it was good," I said angrily, "I proved that temporal gravitational pull can convert the kinetic energy of momentum much like a particle accelerator, thus speeding up the time needed during time travel."

"And he said that was impossible due to the Lorentz Factor, huh?" Dad had gone back to his analysis.

"Yep."

"Yes," he corrected, "Use proper English."

This made me even more furious.

"So you're going to drop out of Time School now," he asked.

"Maybe the School of Psychology is where I should be."

"Looks like the weed out classes are doing exactly what they should."

"What the hell is that supposed to mean, Dad?" I yelled. "Are you telling me I'm not good enough to follow in *your* footsteps? That I should get into Mom's school because it's *easier*?" I was furious.

Dad paused at his drafting table. He took a deep breath and looked me in the eyes.

"Listen. I really don't care what you do. But don't avoid Mom's school because as you walk down the halls everyone looks at you with pity and remorse. Or don't stay in Time School because everyone in the world expects you to follow in my footsteps. And certainly don't drop out because some asshole professor trashed your groundbreaking paper on momentum. Whatever you do, do it because that's what you want to do." Dad turned back to his drafting. "No daughter of mine is going to be forced into something by the memory of her dead mother, the legacy of her father, or some know-it-all professor."

"My paper was really that good?"

"Professor Fatica couldn't tell the difference between the Lorentz Factor and de Broglie wavelength if it smacked him upside the head."

There was a long pause as I waited for Dad to say something else. But he was a man of few words, when he made his case for something he was clear, concise, and always right. I could tell he had said everything he wanted and the conversation was over.

"Are you going to be home on Christmas morning?" I

asked.

"Yes."

I headed for the door and turned the knob.

"Alexandria?" Wow. Dad only used my full name in the rarest of occasions. I turned to find him looking at me right in the eyes.

"Don't ever let anyone tell you what you can or can't do. Anyone. Anything. Any set of persons. Ever. Understand?"

"Yes, Father."

He continued to stare me down and added, "That includes you."

I went back to school that day and marched right into the Time School's Department Head's office. I petitioned for a full review of my paper and my final grade. I argued my theories on momentum and temporal gravitational pull in front of a panel of five professors. Today that theory is known as Alex's Law. Someday I plan to call it Alex's First Law.

I woke up the next morning and knew the bomb shelter was not for me. I couldn't sit on the sidelines anymore. I looked around and found Frank and Mojmir eating bowls of Rice Krispies.

"I can't stay down here isolated from the rest of the world while someone else decides our fate," I announce. "I asked to stay in 1989 and this was the hand I was I dealt. I've got to fix this."

"Do you even know what we're up against?" questions Frank. "There could be a huge Nazi army up there waiting to capture us and then do who knows what to us. One wrong move by any of us can mess up anything Central Command has planned."

"There is no Central Command," I argue. "For all we know it's us and no one else. I'm leaving here after breakfast. You can come with me, or stay here, but I'm gone."

"Where are you going to go?" asks Mojmir.

"I haven't thought that far ahead, yet." I add. "I'll see where my feet lead me. I figure I'd start by heading to the National

Mall to see what I can find."

"Bad idea," counters Mojmir. "Nazis are probably patrolling there by the dozens. You'll get captured instantly and tortured soon after."

"I'll be fine," I say.

"No, you won't," he says solemnly. "I know how the Nazis operate. They don't just inflict pain, they destroy your soul." I look down and see Mojmir rubbing the numbers tattooed on his arm. Frank notices as well.

"You can't go out there alone," argues Frank. "I'm coming with you. You're all I've got now and I'm not going to let you out of my sight."

That's the Frank I know and admire. He's always got my back.

"What about you, Mojmir?" I challenge him, "Care to journey back into the lion's den for one last hurrah?"

"Do you even realize what you're up against?" he snaps back.

"They are Nazis," responds Frank. "Pure evil."

"You don't understand the half of it." Mojmir pushes his bowl away and puts his head in his hands for a moment. He looks away and stares off into space. "I saw hundreds of Jews march off to the gas chamber every day. Men, women, kids, whole families, being led by gun point to their death. Long lines of them. They all knew where they were going. I could see it in their helpless faces. There were days I wished they would have picked me so I wouldn't have to endure the anguish of watching others walk to their death and experience the self-pity of wondering why I survived. When I finally escaped, I promised myself I'd never go back. I'd live out the rest of my days listening to distorted guitars and songs about sex, drugs, and rock 'n' roll. You guys can fight against the Nazis. My time is done." Mojmir begins to walk away, but I grab his arm.

"You don't think there is someone up there on the surface, right now, suffering the same fate? Who knows how many concentration camps are on American soil? Where Jews,

Catholics, Muslims, Blacks, Hispanics, whoever are being killed en masse on a daily basis." I look Mojmir in the eye. "You may be able to hide here away from the Nazis, but can you hide from your nightmares? You have memories of all the people you watched go to their deaths. Now you'll have more if you don't help us. Can you live with the regret that you had the chance to save more people but walked away?"

"I'm not going," he says and pushes my arm away.

"You were once the greatest inspector in the world," I say. "I wonder what happened to that man."

"He died in the gas chamber in Auschwitz," Mojmir solemnly responds.

"I don't think that's how you want to be remembered," I argue. "Come on, Frank. Let's pack up our stuff and go."

Mojmir stares at the numbers tattooed on his arm. Frank finishes his cereal and gets up to go. He pauses and puts his hand on Mojmir's shoulder.

"I guess this is good-bye, my friend," he says.

"My number was 136703," speaks Mojmir. "The day before I left they called up numbers 136200 through 136700. I knew I was next. 136702 was a mother I had met in the laundry room. 136704 was an eleven year old boy whose birthday was that day. I was able to escape, but left all those people behind."

Mojmir pulled his sleeve over his tattoo and looked up at me. "You're right, the nightmares will never go away, but maybe I can replace them with pleasant memories. It's not that I want people to remember me as the best inspector ever. It's that I want them to remember me as the noblest human being ever."

"So you're coming with us?" grins Frank.

Mojmir took a deep breath, "If we're going to do this, we can't just jump at it like a mouse going after cheese in a trap. We need a plan."

EIGHT

After much deliberation, we decide our first move is to make it up to Canada. It probably isn't as bad off there as it is in the United States. Plus, I could see in Frank's eyes that he wants to get back to his homeland. Mojmir pushed long and hard to stowaway on a boat to Europe, but once we reminded him that Canada is home to the greatest progressive rock band ever, Rush, and that there was a good chance of him seeing them play live in the Great White North, he was totally in.

When we get there, Frank's pretty sure he can find someone from his family and somehow explain who we are so we can take refuge there. I have to admit, at first I was very anxious about this. We'll be breaking some International Time Travel rules by telling them we're from the future. I've broken rules before and had to pay some heavy prices for it.

But Mojmir convinces us that it is for the greater good. Besides we're pretty sure the United Nations are more concerned with all the rules the Nazis are breaking.

There are a couple of things we need to get to Canada. First, we need Nazi American money. Except for the few German coins I have, we are without current currency. Second, we need proper identification. We figure that all Nazi Americans have some form of ID they have to show, just like people did in Nazi Germany. We just don't know what that is. The third thing is we have to find safe passage to Canada.

Passage to Canada probably comes out of New York City, or whatever it's currently called. We know we need train tickets from Union Station in D.C. to Penn Station in Manhattan. This again, is going to cost more than the few Nazi coins I have.

Once we get to New York City, we all have access to a large sum of money at safety deposit boxes in the Swiss International Bank. You see, a long time ago, the Swiss declared neutrality among all the nations and became the world's banker throughout time. They established branches in every major international city and connected them throughout the time continuum. That way a country could purchase a temporal bank account for every inspector. They could deposit money in 2050 and the inspector in 1923, 1945, 1989, whenever, could go to the Swiss bank and make a withdrawal. And the beauty is when you overdraft on your account, you just have your country wire more money to the month before the overdraft and you're covered. Once we make it to the Swiss Bank we'll be golden. Any of us can make a withdrawal and we'd have more than enough to get us to Canada.

With passage to a safer country figured out, we now have to solve for getting a little bit of money in order to travel to New York, and find some proper identification. Mojmir proposed an idea.

"I have a friend named Fat Tony that, let's just say, 'can get things'. In the past, he's been able to provide me with things that are a bit illegal," offers Mojmir. "In fact, some of the items down here and some of the steel re-enforcement upstairs he helped acquire."

"That was yesterday. Today's another time. Who knows if this guy even exists," Frank argues.

"Chances are his destiny hasn't changed," I counter, "Even though the world around him is drastically different, at his core he should be the same."

"Fat Tony used to have an affinity for Russian Standard Vodka," explains Mojmir, "I'm sure I can exchange a case of Imperia for whatever we need."

"Alright," says Frank, "It looks like either Fat Tony or nothing. Let's get this done; the sooner I'm back in my homeland, the happier I'll be."

We gather the case of Imperia and head up to the surface. We leave Mojmir's apartment and go around the block to Fat Tony's place. The good news is it's not that far.

Fat Tony used to hold court in the backroom of an Italian Restaurant called *LaMarca's Pasta and Pizza*. It's now a general store called *Mussolini's*. We walk in with the case of liquor under our arm. The person at the front counter sees us and simply points us to the back of the store. It seems this is a standard way of doing business in Nazi America, or at least with Fat Tony.

We get to the back of the store and find a door marked *Non ci sono stronzi* and assume that means the door to see Fat Tony

"This is the door I used to use," Mojmir explains and knocks.

The door opens a crack and Mojmir recognizes the guard.

"We have a... gift for Tony," says Mojmir.

"A gift?" the guard says looking at the box, "I only know one thing that a Russian should be bringing as a gift to Tony. And that box would definitely fit many."

"They're for Tony," adds Frank, "if he wants to share, you can ask him."

The guard scowls at us and lets us in. It's a dark room that's lit by a lamp in the corner, a neon sign behind a small bar, and the glow from a television set playing a soccer match. Fat Tony is visibly pissed off and yelling at the screen in Italian. I don't know what he's saying, but it doesn't sound good. On the set I realize the Italians are playing the French in some type of championship game.

"*Fermo! Fermo! Fermo!*" shouts Fat Tony.

The French forward drives ahead of all the Italians, kicks the ball with all his might and BAM!, off the goalie's hands and into the net. Fat Tony turns beat red as if he's about to explode out of his skin.

"*Va' All'Inferno!*" he yells at the top of his lungs and hurls his bottle of wine at the TV. There's an explosion of glass, red wine, and electricity as the TV shatters and fizzles out. I jump back several feet out of instinct and the room goes suddenly quiet. It's as if someone sucked all the sound out of the room.

Fat Tony stands, takes a deep breath, and calmly slicks back his greasy hair. After another deep breath, he visibly lowers his shoulders and relaxes, suppressing his anger and taking complete control of his emotion. One of his lackeys gets a broom and begins to clean up the mess.

"Looks like we need another TV," chuckles Fat Tony.

The rest of the guys in the room take this as a cue to finally let go of their tension and laugh along with him. Tony looks around the room at his men with confidence and camaraderie. That's when he sees us and realizes something may be wrong.

"Hey," he shouts, "who let these *fessacchioni* in?" A few of the guys reach into their jacket for their guns. I'm ready to make a bee-line out of here. There's no way I'm ending up dead in a backroom of an Italian restaurant like the crooked Irish cop from *The Godfather*. That's when the guard who let us in smiles and speaks up.

"Boss, make him say something," he says pointing to Mojmir.

Fat Tony pulls out a gun and aims it at Mojmir's head. "You heard the guy, say something."

"Raise your hand if you like the French. Raise both hands if you are French," says Mojmir, laying his Russian accent on very thick.

Fat Tony stares straight at Mojmir sizing him up as he points his gun at the top of Mojmir's forehead. Tony weighs about 350 pounds, and there's no way I can tackle him and save Mojmir. But I look out of the corner of my eye at Frank and I can see him lean a bit forward as if in attack mode. I'm sure he's checked at least a dozen hockey defenders Tony's size and knocked them off the ice. Just when I think Frank's going to leap and all hell is going to break loose, Fat Tony notices the box under Mojmir's arms and starts to chuckle. He lowers his gun and turns to his lackeys.

"Jackpot!" yells Fat Tony excitedly, "We got a Russian! What's in the box, Commie?"

"Imperia. Whole case," smiles Mojmir.

Fat Tony's face brightens as if he's been chosen as the next Pope. He holsters his gun and slowly retrieves the box from Mojmir as if he was handling fragile antique crystal. He carefully places the box on the coffee table. He opens it and pulls out a bottle looking at it in the light, examining the liquor through the bottle. He gently breaks the seal and unscrews the cap. He first places the bottle under his nose and deeply inhales the aroma. His face folds with deep pleasure like he's a child that's found a long lost toy. He takes a swig and lets the Vodka drizzle down his throat. His eyes roll back into his head and he closes them. A tear forms at the edge of his eye and he smiles.

"*Paradiso*," he silently exclaims and holds his pleasure for several moments. He finally turns back to us in total awe. "A whole case of this stuff? I want to ask where you got this, but you know that's not how I do business. You've come to the right place, Ruskie. You and your friends."

Fat Tony nods to his guard who then takes the case from Mojmir and puts it behind the bar. He sits back down on the couch and motions for us to sit near him on a few chairs.

"It's not often a case of Imperia shows up at my doorstep, my friend," explains Fat Tony, "In fact, it's a rarity. Name your price."

We hadn't planned this far. We figured what we needed, but we didn't know really what we were asking for. "We need passage to..." Mojmir pauses realizing New York City may not be New York City anymore. "We need to get to Penn Station."

"Penn Station? In New Himmler City?" Fat Tony looks at us suspiciously. I'm sure we've piqued his curiosity on how we came across a case of Imperia. A man like Fat Tony may want to know what we're up to so he can get into the action.

"No questions asked," I add.

"Finally the Irish Rose speaks," smiles Fat Tony. "Of course, no questions asked. I can get you tickets on the next train out." I'm sure Fat Tony has lots of questions, like what's an Irish woman, Canadian, and Russian doing hanging out together in Nazi America.

"We need more than tickets," says Frank.

"Ah... now I know why you come to me with Imperia," laughs Fat Tony, "You need Identification Passes."

"Yes," I say.

"I can make this happen," says Fat Tony. "Passes for all of you, tickets on the next train tonight, and even spending money for the bar car. But that's all I can give you. Your personal protection is your own. And you never knew me, *capasce?"*

"We understand," that's the little Italian I know.

"Joey!" Fat Tony yells to a lackey across the room. "Take these three up to the fifth floor to see Angelo. Tell him I said to do his best."

Joey's a short burly Italian who's about six inches shorter than me, but wider than Frank at the shoulders. He's the type of guy that could wrap his arms around you, lift you two feet off the floor and squeeze the air out of you before you could scream for help. He leads us further into the back of the store and into a freight elevator. Without speaking a word, he takes us up to the fifth floor. We get out and I'm blown away by the operation. There are large computers everywhere, with monitors, keyboard stations, and printers. Several wise guys are running around monitoring computer screens and calling out phrases in Italian. Joey leads us to Angelo.

"Tony says hook these guys up with passes and tickets to Penn Station tonight. Take special care of them." Joey walks away and I hope special care means good care, not the kind of special care where you end up dead in a trash dumpster.

Angelo looks us over and then yells across the room, "Ronnie. When's the last train to Penn Station go out tonight?"

"In about 23 minutes," he yells back.

"Mannaggia. That's not enough time," Angelo says under his breathe. "Ronnie," he yells, "Push it back about two hours."

Ronnie sits down at a computer station, types a few things into keyboard, and shouts back to Angelo, "That train now needs new brake pads on its rear car. It will buy you at least an hour and a half. I'll call our guy at the station and make sure they take their good ol' time." Ronnie wheels his chair over to a bay of phones and starts to call.

"Alright, here's the deal," says Angelo. "We don't use your real names or addresses, but you have to come up with the fake stuff so you can remember it if need be. We'll start with pictures. Who wants to go first?"

"One of you guys are going first," I say. "I got to do something with my hair." The boys roll their eyes at me as I head off to the bathroom. I look in the mirror and grimace at my hair just like I do every morning. It's a big huge curly mess. The quickest way to tame it is by finding a hat to wear, but then I'll always have to be wearing hats where ever I go. I open the vanity and find some Italian pomade. It should give me just enough weight in my hair to control it. After about a third of the can, all I managed to do is take out the frizz. It's not what I want, but I look more normal. It's respectable and I can fit in without being noticed.

I emerge from the bathroom and end up turning a few heads, including Frank's. One of the Italians at a computer desk whistles as I walk by. So much for not being noticed. I sit down for my picture and then we wait around for them to process. It seems like forever, but in less than 30 minutes from when we first started, we leave Fat Tony's with IDs, tickets, and German Marks. They actually did it in record time. I'm now Tricia Miller. Frank is Anthony Huefner and Mojmir is Vladimir Alexoff. We have about an hour and half until our train leaves so we head back to Mojmir's to make sure we have our plan ironed out.

"If we want protection," says Mojmir, "I have a PM stashed away somewhere."

"If there ends up being a metal detector then we're screwed," says Frank. "I say we take our chances without a gun."

"Maybe it's a good idea. We just got lucky with Fat Tony," I say. "If we didn't have that case of Vodka to negotiate with, we would have been dead."

"If any Nazi guard finds us with a gun, we'll be jailed and left there to rot," counters Frank.

"Only if we appear together," says Mojmir, "if we don't look like we're a group and the Nazis find a gun on me, then I'll be the only one to be hauled off. It's just on me. The Daughter of Time Travel can move on."

I think about this for a moment. I don't want to get caught with a gun, but Mojmir's willing to sacrifice his safety for ours. I'm not sure if I want this. First, I hate being indebted to anyone and second, what would this do for international U.S. – Soviet relations if he ends up sacrificing himself for me. Lastly, we need Mojmir? He's obviously more experienced than the two of us. Who knows where and when he's traveled to in his lifetime? He'll be useful in New Himmler City, or whatever it's called. We're better as a team.

"No guns," I say to Mojmir. "We need you too much. We have no idea what we're getting into and we'll need you to help us strategize as we go along. We don't have a plan after we get through the Swiss Bank. You're the man that got us to Fat Tony, I'm sure you'll be more than resourceful further down the line. We can't afford to lose you, and I'm not going to let you be captured by the Nazis to be tortured for eternity. We'll take our chances without fire arms. We've been able to survive this long without them, we don't need them now."

"Okay," says Mojmir. "Our train leaves in an hour. Let's get out of here."

Mojmir looks out of the peep hole in the door. I'm waiting for him to release the bolt so we can get out of this hellhole, but he just stands there staring. "We have a problem," he calmly explains. "There's a Nazi patrol right outside my door."

"Figures," exclaims Frank. "They went looking for Alex, then me, now they are waiting for you."

"We're trapped in her," I say. "There's only one way out and it's right into the lion's den. So much for Fat Tony's help."

"We should have never come back here," laments Frank. "We should have gone straight to the train station."

"Silly Americans," Mojmir smiles at us. "Do you really think I'd build this place with only one way in and out? Let's head back down to the shelter."

We follow Mojmir back to his room and into his Bon Jovi closet, closing the trap door behind us. We climb down the ladder and arrive back down in the bomb shelter.

"An old Russian military rule is to always have two options," Mojmir explains. "If this place had only one entrance, I'd be stuck. I think your expression is, 'Paint myself into a corner.' I knew that if a nuclear blast hit here for some reason, that one day I'd need a way out. That's why I built this out of an old subway station."

Mojmir leads us to the Northern edge of the shelter. Fastened to the floor-to-ceiling lead walls are a number of wardrobes. He opens one and begins to rummage through it. He passes black coats to Frank and me, "Here. It's going to get cold where we're going." Mojmir grabs one for himself. "Plus, it will help us blend in." I put mine on and catch a glimpse of what else is in the wardrobe: biohazard suits, tactical gear, rifles, guns, knives, you name it – Mojmir has it. A lot of it is new technology from 2085, which it a huge violation of International Time Travel laws. You're not allowed to bring any new technology back in time except your communicator.

Mojmir then closes that closet and opens the far one on the right. He steps in and motions for us to follow. We've actually stepped into a hallway. At the end is large metal door that looks more like a submarine hatch than a door. Mojmir flips a latch and disengages a bolt which runs into the ceiling and floor. He turns the wheel and pushes the door open. "This came off a Russian nuclear submarine," he proudly describes. "I put it on the outside of the shelter so if there was a blast, it would stand firm."

We step through the door and into a second small chamber with another metal door at the end. This one looks more like his apartment door with a horizontal bolt. Mojmir lifts the bolt out of the brackets and puts it aside. He reaches into his shirt, pulls out a key on a necklace, and unlocks the deadbolt. He opens the door and we step out onto an old subway platform. The door closes behind us and we're in the dark. Mojmir presses a button on his jacket and it begins to slightly glow, projecting enough light for us to see a few feet in front of us.

"Your jackets can do the same," he explains. "There's a switch in the inside left pocket." Frank and I light our jackets, too. The platform drops off to train tracks that lead uphill.

"These tracks go straight to Union Station," Mojmir points out. "All we need to do is follow them and then get on our train to New York City."

"It leaves in 45 minutes. How long of a walk is it from here to the station?" I ask.

"We're not walking," smiles Mojmir. He goes over to the far end of the platform and pulls back an old brown tarp to reveal a handcar. "Hop on."

"Both of us are going to have to pump that for at least 15 minutes straight," Frank complains. "I'm going to be exhausted when we get there."

"Don't worry, my friend," Mojmir announces. "The Russian has this covered." Mojmir reaches into his jacket and pulls out a black box with a wheel on one side and a key on the other. Mojmir winds the key as far as it goes. He clicks the box into place on the bottom of the handcar and readjusts the chain so it wraps around the wheel.

"Is that a sonic generator?" Frank asks. "Those haven't been invented, yet,"

I recognize the box as top end technology that is still being theorized in 2085. It's a mini generator that's powered by sonic energy. The key actually winds a rubber band that slowly releases a high pitched sonic wave. The wave is converted to kinetic energy that can power any machine it's hooked up to.

"The Russians keep a lot of secrets," Mojmir grins. "Where the nuclear bombs are pointed is just one of them. I have lots more."

"Well, thankfully, the Russians are on the forefront of Sonic Engineering," I commend.

"Hang on everyone," Mojmir flips a switch. The mini generator engages and we're off, traveling about 25 miles per hour along the train tracks.

"At this rate, we'll be there in minutes," Frank exclaims.

"You can thank the Russian scientific community later," laughs Mojmir.

NINE

I feel like I'm in a scene right out of *Indiana Jones and The Last Crusade*. It was the summer blockbuster of 1989 and here I am reliving the moment where Indy and his dad are the only Americans in Berlin and they get on the German blimp.

Except I'm standing at Train Track number 62 instead of a blimp, with Mojmir instead of Sean Connery, and planning on going to New Himmler instead of New Jersey.

We are waiting on Frank. Mojmir and I ditched the handcar on a deserted track while he went ahead. Mojmir thought it would be a good idea for us to learn as much as we could about the current time. So he sent Frank off to a newsstand to pick up as many newspapers and magazines that seemed appropriate for him to carry. At first, Frank was convinced that it was all going to be Nazi propaganda and a waste of our money, but Mojmir insisted we needed to assess the world around us. Then Frank remembered one of the things his college hockey coach always said was to know your environment. If you want to win at your enemy's hockey rink, you gotta know what the fans are going to throw at you when you're on the ice. Apparently Canadian hockey fans are pretty brutal because Frank says he's been hit in the head by many D cell batteries and lived to tell about it.

I admit that Mojmir and Frank have a good point. We have to know what we're up against. So while I'm waiting for him, I start to look around and take it all in. The train station itself doesn't look much different. It was built in 1907 and the construction is totally pre-World War II. The lighting is a bit different, lots of cheap halogen lighting – think warehouse or high school gym - so it casts a weird yellow-green haze everywhere. The biggest difference is the clothing. Things are cut the same way as they were back in 1989, baggy pants, loose tops, tight lines. But the sexual overtones are completely gone and everything is gray or earth tones. No bright Day-Glo colors anywhere. In fact, nothing has any color to it whatsoever. It's like film noir on a rainy day.

The other thing that's missing is the hustle and bustle of any major city. It doesn't matter where you are on the globe, a large metropolis has a hum to it. It's alive and breathing on its own. There are sounds that almost seem animated and the people don't just saunter somewhere, they strut to where they're going. They are important and every resident thinks their city is the epicenter of the world.

But the city I'm in feels like one of those small towns that used to be a crossroads between two other important towns then got bypassed with a new freeway. No one walks with purpose. No one has any energy. It seems no one wants to be here, but have no means to leave. It's depressing.

I can't wait for us to leave this place because I think it's slowly changing us. Mojmir has been pretty quiet since we've left his apartment. He's definitely a fish out of water. Think "Slash died and woke up in Aryan hell." Every boy and man has tight crew cuts, parted to the side, and oiled down. Mojmir's frizzy hair stands six inches off his head, hangs over his shoulders to his chest and is so long in the back it almost touches his butt. We considered dressing him as a girl, but he would have none of it. Mentioned something about refusing to look like the cover of *Look What The Cat Dragged In*. We wanted to cut it, but again he refused. So now I'm left standing with Ted Nugent on the train station, sticking out like a sore thumb.

Frank finally shows up with a handful of newspapers: *New Himmler Times*, *Nazi America Today*, *Adolf Post*, but also some recognizable names – *Boston Globe*, *Baltimore Sun*, and *The Atlanta Journal*.

"I guess the Nazi's didn't change everything," I say.

"Reading material for the train," Frank directs as he passes them out, two to each person. "We'll read through them, report back and give a data dump when we get to New York City."

"I want *Nazi America Today* and the *Baltimore Sun*," argues Mojmir, "English is my second language and I need the easy reading."

"Sure," says Frank as he switches them around, "The train

leaves in 15 minutes. Let's get on and settle in."

"We should see if we can get a private car," I say. "That way Ted Nugent doesn't call so much attention."

"Listen," says Mojmir, "I haven't cut my hair in twenty years, I don't plan to for a bunch of tight ass Nazis."

"Well, then we're going to need to get you a hat or a wig or something," offers Frank. "Because this isn't *Headbanger's Ball* anymore. We have to figure out a way for you to fit in."

We get on the train and it doesn't look that bad. Apparently the Nazis pride themselves with technological innovations in transportation. While the upholstery is a bit bland, the train as a whole is well-crafted. We move to the back cars and find a private car. We settle in and start reading our newspapers. As the train pulls out of the station, the conductor raps his knuckles on the door. After a moment, he enters.

"Tickets," he announces and holds out his hands. We all pass our tickets to him. He inspects them, punches them, and hands them back. He stares at us for a few moments, waiting. He spots Mojmir and is taken aback a bit. Then continues staring at the rest of us.

I have no idea what the etiquette here is. Do we tip him? Have we been caught? Is he just stalling until the Gestapo get here?

"Papers?" he asks.

We all pull out our identification, freshly minted by Fat Tony. The conductor makes a cursory pass at my papers and Frank's, but pauses on Mojmir.

"Vladmir," he says to Mojmir, using the fake name on his papers. "You seem to be a long way from home."

"I'm spending time with family," Mojmir explains.

"Well we have standards here, even in this god-forsaken colony of America. Cut your hair," he commands. "You look like an animal. Like a dirty, starving Soviet bear."

Mojmir looks more like the cover of *Cat Scratch Fever*, but I'm not going to correct the conductor. The guy hands back his papers. We've passed the test.

"Enjoy your ride," he says, but obviously doesn't really

mean it. "We arrive in Penn Station in 3 hours." The conductor steps back into the hallway and closes our door. We breathe a collective sigh of relief.

"I swear to God, the first wig shop or barbershop we find you're going into," argues Frank, "and for your sake, I hope we find a wig shop. Because any Nazi barber is going to cut you so close that you'll be a skinhead."

"I hate skinheads," chuckles Mojmir. "We better find a wig shop. Because if we hit a barbershop, the both of you will get your hair cut along with me. We'll all look like Hitler wannabes." He kicks up his feet on the couch across from him, opens up a paper and begins reading. Frank dives into his reading as well. So it's either look out the window at the debilitating shacks of houses, or get to my reading assignments. My hope is the that the newspapers are less depressing. Unfortunately, I have the two thickest newspapers, *The New Himmler Times* and *The Adolf Post* – both former New York City papers.

An hour later, I'm the last to finish the reading. Mojmir and Frank have been occupying their time with some Russian card game called Durak. Mojmir has been easily winning. As I fold up my newspapers and put them away, Mojmir beats him again.

"You silly Canadians," laughs Mojmir. "All you're good for is Maple Syrup and Hockey. And we even kick your butt at hockey."

"Thank goodness you guys have one of the biggest land masses in the world. You need that much space to make room for your egos," jokes back Frank.

"Are you boys done with your pissing match?" I ask. "Because we have some serious stuff to talk about. I'm mean, unless you want me to bring the conductor back in here. I'm sure he can explain how the Nazis are the superior race."

"Alright Princess of Time," smiles Mojmir. "You're the serious one. No more fun and games for the Commie and the Canuck. What'd you find out from your newspapers?"

I can be fun, but this is no time to argue that. We begin our data dump and determine that the Germans have totally manipulated time and we're in some type of amalgamation of World War II and modern day 1989. It's a complete alternate reality. But we've only been able to piece a few things together about this reality and how it came about. All the papers are filled with Nazi propaganda, a lot of the articles are just reprints from the German News Organization, or GNO. But there are some facts we've been able to determine.

First off, World War II ended much differently. When America focused its efforts towards Japan and put its resources in the Pacific, Japan continued to attack our Western shore. We had to put every ounce of energy against defeating the Japanese, and we weren't able to lend a hand helping Europe. After Germany conquered France, they decided to leave Britain alone and instead attacked our Eastern shores.

With all our military in California, Oregon and Washington, we couldn't move them quickly enough to defend our Eastern cities. One by one Germany bombed the Atlantic shore to smithereens, taking Boston, New York City, Charleston, and eventually Washington, D.C. – all within a month's time. As our ships left the Pacific and tried to come around Cape Hope to fight in the Atlantic, Japan attacked Seattle, San Francisco and Los Angeles, all at once. When our fleets reached the Atlantic shores, the Nazis were waiting for them and crushed us. Then the German Army marched West, and the Japanese East until they met at the Mississippi.

But Germany wouldn't share their new colony with the Japanese. So to demonstrate their rule over all of America, and to subjugate the Japanese, they took one of their newly developed nuclear bombs and dropped it on Denver. After the destruction of one of the biggest U.S. cities west of the Mississippi, they gave us a simple choice: all of America must submit to the Nazi power, or die. We unequivocally surrendered. Germany fortified its strength and made America its largest colony.

Conversely, the Soviets supported the remaining allies in Europe, aligning with the British Isles, Norway, Turkey, Israel and others. Germany focused their hatred against the Soviets, much like the Americans did during the Cold War. No wonder the conductor didn't trust Mojmir.

In the fifties, Germany moved their attention to the Middle East and dominated the oil producing countries like Iraq, Iran, and Syria. Over time, Germany became the world's sole superpower, controlling interests and resources in many parts of the world. They held half of Europe, parts of the Middle East and Pacific-Rim, and most of North America. It seemed in many cases they were one step ahead of history, and exchanged their manipulated time for reality.

"What amazes me is how quickly these changes were made," observes Mojmir. "A Level Five Temporal Shift should take years; there would have been signs, aberrations, smaller shifts. Many inspectors should have noticed over a several year spread. Level Five's don't happen with the flip of the switch."

"What confuses me is the length of the shift," adds Frank. "Think about it, the Fritz Lang movie, that was made when?"

"1927," I say.

"Exactly, the aberrations started over fifty years ago. Fifty years!" continues Frank. "It's been five decades without any course correction, from a simple change in war tactics. I just don't get it. Temporal Gravitation Pull should have righted itself by at least 1952."

"It could go even further back," adds Mojmir.

"What do you mean?" I ask.

"All we know is what we saw from the Madonna video that was reflective of 1927. The aberrations could have started much earlier, say 1910, 1890. Did anyone read a reference to an American Civil War? This could have started before 1850!"

"This temporal time shift could be over a century old," says Frank.

We all knew what happens the longer a Level Five Temporal Shift continues. VanVliet Theory states a shift can happen that's so divisive that temporal space actually splits, being forced into two separate gravitational pulls. Common analysis might surmise two different times are created or alternative destinies, within space. But that's not what VanVliet concludes. He believes that time starts to split backwards until it reaches its core, much like a lightning bolt splits a tree in two. And once temporal mass is split, it explodes with a force greater than anything the universe has ever seen. Well, except for the Big Bang.

"Guys," I say, "If this continues, it can destroy not only temporal space, but the universe as we know it."

We sit in silence for a few moments, taking it all in. We're talking end of the world scenario here. Why would the Nazis want that? I know they are crazy, but destruction of the universe is really not a "win" situation for them.

"Well," claims Mojmir, "You're the Daughter of Time, looks like it's on your shoulders to fix it." Mojmir stretches out his feet and yawns. "I'm taking a nap. Wake me up when you have a plan and we get into Penn Station." He closes his eyes and starts to snore loudly.

"Any ideas?" I ask Frank.

"Mojmir's right. If I'm going to be alert in New York City, I need to get some rest. I'm sure you'll be able to figure something out." Frank moves some of the cushions around and takes a similar position as our Russian friend.

The two men are quickly asleep and it's up to me to solve our big problems. As we make a brief stop in Philadelphia, I pause to consider the irony of being in the city that birthed our freedom while I try to come up with a plan on how to free us from Nazi rule.

We pull out of the station and I try to figure out how one woman can overthrow the German political machine and an army with unimaginable strength. I'm not a political leader, or a field general. I'm simply a time inspector. I'm a girl that's done a lot of research and can observe things to see if they changed.

I look out my window and see hundreds of tents, shacks, and make shift barns dotted along the countryside. These are the houses of American families trying to get away from city life, the everyday control of the Nazis. Who knows how warm they stay in their houses or what type of electricity they have to read by at night? I imagine their world is very much like pioneer days, farming the land and using whatever they can to feed and clothe their families. They have not let the Nazis beat them down. They are resilient and have figured a way to survive.

Americans have always been the masters of their own destiny – that's our culture's constant. If that's true, then I'm in charge of my own fate. I can change this, can't I?

I look down at Frank and across to Mojmir and they are completely out. "Looks like you two had a tough day," I say knowing they can't hear me. "You're sleeping like babies."

"Some babies don't sleep well," snickers Mojmir. He opens his eyes and smiles at me.

"You've been awake this whole time?" I question.

"I'm a very light sleeper," he explains. "When you put in as much time on the job as I have, your body learns to always be on alert. You never know when you have to move from just observing to taking action. I never slept in Auschwitz. In fact, I haven't slept much since. Just a nap here and there. Close my eyes for a while. Sleep leads to dreams, dreams lead to nightmares."

"How old are you?" I ask.

"I'm wise beyond my years, and I'm very, very old," grins Mojmir. "I've seen ages and ages of time over the decades. Things I want to forget. Things I can't."

"How'd you keep going?"

"At first, it was easy," he says, "but then over time it became tougher and tougher. You learn to live your life in isolation. Not because it makes the job any easier, it's for your own personal self-defense."

"I can't do that," I reply. "I have to have some connection."

"Human connection?" he laughs. "Frank's just about your only real human connection. And from what I hear, you keep your distance."

"What's that supposed to mean?" I challenge.

"You've been here for five years… you don't go to movies with him, concerts, hockey games, whatever. You keep your distance."

"I'm being professional," I argue.

"You're isolating yourself," Mojmir explains matter-of-factly. "Just like I do, like we all do…. Like your father does."

"All you know about my father is what you read," I snap back somewhat defensively.

Uncomfortable silence fills the air. Mojmir called me out and I don't like it. So what if I've lived my life on my own for five years? I'm all I can trust. I'm all I can rely on.

"You know, I've met him," Mojmir says softly.

"My father?" I'm shocked. "You met my father?"

"Yes," confirms Mojmir. "I heard him speak once at Leningrad University. He was discussing some of the finer points of Temporal Gravity Theory, explaining how an object could re-enter at different points in time rather than return to its original state."

"Yes. The Law of Return," I say rolling my eyes. "Trust me, I know it well."

"Exactly – the Law of Return," Mojmir confirms. "Now I agree with most of Evistonian Physics. For example, obviously once you time travel you become an independent mass and anything that happens to your past doesn't have any effect on you now. I actually had an enemy from Afghanistan go back in time and kill my father before I was born and I'm still here. So I'm living proof that theory is correct."

"Yes, yes, the Law of Independent Mass," I agree, "I used teach it as a graduate assistant. It doesn't matter what your grandfather discovered, did, or changed, life will continue on and eventually the same thing will be discovered, the same action will be done, or the same element will be changed.

"But the Law of Return," Mojmir hesitates, "I believe some of his theories are quite not as accurate so after his lecture I told him I saw some fallacies in his work."

"You told my father he was wrong?" I'm shocked. No one questions my father, not even my mom did.

Mojmir chuckles. "Remember, before your dad came along everyone thought Einstein was right. It was your dad that questioned his theories. What's so wrong about me questioning your father?"

"I can buy that argument," I acquiesce. "But you and I are sitting here right now in a different time, how could my dad be wrong?"

"I'm not questioning time travel in general," says Mojmir. "I'm just questioning the process."

"What do you mean?" Now he's caught my curiosity.

"When you've done this job as long as I have, you've seen and experienced things that you never thought possible," Mojmir whispers. "Do you really think governments established inspectors to avoid small simple aberrations? What's the big deal of an aberration if we know it's going to pull back together?"

"What do you mean?" I question.

"There are some out there who think we have more control over our future than your father theorized we do, that we have our own personal destiny. We control our own future, not temporal gravity."

"Well, if that's the case, then how is it that history reverts back over time? How is it that you can remove one or two things and decades later it's all the same?"

"That's the billion dollar question," Mojmir smiles. "One that maybe the Nazis are trying to figure out. Maybe they've theorized a way to change time forever."

Mojmir yawns and nestles himself back into the corner of his couch. "Just remember, young one," he yawns again. "You are in charge of your own future – not some gravitational pull."

I lean back thinking about his sage advice. He's been around the block a million times. Maybe he's right. Maybe my dad doesn't know everything. But then again, my dad's theories have been tested over and over again. All I know is that I'm going somewhere. Is it temporal gravity that's taking me there? I have no idea. For now, I close my eyes and fall asleep.

TEN

An hour later we pull into Penn Station and I'm woken by Mojmir.

"Seems like you got a little comfortable," he says to me with a sly Russian grin.

I look around and realize I had snuggled up to Frank and fell asleep with my head resting on his shoulder.

"He took all the cushions," I blush. "How else was I going to get comfortable?"

"Sure and I'm next in line to be the Russian czar," laughs Mojmir. "You should wake him up. We need to get out of here as soon as possible, just in case the Nazis are looking for us at the train platform. We can't have anyone see us on our way to the Swiss Bank."

I nudge Frank who gets up groggily. He stretches and asks, "What's the plan after the Swiss Bank?"

Was he awake the whole time? Did he hear Mojmir's and my conversation about falling asleep in his lap? We're at war now and both Frank and I have to stay focused. We can't afford to be wasting our time wondering about flirtatious comments from one another.

"I have some connections in Chinatown," says Mojmir, "or I used to. I was friendly with the Chinese Inspector in town. I'd come to visit, get great Chinese food, and drink Mao Tai jiu until the sun came up."

"So we'll get to the Swiss Bank, get a stash of money, and look up your friend in Chinatown," I say.

"Sounds like a solid plan," confirms Frank, "Let's go."

Frank's the first one off the train. We figure he fits in the most and maybe the less likely to get noticed. Plus, he mentioned something about being best in class in his "Recon" training, and he stepped off the train before really asking Mojmir or me anyway.

We watch him through the train window. After a few moments, Frank waves us on to follow. I step onto the platform. One would expect Penn Station to be fairly clean and well kept, even for a New York City train station. But this place is disgusting. Trash piled high to the ceiling, covered with huge rats and cockroaches the size of baby shoes. Water leaks from the ceiling, and pools in cracks speckled across the floor. Foul smell seems to radiate from everywhere, fouler than the usual urine filled subways. It stinks. Worse yet, no one else is sickened by it. They all go about their business as if they expect it to be that way, as if this is daily life for them. I look at Mojmir and he's turning a bit green.

"This is what London smelled like during The Great Plague," he explains, trying to keep down what's in his stomach.

"There's a staircase to street level," Frank points. "Let's get out of here."

We emerge from the underground onto 7th Avenue just south of 31st Street and I immediately feel like heading back down to the train and going home to D.C. The stench up here isn't any better than down below. Trash is strewn everywhere. It fills up the gutters and sewers, overflows every trash dumpster, and is piled high in every vacant area. I look around and see a city in ruins.

Hotel Pennsylvania is barely discernible. The north half of the building has been bombed and is gone. It looks like a huge Lego set that hasn't been completed. Windows are missing or shattered and the entrance way is boarded up with rubble and broken wood. As we head up 7th and circle around it, we can see right into the building. The destruction goes up diagonally to the roof about 20 floors and at the top, it makes its way to the center of the building.

The hotel is now being used as an apartment building and you can see right into everyone's unit. The tenants are using the open rooms as living quarters, with destroyed walls as balconies with a view. Tattered clothing hangs from rope as people try to dry them. I see a mother preparing a meal of potatoes and lettuce while a baby cries at her feet. Blue tarps shelter one apartment that doesn't even have a roof. A few kids play catch in one open room, far too close to the edge for my comfort.

Macy's across the street is not much different. A bomb has destroyed its outside southern wall giving view to a whole open floor of apartments. People have stacked up whatever they could to create their own living space, using shelving units, mannequins, and display cases. In some instances, they've piled the garbage to the ceiling to get some privacy. Those that have their space on the edge of the building don't have protection from the weather. Those on the inside are safe from the storms, but sacrifice any light. Parts of the building have collapsed, and somehow tenants have made those crushed beams and concrete their homes as well.

Many of the buildings we pass have also been bombed, being left with crumbling facades, stone rubble piles, and protruding steel girders. Garbage continues to be piled up everywhere.

There is a defining silence to the city. No traffic, no hum of engines, honking of horns, or clickity-clack of dress shoes on concrete.

The people we pass by have faces of despair. Even the youth look as if they are aged decades beyond their years. They all shuffle down the street, dragging their heels as they walk slowly through the drudgery of their life. There are no smiles. No hope. They are just going through the actions. Walking to somewhere to do something. Quiet sheep, meandering to their destination, never looking up, staring at their feet.

This city has no pulse; it is dead.

As we reach 34th and Fifth Avenue, I see a new shocking sight. The Empire State Building is gone. What was once a glimmering shiny steel marvel and the tallest building in the world is now a pile of rubble, twisted metal, concrete, and glass that rises only five stories from the street. It used to be the jewel of Midtown Manhattan. It's now a memory and constant symbol of Nazi destruction to those who live here.

The Big Apple was hit hard. Evidence of air raids is everywhere. On one block there's a pristine building, and on the next a pile of metal and concrete. We need to walk up to 50th Street where the Swiss Bank Tower is, and now I wonder if it even still exists.

But as destiny would have it, the Swiss Bank Tower has been untouched. The common observer would think this was luck, a miracle, or even coincidence. But I know better. It has to do with the Swiss. It's their temporal nature to remain forever neutral as the other historic super powers battle it out. Germans would never bomb their buildings, they need the Swiss.

You see, each country has its own temporal pull as well. In graduate school, I took a class under a well-known Professor Tim Spradling. Professor Spradling was not a Temporal Engineer, but was housed in the Department of Arts and Science. His area of expertise was rather unique, studying both History and Social Psychology to better understand the trends complete cultures had over time.

He developed a theory that became widely accepted called the Cultural Destiny Theory. This states that a set of people held together by cultural ancestry maintains the same trajectory of fate. Much like temporal gravity pulls events in a specific direction, cultures are pulled as well.

For example, Chinese ancestry can be traced all the way back to *Homo erectus* Peking Man. These fossils were discovered outside of Beijing, along with evidence of fire, animals, tools, and most importantly the manufacturing of tools. Comparing the carbon data to similar fossils in Georgia, Africa, Indonesia, and India, the Peking Man was much more developed in terms of tool usage than his counterparts.

This advanced behavior is very typical of Chinese culture throughout history. They were the first to develop gunpowder, the compass, papermaking, printing, the wheelbarrow, the suspension bridge, and advancements in medicine. They are certainly a country, and people, to be respected and admired.

Some would claim that the Chinese succeeded beyond others because they had money and power to do so, but the Cultural Destiny Theory states they are being pulled in that direction by temporal gravity. China will always have a preferential state compared to others, no matter what the circumstance or what happens with a temporal shift.

Spradling identified other cultures with similar fates: the United States, Soviets, Germans, Romans, the Egyptians, along with the Chinese, have shown unique superiority over the course of time. Other countries have opposite fates: Afghanistan, Somalia, and Zimbabwe will always end up with misfortune or a poor outcome no matter how the cards of time get shuffled. They are just unlucky.

One culture that has been studied in great detail from a temporal perspective is Switzerland. This country's destiny is to remain neutral in all situations. No matter what occurs or changes there are in time, this culture will not take sides. They maintain the same demeanor and attitudes towards all superpowers and counties, dealing with the Nazis the same way they deal with the Soviets.

Because of this, countries have used them as their bank over the course of time. It's been a great way to exchange money through temporal space. In fact, it's how I get paid every two weeks. In addition to direct deposits from 2085 to whatever year you live in, most countries set up an emergency account so an Inspector can withdraw any sum of money and it's credited to the corresponding country. That's the account we're going to tap into. We'll take the money to Mojmir's friend in Chinatown and find safe passage to Canada.

The first floor of the Swiss Bank Tower used to be Saks Fifth Avenue. Today it's a textile factory that makes all the drab clothing we've seen since the Level Five Temporal Shift. We pass by the factory entrance, take the stairs to the upper level, and enter the Swiss Bank.

ELEVEN

We pull open large wooden doors to reveal a dimly lit hallway gilded in gold leafing. Fine Italian marble is laid on the floor in diamond patterns, leading your eye towards the opposite end. Beautiful oak paneling covers the walls with carvings of Swiss lore. The panels on the left side depict a scene of a long passage way carved between two stone mountains. The section closest to us shows a military man falling off a horse with an arrow sticking from his chest, and at the far end is a large strong man aiming a crossbow.

"William Tell," I say. "He led Switzerland's independence."

On the right side is a stone bridge high above a winding river. Standing at the opposite shore is a fiery but cowering devil lifting a boulder into the sky with an old feeble woman holding a wooden cross in his path.

"Teufelsbrücke," I acknowledge, "Devil's Bridge."

Both Frank and Mojmir look at me oddly. "And you know this, how?" asks Frank.

"I took Swiss Culture as an elective in undergrad. There was a cute boy in my dorm room who took it and I tagged along," I explained. "Never thought I'd put it to use."

"Congratulations," says Mojmir, "You just correctly identified two old wooden carvings worth more than all our yearly salaries combined."

At the end of the hallway is a marble desk with an older white-haired gentleman sitting at it. He stares at us with disdain and doesn't speak until we are right at the edge of his desk.

"Are you lost?" he asked.

The three of us had thought long and hard about this moment. We knew that the gatekeeper would consider us citizens of the current time since we were dressed as ones. The quickest way to identify oneself as an Inspector is to provide the gatekeeper with your bank account number.

Two things we had to consider. First, which of our bank accounts should we use? Mine was absolutely out of the question as the U.S. emergency bank account probably doesn't exist. Equally, providing Frank's bank account didn't make sense because his account relies on U.S. sharing time travel with Canada. This most likely hasn't happened since the Nazi's now control the U.S.'s particle accelerator. On Mojmir's recommendation, we decided the safest bet is to use his account.

The second thing we needed to consider is whether or not the Swiss Bank actually works in this temporal space as it did in our historic temporal space. This we would not know until we actually attempted a withdrawal on an account. If we were refused, no foul no harm. If we were approved, well then, we're in the money.

"If you are lost," the gatekeeper says, "then I can have you escorted back down to the factory."

"Six five two, seven nine eight, twenty-two, twenty-two, A, four, twelve," exclaims Mojmir.

"Excuse me?" he questioned.

"You heard me gatekeeper," Mojmir stated, "Let us in."

The gatekeeper pushed a button on the desk.

"Access granted," spoke an automated voice from the desk.

"You can go in," says the gatekeeper, "but they need to stay behind."

"Nyet!" Mojmir says boldly, "They come with me."

The gatekeeper scowled, got up, and walked up to the gold doors several steps behind his desk. Carved in each door was a large mountain.

"That's Monte Rosa," I say, "and that's Dom."

"Stop it," whispers Frank, "you're freaking me out."

The gatekeeper places a key into one of the door locks and turns it. He bangs three times, pauses, and bangs again twice. The doors push in from the outside.

"Go down the hall and make the second turn on your right. You'll come to a desk. Speak with Fadri." The gatekeeper turned around and sat back down at his desk as if we weren't there anymore. As we step into the hallway, the doors slowly close behind us.

The new hallway is more spectacular than the previous one.

Stained glass windows on both sides reflect in color lights of the Swiss Alps. The fine Italian marble walkway continues, and throughout the hallway are several golden doorways, each with a carving of a different mountain dwarf adorning its entranceway.

We find the second right and turn into a smaller hallway that continues in elegance. This time the stained glass has been replaced with murals of expressionist art - dark and rich colors creating emotionally powerful images.

"Paul Klee," I say.

"Enough with the Swiss culture stuff," says Mojmir, "You win. You're the smart one."

I smile, "It's not about winning, it's about knowing more than you two."

"That sounds a lot like winning," jests Frank.

At the end of this hallway, sits a man at a desk. Remarkably, both look exactly like the man and desk we just left.

"Either this guy is his twin or all Swiss look alike," jokes Frank, whispering under his breathe.

This man stares at us with same exact distain until we are about foot away from him. I assume he's Fadri. I let the Russian do all the talking.

Mojmir rattles off the account number, "Six five two, seven nine eight, twenty-two, twenty-two, A, four, twelve."

"Clarifying statement?" asks Fadri.

Every Inspector account number has the common final numbers: twelve. As to ensure authenticity, the Swiss and the account holder agree to a clarifying statement to help identify the proper owner. It's kind of like a secret code, and I can't wait to hear Mojmir's.

Mojmir turns to the two of us, pauses, and then turns back to Fadri and mumbles something.

"I'm sorry, sir," Fadri says loudly, "You'll need to speak up. I can't hear you."

Mojmir sighs then begins his clarifying statement, "Look at this stuff. Isn't it neat? Wouldn't you think my collection's complete? Wouldn't you think I'm the girl, the girl who has everything?"

Fadri pushes a button on his desk. "Clarifying statement confirmed on account six five two, seven nine eight, twenty-two, twenty-two, A, four, twelve. Okay to proceed."

Fadri steps from his desk and leads us around the corner to a bank of elevators.

"Aren't you a little old for *The Little Mermaid*?" says Frank.

"I have a thing for Disney movies," confesses Mojmir.

We step into the elevator. It's definitely 2085 technology. The floors, ceiling, and walls are made of titanium glass injected with seawater. Living within the seawater are millions of two distinct bioluminescence creatures that are normally found deep below the ocean's surface. These creatures give off a whitish-blue glow, very similar to mid-day sun, and put off enough lumens to light the entire elevator. They are some of the heartiest animals on the planet and survive through a symbiotic relationship, feeding off each other's waste. No need to change any light bulbs.

Another technological advance is the understanding and use of sound. It started with voice activation. For example, there are no buttons in this elevator. It's all controlled by voice command. Physicists at Stanford thought there were more exciting aspects to sound than just machines reacting to humans. They discovered the inherit power of sound waves and how it could be used for many things. Most of the research when I left the future centered around how different sounds could alter human mood. That's why the elevator is pumping the sound of a low humming whales through its speakers. Studies show this is one of the most calming and relaxing sounds to the human ears.

While the whale sounds are comforting, I'll feel more at ease once we have money in our hands and are far away from the Swiss. There's something about them that gives me the creeps.

"Account six five two, seven nine eight, twenty-two, twenty-two, A, four, twelve," declares Fadri.

"Account six five two, seven nine eight, twenty-two,

twenty-two, A, four, twelve," says a soothing female voice. "Level 3."

We're ready to move upwards, when the elevator suddenly dips downward.

"The vaults are in the basement," explains Fadri.

The ride is smooth, quick, but light as a feather, using 2085 technology. Transportation is all about the displacement of air using sound waves. We're not traveling on a cable, or magnetically propelling ourselves through a concrete tunnel. We're rebalancing our physical space against the air molecules we're going towards. Basically, someone from the past would think we were flying. It's the simplest, quickest, and most efficient way to travel. We are three floors down within seconds.

"Welcome to the Velvet Floor," says Fadri, but in an unwelcoming voice. The doors open quickly and we are once again met with opulence. Everything is covered in velvet: brown velvet carpet, red velvet draping on the wall. I reach out to touch a drape and it's the smoothest cloth I've ever touched.

Fadri walks us down the hall to a door marked, Twelve Accounts, and leads us in. There is an oak table with six high back chairs.

"How much would you like to withdraw?" asks Fadri.

"The equivalent of 300,000 rubles in current currency," explains Mojmir.

"Wait here," instructs Fadri as he steps out of the room and the door click shut.

"You know what I like about banking with the Swiss?" Frank turns to Mojmir and eyes him oddly, "It's like you get your money for nothing."

Mojmir's eyes dart around the room and for a brief moment he smiles but returns to a casual demeanor, "Yes, but even though I work hard for my money, I still feel like I'm living on a prayer."

Why are Frank and Mojmir quoting 80s songs about money? What are they hinting at? I catch Frank's attention and his eyes quickly dart to the corner of the ceiling then back at me. I look up and notice a small camera pointed on us. We're obviously being monitored.

Much time passes as we sit and wait for Fadri to come back. Frank and Mojmir amuse themselves by quoting more 80s rock songs while I take a look around the room. Except for the table, chairs, and shag carpet, the whole room is velvet. Who makes a whole room, a whole floor, out of velvet? The Swiss do, that's who. They are strange people. It's obvious they're taking their good old time getting our money.

"How long does it take to withdraw 300,000 rubles?" Mojmir banters, "Are they counting it by abacus?"

Math comes easy to anyone involved in Temporal Science, and as an inspector you have to study Temporal Science, Physics, History, and Criminology. It's a very demanding field to get into and many people take electives along the way so they can flaunt their knowledge.

Which is one of the other reasons I took Swiss Culture. Did I know that I'd be holed up with a Russian and Canadian in the basement of a Swiss bank one day? No. But I knew that at some point in my life I'd have some interaction with the Swiss, and have an opportunity to impress someone.

"Did you know the Swiss had many famous mathematicians?" I ask.

"Here we go," sighs Frank. "Please, begin this afternoon's lecture."

"They had a revered School of Mathematics at the University of Basel," I add. "There were many great mathematicians and physicists that graduated from there. One of the most famous was Leonhard Euler who developed several of theories of mechanics on which my father based his early work. We actually traveled one summer to the Berlin Academy where Euler did a majority of his deepest research on the topic."

Then it hit me. The Swiss are highly influenced by three other cultures: Italian, French, and German. This is a trap.

"Guys," I say as I get up. "We've got to get out of here."

"What are you talking about," says Mojmir, "We don't have

our money."

"We're not going to get our money," I explain. "They're not counting it. They are keeping us waiting as prisoners until the Nazis get here."

"The Swiss are neutral," reminds Frank.

"The Swiss have German blood, they are part of their culture," I continue to explain, "Remember all those bank accounts they kept for the Nazis during World War II? I'm telling you, they are aligned with the Nazis."

"We are not prisoners, all they are doing is monitoring us," argues Frank. "Watch, we can leave at any time." Frank gets up and tries the door. It's locked shut. "Damn it," yells Frank. "How long have we been sitting here?"

"Long enough for them to alert the Nazis and for them to send a unit to apprehend us," Mojmir pulls out his PM, loads it, and pulls back the slide. "They ain't gonna take this commie alive."

"I thought we said to leave the guns at home," I say.

"You want to argue whether that was a good idea or not now?" smiles Mojmir.

With a running start, Frank gives the door a strong shoulder, checks it as if it was a hockey player, and he busts through.

Mojmir joins him in the hallway and yells back, "We're clear, no Nazis."

As I step through the threshold sirens go blazing through the whole floor.

"Fräulein," commands a voice with a thick German accent over some type of loudspeaker system. "We have you trapped. There is only one way out, the elevators. We will be down to capture you momentarily. Your companions will die."

Stanford sound wave researchers also determined that thick German accents were the most annoying accents in all of Europe.

"This way," says Mojmir who starts heading in the direction opposite the elevators.

"You're going the wrong way," argues Frank. "The only

way out is the elevators. If we can get on them before the Nazis do, we can take them to roof and find a way out of here."

Mojmir grabs us both and pulls us in his direction. "My specialty, besides Music History, is Urban Archeology," he explains, practically dragging us down the hallway. "Most major cities are layered with several different levels of history. They have caverns and catacombs that cross over and run parallel to each other in places you'd never expect. New York City is just like that, you never know where a subway line may be or how close another building or catacomb is when you're underground. It may be right next to you and you'd never know it. We're not going up, we're going over. All we need to do is find an exterior wall."

The hallway ends and we suddenly stop. Mojmir examines the wall with his hands.

"Cold brick is behind this velvet," he claims, "This is it." Mojmir reaches into his pocket and pulls out a compass.

"North, we're facing towards Fiftieth Street. I was hoping for Madison Avenue, but I don't think we have a lot of time."

"I can't bust down that wall like I did the door," says Frank. "I hope you got a plan Mojmir."

The sirens change to a piercing tone and the ability to think is becoming more and more difficult. Even with my hands over my ears, my body naturally begins to crouch down at my knees from the pain.

"Fräulein," says the German voice blaring over the sirens, "There is no chance for escape. Surrender now and we may let your companions die quickly instead of being tortured."

"I think we have an alternative," Mojmir yells as he pulls from his pocket two small discs. "These are seismic explosive plates – high end Russian technology." Mojmir affixes the two plates to the wall about 3 feet from each other. "They work like an earthquake does, but much more concentrated and directional, focusing their destructive energy forward and away from you. All you do is set the trigger, wait 10 seconds and KA-BOOM."

"Well," yells back Frank, "I can't take this pain much longer. Set the trigger and let's hope there's something beyond this wall."

Mojmir presses buttons on both discs and we step back several paces waiting for impact. I brace myself towards the ground, cowering from the piercing siren and anticipating the explosion ahead. Out of the corner of my eye, I see the Nazis at the end of the hallway. They are yelling for me, but I can no longer hear them over the sirens. They aim and shoot.

Bullets start flying past us as a huge explosion emits from the wall and shocks the whole hallway. There's light coming from the hole so we head in that direction. We duck our heads and enter a catacomb of some sort. The sirens are fading away, but we know the Nazis are reloading their guns and will follow us through the hole.

As we climb out of the catacombs into a chamber, Mojmir grabs my hand and stops me. He turns to Frank.

"You must keep her safe. The Daughter of Time Travel must survive," he explains, "She is our only hope. She is special."

He pauses as a tear comes to his eye, "Tell my Chinese flower that I love her. I go now to confirm Mott's law." Mojmir disappears back into the catacombs, heading straight for the Nazis.

Phillip Mott was a famous Temporal Philosopher. His studies were in the area of destiny and temporal gravitational pull. He theorized that a mass can create its own destiny, separate from temporal gravitational pull and claimed that man could control his fate and that he had ultimate choice to do whatever he wanted. Man was not subjected to whatever forces were around him; his destiny was in his own hands. He proved man's independence from fate by shooting himself, thus showing the ultimate control he had over his own life.

On the other side of the hole, we could hear Mojmir screaming, "You're in the jungle, baby! You're gonna die!"

"Come on," Frank says as he pulls me forward, "We gotta get out of here."

We take a few steps into the next chamber. With my understanding of my Irish-Catholic heritage, I know exactly where we are. We're deep underneath the high altar of Saint Patrick's Cathedral in a tomb where they bury all the Cardinals of the New York Diocese. Here are the highest ranking priests that walked through this church. Holy men, whose spirits I hope are watching over us, and Mojmir.

There's no time for prayer now. At the top of the stairs, there's an old iron gate. Frank throws his weight against it and we break through into the Sacristy.

As we burst onto the altar, we disrupt the start of an early evening Saturday mass and have to work ourselves through the procession. It seems the only thing for poor people to do in New York City these days is to go church and pray, because just about every pew is packed.

We head for the North Transept, the one place where we can see outside light. As we reach the door, the Nazis come from the tomb, blowing whistles and shoving the congregation, priests, and nuns out of their way.

"FRAULEIN!" yells the chief Nazi. "You cannot escape. I will find you!" He fires his gun into the air. A cardinal's mitre falls from the ceiling along with some plaster.

Panic ensues and people pour out of the pews and head for the exits, pushing Frank and I out the side door and onto Fifty-First Street. The streets are flooded with other New Yorkers going somewhere. Our wave of people from the church meets those on the street and we meld into them. Frank and I snuggle together and head east. We don't look up. We don't look back. We just keep on moving forward, hoping we won't be seen. For now, we blend in.

We don't speak a word to each other until we make it to Third Avenue, partially to avoid calling attention to ourselves, but more so from the shock of losing Mojmir. As we round the corner at Third Avenue, we step into an apartment vestibule for a quick breather.

"What's next?" I ask Frank.

"We move forward on the plan and find Mojmir's Chinese

contact," Frank offers. "With or without money, he's our best bet."

"Manhattan is huge," I say, overwhelmed by the notion of trying to find a needle in a haystack while being hunted by Nazis. "Where do we start?"

"Let's start with the obvious," smiles Frank. "Chinatown."

TWELVE

Third Avenue is eerily quiet. It's a residential area of Midtown Manhattan with the typical hustle and bustle of a New York City street but today it's as desolate as if we're traveling through a Wild West ghost town. Every now and then, we see some semblance of life, a few people walking here or there, but no cars, and just a handful of trucks. Everything is in disrepair. Buildings are crumbling and broken glass windows are covered in plastic or old sheets. Awnings above store fronts are torn and flapping in the wind. Likewise, signs are faded, with some hanging by one or two nails. The city has been left for dead.

The effects of the war are dotted along our journey south. On the corner of 34th Street stands the shell of a building, bombed to all hell. Steel girders jut out in all directions like an unfinished erector set. Brick and concrete, still black with burn scars pile high into the street making it impossible to navigate. Frank and I have to cross over to the east side of the block to get through. As we pass by, I notice mold and other growth creeping up several feet on the lower bricks. This building must have been standing this way for several decades and left undisturbed. There has been no rebuilding here after the war. Maybe there's been no desire, maybe there's been no money, or maybe this has been left here as a reminder by the Nazis. "Don't mess with us," it says, "or we'll destroy your whole city."

I've yet to fully take in the loss of Mojmir. As an inspector they train you to suppress your feelings, to not make any friends and remain a loner. In the past several years, I've only allowed myself to get close to Frank. But in the past few days, I've taken a liking to Mojmir.

He started off as my enemy, and in a different situation I would have never trusted him with my life or well-being. But that crazy Bon Jovi loving Russian grew on me. It's amazing how just a change in history gave us a common goal. In the end, he was my friend and gave his life so that I might live. World domination presents itself with many strange situations, and throughout history there have been some instances of enemies strategizing together against a common enemy.

But this was more than just shared interests, I actually liked Mojmir. He would have been a great ally and a huge help to strategize our future, but it would not be. Time travel could not change this moment.

Mojmir is gone and unfortunately there is no time to cry. I'm being hunted by Nazis and we have to move on.

"I wonder what they'll do with his body," laments Frank, "maybe they'll return it to the Russian Embassy."

We both know this will not happen. The Nazis want no evidence of Mojmir's death. If the Russians knew what happened, it will infuriate them and their relationship will get even worse. I don't know exactly how amicable the Nazis and Russians are in this temporal shift, but if there's any good-will between two it will be gone knowing they murdered Mojmir. The last thing the Nazis need is both America and Russia to be upset with them.

"I've never imagined New York City like this," offers Frank, trying to break the uncomfortable silence.

New York City is amazing. It's always changing but always stagnant at the same time. You can leave the city, not comeback for 10 years, and still have this huge sense of familiarity, even if shops have changed. St. Patrick's will always be on Fifth Avenue. Little Italy will always be on Mulberry Street. Central Park West will always be the elite place to live.

This is a different New York City. It's seems less like the epicenter of the work and more like a forgotten Midwestern steel town. As we reach 14th and Third Avenue, we can see some of the biggest devastation in the city. South of 14th Street is the East Village and another residential area. It makes the section of town we just left look like paradise. Either this neighborhood was a favorite target of the Nazi bombers, or the Germans never took the effort to clean up anything here.

To describe the East Village's current status as a shithole would be a compliment. The smell of rotten trash and urine waft through the street and I need to cover my nose to keep from vomiting. There are big gaping holes in the middle of the street looking down into the subway tunnels, some with old rusted out buses that have fallen in decades ago. Apartment buildings have collapsed into the street all over. Children play in the alleys chasing rats for fun, instead of playing with dogs or cats. People drudge down the sidewalks aimlessly walking somewhere, as if it doesn't matter.

The traffic is a little more active than Midtown, but that's because of the military vehicles. They drive down the streets, and every now and then stop. Through a megaphone, they yell at the children, laugh at the adults at the corner, or whistle at the teenage girls.

"We are the superior race," they repeat over and over. "We defeated you in battle. You serve us now."

Across the street, a mother and young daughter step out from a grocery store. The mom notices the Nazi patrol and instinctively pulls the girl and herself back in the store until they go by. Once they are in the clear they step back out and return to where ever they were going. Is this normal for them? I imagine how these people must live. They have nothing and are surrounded by desolation. What makes them happy? Do they go day to day in complete drudgery? Is there hope? Is there a feeling within them that this can get better, that things can change? Or have they accepted this world as the new normal? That this is what they have and they should be content, that things could be worse? To deal with the pain, they've probably isolated themselves from the world around them, from all the major problems that exist. They've most likely created their own reality so they can just mentality survive. While all this is new to Frank and me, this is their everyday.

Frank and I try hard to hide and look as if we live there. We know the Nazis are hunting us. If we're even pulled aside for looking different, they may arrest us and it will be over. Frank is watching everywhere, every one. I can see him out of the corner of my eye, as if he's a wolf ready to attack anyone that touches me. It's Frank and me now, and he's willing to lay down his life for me. Hopefully, it won't come to that.

"We need to find Mojmir's friend," he says. "Did he give us any clues?"

"Well, we know he's from Chinatown. They drank Mao Tai jiu together," I remind him. "It's Chinese liquor.

"So all we need to do is find a Chinese man in Chinatown. Awesome," sighs Frank, "Why didn't Mojmir tell us more?"

"He knew they were listening to us," I say, "he stopped giving any details of what we were doing just in case they overheard."

"Do you think maybe Mott's Law was a clue?" Frank asks.

"What do you mean?"

"Well, of course Mott was a Temporal Philosopher," states Frank. "But Mott is also a famous street in Chinatown."

I hate playing the game Clue with Frank. He always figures out the answer in the first fifteen minutes. Never fails. Looks like it's Mojmir's friend, with the liquor bottle, on Mott Street.

"There has to be a liquor store on Mott," he says. "We find it and camp out until someone recognizes you. I mean, you're the Daughter of Time Travel. If there's an inspector there, they will know you."

"Sounds like a plan," I say.

"Here's Mott Street," announces Frank.

"And there's our liquor store," I point out, "On the corner of Pell Street."

In front of us is a small store front with the words, "Fu-Xing's" written on it.

"We don't have any money," Frank reminds me.

"But we have luck," I say, "And it's gotten us this far. So I'll keep on counting on it. Follow me and keep your eye out for someone staring at me."

"I got your back," says Frank.

I smile to myself. If there's one person that can help me get through all this, it's Frank. He's a great partner.

"One more thing," I add, "This encounter may not be friendly. The last time I checked the Chinese weren't all together happy with Americans."

If Frank and I stuck out like a sore thumb in Nazi New York, then in Nazi Chinatown we must now look like a blinking Neon sign that says "We're Not From Here." Fu-Xing's is more like a Buddhist Temple than a liquor store. A large laughing Buddha sits opposite the door, and other statues, including a monk warrior, are riddled throughout the store. The smell of incense and fruit linger in the air and everything is dark, with shafts of light peeking in here and there.

The shelves are lined with Chinese food products, sauces, marinades, and yes, liquor. Everything is written in Mandarin. An old, old man looks up from the counter and stares at us for a moment, then goes back to his prayer beads. We go through the store, looking at the bottles, seeing if we can find Mao Tai jiu even though we have no idea what it looks like.

We are the only customers in the store, which is about 250 square feet, and have been wandering around for at least 30 minutes. The whole time the old man behind the counter has been chanting and meditating with his prayer beads. Frank and I are at an impasse. We've checked every bottle on the shelf and haven't been able to find anything called Mao Tai jiu. I finally get the nerve to ask the man behind the counter.

"Excuse me kind sir," I say. He says nothing for several moments. About the time I think he's deaf, he finally responds.

"What do you seek?" he asks without opening his eyes, still deep in meditation.

"Mao Tai jiu," says Frank.

The man's eyes open and he stares at us with deep curiosity. "Do you understand what you seek?"

"Yes," I respond, trying to sound confident.

The man laughs out loud, "You are a lost flower in a field of thistle. Come. See what you seek, Daughter of Time Travel."

The man stands up and moves the chair he was sitting on. He bends over and lifts open a trap down in the basement. I can see rickety stairs leading to a basement.

"You will not find Mao Tai jiu on any of my shelves," he

declares, "you will find it beneath because it is the foundation of everything we do. Go down and find what you seek."

I thought Mojmir was strange at first, but the Chinese are so over the top. I look at Frank for what to do. He gives me a look of confidence knowing that he's got my back. I head down the stairs with Frank behind me. As soon as he clears the floor, the trap door gracefully closes and we can hear the old, old man put his stool back in place. We're stuck down here.

"I'm right here," whispers Frank in my ear. He's in high gear protective mode.

Light and shadows flicker throughout the basement. In the corner I see a figure sitting in a Lotus Position with its back to us, surrounded by several lit candles and burning incense. We quietly walk up to the figure.

"Baojia has shown you the way, but do you know what you seek?" a woman's voice breaks the silence. It sounds vaguely familiar.

"We are looking for a friend of Mojmir Ivanov," reveals Frank.

"Ah, Mojmir," she responds, "I know him well."

I have heard this woman's voice before. It has a distinct gravel to it, with a thick, thick Chinese accent. She has a slowness to her delivery as if she's contemplating each consonant and vowel to make sure it's phrased to perfection. There is much deliberation to her words.

"I know you," I say, "I have heard your voice."

She turns to me, pauses, and slowly smiles with recognition in her face, "And I have placed my eyes upon your face, Daughter of Time Travel."

How absolutely foolish of me. Mao Tai jiu is not liquor. It is a person – she is THE Mao Tai Jiu, the most famous Temporal Philosopher of the East. By the look on Frank's face, he recognizes her as well.

"Welcome to my world," she says, "It has changed, but will revert in time. I'll make some tea. We have lots to talk about."

Assignment 1989

THIRTEEN

Temporal Philosophy is a field that quickly grew after the
evolution of Temporal Physics and Temporal History. Man
frequently goes through three phases with a major invention or
discovery. First - what is it? Temporal Physics answers this. It's
the creation phase, a moment of awe. Discovery is so new that
there's no time to understand it. That's when the second phase
hits - what happens? You begin to learn everything about the
physical state of the discovery and how it changes the world
we live in. The study of Temporal History covers this. But it's
only until the last phase that we ask the most difficult question
to answer - how does it affect man? This is where Temporal
Philosophy comes in.

It's the contemplation of questions like, if I've been abused
by my parents, is it okay for me to get revenge and go back in
time to abuse them when they are little kids? If nuclear war is
so destructive, should we go back in time and stop the creation
of the Atomic Bomb?

All these dilemmas were just conversation until 2042. That
was the year they discovered that wheat was a slow acting
poison and the root cause of everything from autism, heart
disease, erectile dysfunction, infertility and cancer. Scientists
learned that it slowly destroys your immune system, letting
down your natural defenses, allowing for infections and
diseases to easily take control of your body. For centuries,
doctors tried to cure symptoms of each disease and finally
discovered why all of them were happening in the first place –
people were eating wheat.

It took two full years to get it out of the food supply and
while the effort took place, another estimated 50,000 people
around the globe died from wheat's toxic effects. It was the
first time after the discovery of Time Travel that a major
worldwide pandemic was uncovered – one that could be
avoided with a simple trip back in time. There was feverish
debate over whether or not we should go back in time and
eradicate wheat from our ancestral diet. There were those that

were "Purists" and believed that time should continue as is and not be tampered with. There were "Humanists" who wanted to go back and switch out wheat for a safer grain. There were the "Choice" group who simply wanted to go back in time and explain the science to all and let them choose between wheat and an alternative.

It was a complete mess, with more opinions than a political race. Thankfully, the particle accelerators were in the hands of the governments and not the people, or mass temporal chaos would have ensued.

Protests exploded across the globe and countries took positions. The U.S. offered to pour billions into agriculture of Third World Countries to help them develop new ways to farm other grains. Russia had a laissez-faire attitude, letting others deal with the problem in their own way. Many of the Third World countries demonstrated strong hatred to the U.S. and Russia who both sold them cheap wheat for decades. Embassies were stoned, flags were burned, politicians were lambasted, and celebrities who ended up on the wrong side were ostracized. No one could calm the masses down, not even the Pope.

That's when Mao Tai Jui appeared. She was already a prominent Temporal Philosopher, advising the United Nations on the ethics of Time Travel and counseling the Chinese government. During a global submit at the United Nations, she was scheduled to speak for a full two hours on this topic. Instead, she spoke for 10 seconds. She simply said, "Time moves forward, so must we. Look to the past to learn from your mistakes, but look to the future to live."

There was a collective pause around the world when she said those words. Everyone expected a long philosophy session and was ready to take whatever she said to use as support for their cause. Instead, she spoke only twenty-two words and changed people's attitudes towards time travel forever. The world indeed moved on, but we all took more care about the foods we ate and shared within our communities.

I now sit in Mao Tai Jui's presence, drinking the most wonderful green tea I ever tasted. Frank has already had a second serving.

"What do you know about the temporal shift?" I ask.

"This is the largest shift I've ever experienced," says Mao Tai Jui. "The Germans have taken great measures to extend it as much as possible."

"How have they managed this?" asks Frank.

Mao Tai Jui steps over to a fountain in the corner of the basement and sticks a chopstick in the water flowing from the top. "When you make a change in time, it splits, but returns much like water in the river returns its course," she explains. Then she sticks a second chopstick underneath it, "But when you continue to manipulate time over the course of its flow, the gap continues to widen," she adds. Then she places her whole hand under the chopstick, "If you manipulate it long enough, the river flow will split creating two separate streams. This is what the Germans are trying to do, and in turn changing time forever."

"So are we in an alternative universe?" Frank asks.

"No," she says, "but they are definitely trying. My fellow Chinese inspectors here have been able to communicate with their leaders at Central Command. We know what they are doing, but we don't know their next steps."

"What's the plan?" I ask, "How do we stop them?"

"I was hoping you could tell me that," she responds, "Daughter of Time Travel."

Here I am trapped in 1989, and once again my enemy is turning to me to solve the problems of the world. Is this typical of the other world powers? Wait for the United States to take action, then approve or disapprove?

"We're looking for safe travel to Canada," Frank says, "Mojmir sent us here. He said you could help us."

"Mojmir! How is my dear friend doing?"

"He's dead," I say solemnly. There's no use beating around the bush or sugar coating it. "He died to save our lives."

Mao Tai Jui bows her head for several moments. "Well,

then he died nobly. You must avenge his death, Alex. We cannot have the Nazis win. One day, there will be a winner to this on-going war. It may be China, it may be Russia, it may be the U.S., but we can't let it be Germany." She steps away from the fountain and back to her meditation position, sitting still for several moments.

"So what do we do now?" asks Frank.

"Silence," says Mao Tai Jui.

We sit still for a few moments, which is not something I am used to doing, waiting for her to finish her prayers. Then we hear a bell in the shop above. Several footsteps walk into the small shop, followed by another pair of heavy boots on the wooden floor.

"Good afternoon shopkeeper," it's the same German voice from the Swiss Bank. When Frank hears him, he pulls me close and stares up at the ceiling.

"We have no Riesling here," says the shopkeeper, "You may want to try some of the shops in Uptown."

There's a smack of leather. "SILENCE!" the Nazi leader yells. "You know why I am here. We've been following the Russian for decades. We know he likes to frequent this shop. Fräulein Eviston is coming here and we intend to find her by any means necessary. Do you understand?"

"I only sell food and drink here to this Chinese neighborhood," says the shopkeeper. "I know nothing of Russians."

"Whether you tell the truth or lie, I don't care," says the Nazi. "Nevertheless, someone will stand guard at your entrance until she is found."

"But no one will visit my shop," he responds. "I will make no money."

"Nor will you make any money if I burn it down," laughs the Nazi leader, "Because if we don't find her within three days, your place will go up in smoke." The Nazi leader continues to laugh. We hear his boots on the wooden floor again, and the shop bell rings as his laughter fades away.

I slowly walk over to Mao Tai Jui and Frank follows.

"We need to get out of here," I whisper, "We need to get to Canada."

"I can get you to Canada," says Mao Tai Jui, "But is that really where you need to be?"

"Yes," says Frank. "Once in Canada, we can begin to plan how we're going to fix all this. But while we're constantly on the run, we can't even stop and think for an hour. Or grieve a friend's passing."

"We have a secret way to get to Canada," she says. "It is dangerous and I can't guarantee your safety. But I do ask you to reconsider. I see your fate as here, making change on the inside. Rest tonight, safely here. Tomorrow we will talk more." She motions to a few mats on the floor in the corner of the basement. They look about as comfortable to sleep on as gravel driveway. But Frank and I have had a long day. We curl up next to each other for warmth and fall fast asleep.

FOURTEEN

As I lay there sleeping, I start dreaming of General Custer and my favorite graduate class, History 751: Integrative Situational Analysis. It was a core class for every Inspector which taught how different critical moments in history can affect the course of time for decades.

Furthermore, we were to engage history to help us think on our feet. ISA (as we called it) was a class that partnered with the Theatre Department. Graduate level actors would appear every week and play the role of a famous character in history. As a Student Inspector, we could ask them questions about what they were thinking, why they acted the way they did, and what actually happened vs. what was written in the history books. But most importantly, it was our goal to persuade them to make a different choice that would alter the course of history.

There were some great figures we got to interview: Chairman Mao, Margaret Thatcher, Malcolm X, President George W. Bush, Gandhi, Cleopatra. But my favorite was General Custer.

General Custer led just under 500 U.S. soldiers to their death in the Battle of Little Bighorn, rushing into battle against almost 2000 Indian warriors. They were outnumbered and attacked them on their home turf. No other General is history is known for being so arrogant.

Our assignment that day was to convince General Custer to make an alternate decision that would significantly change American history in a positive way. Many of my cohorts tried to convince Custer to not go into battle, to wait for back-up, to take the offer of extra battalions from General Terry, or take the Gatling Guns through Yellowstone Park and use them as firepower in the battle. None of my cohorts had much success in their arguments. General Custer was full of himself and would have none of it.

Then it was my turn and I had an argument that was much different. "Take your troops only," I told him, "Leave Major

Reno, Captain Benteen, and Captain McDougall's troops behind to guard the rear in case more Indians arrive." This would reduce the death toll from 500 to only about 200.

This gave Custer pause, so I added, "You're the most famous American General in history. You could defeat the entire Indian Village single handedly before Noon."

General Custer smiled. "That's a damn good idea, young lady," he said, "Why should I share all the glory with the other captains? The glory that should be mine alone! I'll do it."

It was the first change that anyone had ever been able to get Custer to make since IAS began being offered 10 years earlier. There was a hush in the classroom, even Professor Stark couldn't speak. No one said a word until Robby Bernstein butted in. Robby was one of those smart ass know-it-alls that couldn't stand being shown up. And since I got Custer to change, and he couldn't, I was now on his shitlist.

"Great job Daughter of Time Travel," he sneered, "You just killed 200 U.S. Troops. Bravo." He clapped sarcastically.

"General Custer was the military model of arrogance," I said. "He's the example all generals present when someone wants to rush into battle unprepared. Without General Custer, U.S. Military arrogance would run rampant and we probably would have made several wrong decisions in World War I, suffering great loss. By convincing Custer to leave 300 troops behind, I've saved American lives, maintain his arrogance lesson and made an even better case for future military leaders to never let pride influence their decisions."

Robby was beet red. I smiled knowing that I finally silenced his wise-ass remarks. Before he had time to come up with something else, I turned to General Custer to ask him a question.

"Are you familiar with the Battle of Normandy?" I asked. All selected historical characters in ISA were well-versed in other relevant situations, no matter what time in history they were made. It would make sense that a General would know about a major invasion from World War II, but I had to confirm.

"D-Day? When we killed over 300,000 stinkin' Nazis? Yes, I'm familiar."

"Good," I say. "Would you have invaded June 5th, June 6th, or postponed the battle to the following month?" The D-Day invasion was a tricky task. They needed to wait for a full moon and clear weather. The full moon would give them high tide and great light to coordinate the air and naval maneuvers. Clear weather was further necessary to aid in the coordination. The battle was originally planned for June 5th but poor weather conditions held it off. Naval troops had to hide in the inlets in the British Island for cover that night, and hope they were undetected by the enemy. On June 6th the weather cleared somewhat so they attacked. Postponing a full month would have meant re-coordinating a quarter of a million troops. I'm curious as to what arrogant Custer would have done.

"You have to take the element of surprise when you have it," says the General, "I would have attacked on June 5th as planned, with or without the help of the British."

That's what I expected. If we would have attacked on June 5th, we'd be battling not only the Nazis, but the elements as well. Gale force winds, waves crashing into the shore, and rain drenching everything would have been just some of the extra things we'd have to deal with. We would have lost many more soldiers that day, especially if we attacked without the British. I'm sure the Battle of Little Bighorn went through Eisenhower's mind when he had to decide when to attack. Without General Custer's arrogant suicide mission as a history lesson, the U.S. may have gone early.

Professor Stark told me after class that I aced his course from just this one session — that I could even skip the rest of the semester if I wanted to. Skip class and lose the opportunity to gloat? Never. What I really wanted to do was rub it in Robby's face, but I'm a better person than that. Instead, I sat behind him for every remaining class and gave him hell whenever I could. I was a big hit with the rest of my cohorts. Even years later when fellow alumni would see me in the halls of Central Command, I would still get high-fives.

I wake up the next morning to the sun beginning to shine through a basement window. During the night, I had snuggled up next to Frank and used his shoulder as a pillow. I have to admit, my crush on Frank is returning and growing bit by bit every day. It's kind of cute to see him balance being my protector with giving me enough space to be the strong woman that I am. Unfortunately, I'm not sure if he feels the same way about me. I sit up, stretch a bit and look down at him. He's still fast asleep with his head resting on a cardboard box. I let Frank sleep in and get up to join Mao Tai Jui in her kitchenette. Describing it as a kitchenette is generous. It's a hearth in the corner of the basement with a short table and pillows to sit on. She's been up for some time, but I really believe she never even slept. As I sit down on the pillows, she serves me some tea and Dim Sum.

"So what is your choice, Daughter of Time Travel?" Mao Tai Jui asks. "Will you stay and find a way to fight or will you leave and head off to Canada?"

"You'll see no Custer's Last Stand from me," I say, "I'm not leading Frank into battle against the Nazis here in New York City."

"So you will run to Canada then," she says disappointedly.

"I'm not running to Canada. I'm escaping to Canada," I correct her. "When I get there, we'll regroup and figure out a way to kick these Nazis out of the U.S. and send them all the way back to Germany. After that, we'll give them a one way fast pass to hell."

"As you wish," she says. "I'll arrange safe passage for you today. It may take a while, but we will get you to Canada."

FIFTEEN

Frank and I never ate so much Chinese food in our lives. And I don't mean American-Chinese food, I mean the real stuff. It was awesome. Mao Tai Jui kept us well fed while we were hidden underneath the general store. The Nazi guard stood outside the front door, waiting for us to show up. But we never walked through that door.

We eventually discovered there was a secret entrance to the basement from the building next door. In fact, there were basement connections all over Chinatown and even into Little Italy. Mao Tai Jui explained that the tunnels were originally created to smuggle liquor and booze during the Prohibition but was repurposed after the war as a way to secretly avoid Nazi patrols in this area of town. Both the Italian and Chinese neighborhoods were anxious to avoid the Nazis, so keeping the passages a secret was easy. This actually accounted for the lack of pedestrian traffic on the streets and gave the Nazis a false understanding of how many people there really were in this part of Manhattan.

Mao Tai Jui was our connection to the current time. She was able to speak with many of the residents and learn about what was going on. We experienced a quick change, as if a light switch was flipped and we were suddenly in Nazi America. But for them, they had decades and decades of a divergent temporal shift that created their current time. We came to find out that the Germans have set up colonies in America, France, Italy and other parts of Europe, as well as Japan and Northern Africa. For each of these colonies, Germany installed a Colonial Governor to rule with an iron fist. Since America was its largest colony, they set up a three tier chain of command. That way, if one leader ends up getting soft, the others will quickly get him back in line. There's the Governor, the Chancellor, and the Prime Minister, but all seem to have equal power that they use to squash every move anyone makes against them.

The United States are now commonly referred to as

America or Nazi America. The country is a shell of what it used to be. Despite its vast resources, it's the poorest of all the colonies since everything of value is shipped to the motherland. All the coal is shipped overseas, as well as textiles, steel, and food. The industrial workers are practically slaves to the Nazis, churning out whatever resources the motherland asks for, with little pay.

Since so much goes overseas, there's not much left for Americans to use for themselves. Many go hungry, especially in cities. In rural communities, people have returned to the pioneer days and began to live off the land again. Rumor has it there are totally independent communes scattered across the country in Appalachia, the Great Plains, and the Western deserts. But none of this can be confirmed.

Mao Tao Jui doesn't have much in the way of food, but she willingly shares what she has. Every evening, she watches as Frank and I sleep. When we awake, she is cooking breakfast for us. We know she disappears in the middle of the night, but always returns before daybreak. I can see Frank watching her, suspicious of her behavior. But I know we need to trust her because she's all we have right now.

On the third afternoon, she excuses herself and heads out the tunnel. "Don't leave here," she warns before closing the tunnel door. "Nazis are everywhere. Above the surface they are like a cluster of spiders, weaving webs at every street corner. They will trap you, take you in, and slowly kill you. They cannot harm you if you stay down here."

When she closes the door, Frank quietly inspects the room. He turns to me, holds his finger over his lips, and signals for me to be silent. He listens at the tunnel door and then looks up the stairs and trap door to see if Baojia is listening. He slowly walks back over to me and motions to sit down on the mats. He leans forward.

"I don't trust her," Frank whispers.

"She's all we have," I remind him. "If not her, who?"

"I've never been a fan of the Chinese," Frank confesses. "There is something about them that's strange. She knows more than she's leading on to."

"There are definitely things she's not telling us," I agree. "But she's hiding us from the Nazis. If she wanted to turn us in, she would have done it yesterday. Remember, we all have a common enemy right now. We'll have more strange bedfellows before this war is won."

Frank pauses to take this in. "Okay, it looks like we'll have to trust her. She is our only ticket to Canada, anyway."

"What's our plan once we get there?" I ask.

"I've been thinking about this for some time," Frank reveals. "My family has been very powerful in Canada for many years. My great-grandfather was Minister of National Defense during the late 80's. We have to get to him to explain the situation. It's our only hope."

"Sure, let's just waltz into the Parliament, let them know we're from the future and everyone will just welcome us with open arms," I say with thick sarcasm.

"Well obviously that's not going to work," chuckles Frank. "But I've got a plan. My family has an estate in Burlington, which is between Hamilton and Toronto. My grandfather spent most of his time there, helping nurse my sick grandmother. We'll go there first and I'll talk to him one-on-one."

This plan still isn't going to work. "Frank, I don't care how enlightened your grandfather is. He's not going to believe you're from the future."

"Yes he will," Frank counters. "First, I bear a striking resemblance to my father. There's no denying I'm family."

"Okay, there's some plausibility." I'm beginning to have a little faith. "So maybe you're a long lost distant cousin."

"There's more," confesses Frank. "I know things. Family secrets. Heirlooms. Hidden bank account numbers. Stories. Secrets."

"Those are things that any detective can find out," I argue. "How's this guy going to believe you?"

"There are things only told to the first born male of every generation. Family secrets that only a few living members of the family know about. My grandfather and father are the only two male living members of the family in 1989. My dad told me a secret when I turned 18. He'll know I'm family."

"So you know a deep dark family secret," I reply, "but will that be convincing enough?"

Frank looked away for a moment, and was deep in thought. He looked back at me, straight in the eyes, with a pained look in his face. "What I'm about to tell you, you can never tell anyone," he said with all seriousness. "This is a family secret we've held for generations and it needs to stay a secret. I'm only telling you now so you can trust me."

"I swear." This is the most serious I've ever seen Frank.

"Remember how I told you my family's fortune dates back to the French Revolution?"

"Yes," I said curiously.

"My ancestor was Baron de Breteuil," announces Frank. "He help planned the failed escape of King Louis XVII and Queen Marie Antoinette."

"They escaped prison to avoid execution," I remember this from my World History class. "They headed to Sweden, except they were spotted in the city of Varennes and taken back to Paris. It was the final straw in the abolishment of the French Monarchy."

"Except the Baron didn't plan their escape," Frank said solemnly. "He planned their capture. He was a traitor."

"Traitor?" I'm shocked. "How?"

"You see the Revolution needed one more mistake by the monarchy to seal the deal on the new government. The Baron had liberal ideas so the rebels turned to him for help. The Revolution offered him lots of money and prestige if he helped planned a failed escape for the King. He couldn't refuse. So he convinced the Queen to take the family and flee to her homeland. The Baron arranged for a Postmaster to spot them in Varennes. The rest is history."

"Your family is responsible for ending the French Monarchy?"

"My family was sworn to protect the King, to protect the

throne. Instead, we were traitors. This is our dark secret," Frank explains. "We've been trying to right the wrong ever since. That's why we fled to Canada. Today we serve the Crown of England, and we will not let down that throne."

"I guess I'm not the only one whose family changed history forever," I joke.

Frank lets out a slight chuckle. "That's why I have to get to Canada. Not just to escape the Nazis here in America, but to help my homeland and make good my family name. I can't desert my people when they need me most, not like one of my fore-fathers did. Once I speak with my grandfather about this secret, he'll know I'm family. He'll believe anything I say after that."

"So that's the plan," I agree. "We leave here and head to Burlington."

At that moment we hear the shop bell ring and heavy boots pace across the floor.

"Shopkeeper!" yells the same German voice from the Swiss bank. "I have not seen your friends."

"I have many friends," says Baojia.

"The American. The Canadian. We know they are traveling here. If they do not show their face by evening, your shop will be no more."

"The existence of my shop," Baojia pauses, "is timeless."

"Chinese are so amusing," the German laughs, "for you let your spirituality cloud reality. Turn over your friends and your shop will be saved. Otherwise, it will be a pile of scorched embers. It will look like every other building in this town."

The boots pace away and the shop bell rings. There is silence again.

"We should get some sleep," says Frank. "I don't know what's going to happen this evening, but I know it's going to be a long night. We'll need our rest."

Frank and I snuggle into the same positions we've been in during the last few nights. My head on his shoulder, and his on the cardboard box.

The smell of ginger and sesame oil wake us up hours later and we find that Mao Tai Jui has made an elaborate meal for us. I feel it's our last with her.

"Tonight, you travel," she explains, "You will tunnel under the Hudson River to the Meadowlands. There you will be picked up by a truck that will take you over the border to Ontario. I have paid handsomely for your passage. But if you choose not to take it, and stay and fight, then I will not be angry."

"We've decided to go to Canada," Frank says. "Why do you continue to try and convince us to stay and fight?"

"Because she is the Daughter of Time Travel and it is her fate to fight," she explains. "If not today, maybe tomorrow."

"I am in charge of my fate. I'll decide whether I will fight or not," I say, "And I choose not to."

"I understand this choice," says Mao Tao Jui, "But I also understand things you do not. I see your Qi and it tells me you're a rebel and a leader."

"Qi?" asks Frank.

"It is the energy inside you," she explains, "It dictates where you are going."

"Wait a minute," I say, "My father proved temporal gravitational pull. We are all going in the same direction."

"Yes," she says, "But how we get there is governed by our Qi. It is the energy within that determines what we do with the time we have. When you live through as many temporal shifts as I have, then you begin to see Qi in everything and everyone."

"There have been more temporal shifts than this one?" asks Frank.

Mao Tai Jui sighs heavily, "It is the egotistical nature of humanity to assume the world around them is the only one that exists. There have been many temporal shifts, especially in the early days of Time Travel. True, it has been some time since we've had a shift similar to this one. But that's only because those with the ability to travel got together and signed a time travel accord, banning the use of it for war."

"So you're saying that we've been through this before, and we've come out okay?" I ask.

"We've had over ten plus Level Four Temporal Shifts since Time Travel was first invented. And each time, it was your father that discovered its existence. That is his destiny, his Qi," she explains.

"And my role, has it differed?" I ask.

"We've never gotten this far before," she explains. "Your destiny has never come to fruition. But I know your Qi. You are a rebel, and you, Frank, I know your story, too. You wear your Qi like clothing and it shows that you are loyal to your family and friends."

Frank glares at her, "My story is my own. You know nothing."

Mao Tai Jui smiles at us both, "You are so young. So unaware. I care not about your past, nor your future. I care about your present. We must focus on the now and move it forward."

"Well, it appears this temporal shift hasn't moved us forward," observes Frank, "But instead backwards. Nazi America sounds a lot like Eastern Europe in the 60s."

"Precisely," Mao Tai Jui agrees. "And Russia is not in a Cold War with the United States, but with Berlin instead. Your father invented time travel. This time it will not be for the Americans, but for the Nazis instead."

This cannot be possible. My father is going to help the Nazis defeat Russia? My dad would never side with the Germans. And Mao Tao Jui thinks I will have a role in how this plays out.

"Well, what's my destiny? Where will my Qi lead me?" I ask.

Faintly, we begin to hear several sirens in the distance.

"It is beginning," announces Mao Tai Jui.

The sirens increase and are coming closer.

"Will you stop speaking in bits and piece and explain what's going on here?" asks Frank.

The sirens are now outside at street level and slowly fade

off. Through the basement window we can see red flashing and we hear lots of boots hit the ground and assemble close to the building.

"FRAULEIN!" yells the German voice through a megaphone. "We know you are here. Come out now and this neighborhood will be saved. If you don't we will burn it all down to the ground. We'll light every building one-by-one, and shoot anyone coming out. Thousands of people will die by the bullet or be burned alive, all because of your cowardice. Will you surrender? Or kill the innocent?"

Through the basement window, I can see a Nazi with huge flamethrower. He pulls the trigger and fire shoots across the street. They are serious about this.

"Mao Tai Jui, I cannot let all these people die," I gasp. "I am surrendering."

She smiles at me. "Such a large heart for a small body. Do you think these people are really home tonight? Did you not think I'd know the Nazis have been planning to burn down the whole neighborhood? This is their trap, their web to catch you with. The people of this neighbor have already escaped through the catacombs. Let the Nazis burn down all these shack tenements. We will rebuild them all one day."

"FRAULEIN!" I hear from outside. "This is your last chance to surrender." The soldier with the flame thrower blasts a few flames in the direction of the door, lighting the evening sky.

"What are we waiting for?" asks Frank. "He's going to burn down this place. Let's get out of here."

"Your escort will be here momentarily," she calmly explains.

"Escort?" I'm shocked. "You're not coming with us?"

"Brennen Sie es," the German voice commands. "Burn it all down to the ground."

Through the window we see the flamethrower ignite, shooting a steady stream of fire. The soldier moves towards the shop. He spreads his flame across the door and the building instantly catches on fire. The trap door opens and down comes Baojia. He races across the floor, amazingly nimble and quick for such an old man. He opens a large cabinet, revealing a blue Samurai suit and begins to put it on. Upstairs the fire is growing and smoke is starting to move down the stairs. The wooden ceiling is starting to smolder.

"FRAULEIN! SHOW YOURSELF!" A round of machine gun fire peppers through the fiery walls of the shop, splintering the doors and shattering most of the windows.

Mao Tai Jui sits still in one corner of the room in the lotus position. Baojia finishes putting on the Samurai suit and stands at the bottom of the stairs. Suddenly, several Nazis bust down the door to the shop and more rounds of machine gun fire spray through the shelves, destroying boxes, cans, and bottles. This is when I realize we have no protection, no guns, no ammunition. We are sitting ducks. But I have to fight. I look against the wall and find an axe handle. Before I can reach for it, there's a banging on the wall behind the boxes Frank's been sleeping against.

"Ahh… your escort," Mao Tai Jui says.

Mao Tao Jui moves a few boxes from against the wall to reveal a small bookshelf. She flips a latch on the side and swings the bookshelf out, revealing a tunnel. A small Chinese boy steps out and whispers something in her ear.

"It is time," Mao Tao Jui declares. "You must go now."

Upstairs the Nazis are yelling. They have found the trap door and are moving furniture around to open it.

"I'm not leaving you here to die," I argue. "You will not suffer the same fate as Mojmir because of me."

She smiles at me. "My fate is my own," she responds calmly.

The Nazis are starting to break through the trap door in the ceiling. I can see their gun butts splintering through the wood.

"I can help you fight," I say.

"We have to go," Frank whispers in my ear. "There's no better time to leave then now." He grabs me and starts to drag me to the door.

"Good-bye, Daughter of Time," Mao Tao Jui says to me,

"Fate will find you."

Then she turns to Frank and adds, "You will find peace and redemption." Taking a long sword from the samurai cabinet, she joins Baojia at the bottom of the stairs.

The Chinese boy grabs my hand and pulls me into the dark tunnel. I can barely see a thing. Frank slams the door behind me and follows, grabbing my hand so I can lead him along in the darkness. We are a human train, moving through pitch black catacombs, and in the care of a 10 year old guide.

The tunnels are carved into the rock and are about five feet high, give or take a few inches. Even a short person needs to crouch as they travel through them. It is mostly dark but every now and then we pass by another doorway with light shining through, allowing us to see a few feet ahead of us.

After we travel for what seems a few city blocks, the tunnel starts to slope down and the moisture seems to increase. Our guide stops for a moment and pulls flint and steel from his pocket. He reaches up to the wall and pulls down a torch. He strikes the flint against the steel, sending a spark to the wood and the torch is ablaze. Lifting the torch in the air to light our way, the guide leads us down the hallway.

We can see about 100 feet ahead and beyond that, it's pitch black. Water has begun to pool on the floor. As we travel farther down the tunnel, the pools form into a stream, then into a river. Our guide points to the right side of tunnel and begins to walk along the wall.

At first, we don't understand what he wants. Then Frank steps too far to the left and almost falls knee deep in mud. Our guide does the wall motion sign again and this time we understand he wants us to walk along the right side of the wall.

After several moments, the tunnel starts sloping back up. Ahead, we see shafts of light coming from the ceiling and our guide no longer needs the torch to show us the way. He places the lit torch in a holder on the wall and continues to lead us down the tunnel.

The path continues to slope up. Rock turns into dirt and the ceiling gets shorter. Then the tunnel suddenly comes to a stop. There's an old rope ladder that leads to a trap door above us. Our guide points to it, waves good-bye, then disappears.

Frank and I clumsily climb the ladder, slowly open the trap door, and climb out. We are surrounded by about fifty Chinese of various ages. There are men, women, children, and babies. But that's not the odd thing. What takes me aback is that without a cloud in the sky, they are all wearing raincoats.

SIXTEEN

"What's up with all the rain gear?" Frank asks, "Do you think the time shift has affected the weather in Canada?"

"My guess is we're getting put in the flat bed of a truck and the forecast tonight is rain up North," I respond.

Our new friends are covered head-to-toe in rain gear. They are wearing coats, pants, ponchos, and boots. The babies are swaddled in small garbage bags and the kids are wearing rubber gloves. Not an umbrella in sight. Everybody stands here quietly in the tall grass of the Jersey meadowlands. Even with the night sky lit by the full moon, we can't see more than 100 feet in front of us since we can't look over the tall grass. I hear crickets chirping everywhere.

After some time, the rumble of a trailer truck fills the night air. The crowd gets anxious and everyone begins to gather their stuff. Some have bags, some have suitcases, and some have nothing at all. A few stare at us oddly, as if they are waiting for us to do something. All Frank and I have are the clothes on our back, and I feel lucky that we're even alive.

Headlights come towards the crowd and light up a dirt road that's been in front of us this whole time. As they take a bend in the road, I realize that it's two large oil tankers. They stop right in front of us.

"We're getting in there?" asks Frank.

"I don't think we have a choice," I respond.

Two lines form, one in front of each tanker. The line to the first formed before we had a chance to figure out what was going on, so Frank and I are stuck getting into the second one. We get in line behind a young father and his five year old girl. He's dressed in a fireman's coat and hat, while the girl is completely wrapped in garbage bags from the neck down, along with a rain hat.

"Where is your rain gear?" he asks in perfect English.

"No one told us we needed it," Frank responds.

"The trip will be about six hours," he explains, "I'm sure you won't suffer that much. I figured that I'd be okay, too, but

I couldn't chance it with my girl."

I look at the front of the line. The truckers have got out of the cab and lowered a ladder into the oil tankers. The passengers are now climbing up the side of the tanker and being helped down inside it. I look at Frank and we both realize the purpose of the rain gear.

"We're about to get covered in crude oil," he says, "We're going to have to bathe in Dawn for weeks after this."

"If this gets us to safety," I say, "then it's all worth it."

One by one we see the Chinese disappear into the tanker. Frank helps the father in front of us with the girl, passing her down to him in the tanker. Frank climbs down as well, and I follow. I am the last one in.

The tanker is pitch black inside. While it's been emptied of all its oil, the walls and floor are still coated in it. Getting around is like walking on fish, your foot instantly slips with each step. People sit down and we take our spot next to the father and his daughter. The truckers lower special containers over the top and close the hatch.

"The special covers allow air down here," explains the father, "But if you open the hatch from the outside it looks as if the oil tanker is empty." He smiles, "American ingenuity."

"I'm Alex," I say, "and this is Frank."

"I'm Paul," he says, "and this is my daughter, Lynn."

Frank extends his hand to Lynn, "Nice to meet you." Lynn's little hand barely makes it around Frank's fingers.

"We are hoping to meet up with my father and mother, tonight," Paul explains, "They are old and traveled up to Canada several months ago. We promised we'd meet up with them on the full moon in November. Do you have family in Canada?"

"Yes," says Frank. "I have family in Toronto."

Paul's face turns ashen. "I am so sorry. How did they survive? Were they outside of the blast radius of the cloud?"

Wow. An atomic bomb hit Toronto. Maybe Canada isn't a safe place to go.

"Yes," Frank responds, "It's difficult to talk about." They

teach us in Inspector School to deflect the conversation if you don't know the answer. I'm always impressed how quickly Frank can think on his feet.

"Yes," Paul says, "I understand. Other than my mother and father, I have no idea where the rest of my family is. After the war, the Nazis split my father's family apart. Some were sent to the South to farm, others to the Midwest for coal mining or steel, and my dad was sent to New York to make clothes."

"The war, I'm glad it's over," I say, hoping to fish more details out of him.

"But the Nazis will never let us forget we lost. Rumor has it that decades ago, we had a chance to align with the English, French, Canada, and even Russia to attack the Nazis. They wanted us to help in the Battle of Normandy. But President Roosevelt wanted nothing of the war. Until, Japan hit us in '45."

Pearl Harbor happened in 1941. The war was supposed to be over in May of '45.

"By then the Nazis had us right where they wanted us," continues Paul. "The Allies were busy fighting the front in Europe. We concentrated our efforts on the West Coast, which left our East Coast vulnerable. The Nazis took our major cities, and we quickly fell under their rule."

I needed more details from Paul if we were to fully understand the temporal shift. "Frank and I were born and raised in Canada," I say, "We never learned much about American history. What happened here after the war?"

Paul continues to look at us oddly, "Do you mean after we were conquered in 1945? Or when they dropped the bomb on Toronto in '79?"

That's how they did it. The Nazis extended the war almost forty years, and probably dropped the bomb on Toronto to end the battle — a little more than ten years ago. That has to be fresh blood. The Canadians must still be pissed off.

"I mean after 1945," I said.

"Americans became slaves to the Nazis. We are second class citizens. Anyone born in the states gets these tattoos."

Paul rolled up his sleeve to show the numbers '25194288'. "I knew you weren't American born because you don't have any numbers on your forearm."

That must be how we were tracked so easily in New York City. This man is a goldmine of information.

"But the Nazis must know they'll be defeated one day," says Frank.

"Who will stand up against them?" Paul asks, "The Canadians have carried the torch too long and have suffered for it. Half of Europe is already under Nazi control, and England is about to collapse. The famine in the Soviet states has desolated their armies and their people. China was our last hope, but their pacifist belief has kept them in isolation. This is the new norm," he explains sadly, "which is why I am going to Canada. As war torn as the country is, there I will have freedom for my daughter. She will be able to choose her destiny, instead of being told what to do, or worse yet, be tortured by their villainy."

Paul looks down at his daughter who has now fallen asleep in her lap. He lays his hand on her shoulder and begins to stroke her back.

"Tortured?" I wondered, "Paul, if I may ask, is Lynn's mother, your wife, waiting for you tonight in Canada as well?"

"Do you believe in heaven?" Paul asks.

"Of course," answers Frank.

"My wife is waiting for us there," Paul replies as his eyes well up. "You see, she worked as a seamstress in the Nazi factories, sewing the Nazi eagle onto their hats. Day after day she toiled in the factories, suffering the heat in the summer and freezing in the winter. She silently did her duty, not looking at anyone and never causing any trouble. But she caught the eye of one of the German Foremen. See, my wife was a beautiful woman, just like my daughter. The Foreman made advances at my wife. But she was an honorable woman and kept pushing him away. I wanted to hunt this man down, crush him with my own hands, and make him pay for his wicked ways. But my wife knew that would leave our daughter fatherless and she and my daughter destitute. So she tolerated what she could, but his advances became stronger and stronger. Then one evening she never came home. Several of us from the neighborhood went looking for her late into the evening. We eventually found her in an alley, her lifeless body leaning up against a trash can. She had been violated."

Frank and I sit in silence as Paul wiped a few tears from his eyes. He looks down at Lynn with deep sorrow in his face, "As a child, you come into this world knowing only joy in your heart. I've tried to shelter her from the pain and agony in the world around her. But as she gets older and older, there are things she sees. And questions she asks. At some point I have to have answers about the evils that surround her. Then her make-believe paradise that I've sheltered her in will become a world of horrors. I had to get out of there and leave for Canada. I have to get as far away from the Nazis as I can. For my daughter."

Lynn rolls over in her father's lap. Her arm shifts and we see the numbers '31013405'.

We sit in silence, and Paul cries himself to sleep. I look around the tanker and see tired faces on everyone. It doesn't matter if they are old, young, male or female – everyone looks tired. These people have been through hell. I realize that just under a week ago I was drinking the best freshly brewed coffee I ever tasted, and took it for granted. Coffee must be a delicacy to these people.

"Frank, we have to do something about this," I say, "This madness must end."

"We get to Canada," says Frank, "And we unleash a storm on the Nazis. They will pay for all this." Frank must have been thinking of his homeland. He's seen the effects of the bomb on Hiroshima and Nagasaki. I'm sure he's been imagining his friends and family as victims of radioactive fallout. His eyes are a bit misty, but I dare not acknowledge it. Instead I pull him close to me, and wrap his arms around me. In his warmth, I slowly fall asleep.

When my mother passed away, hundreds of people came to our house to pay their respects. Mom was well known across the globe and many of her colleagues traveled hours, days, and across oceans to honor her. Likewise, many of the people my father worked with visited as well. Scientists, military men and women, politicians, researchers, and professors were all gathered at my house. They told stories, shared memories, ate food, and drank wine. One-by-one they said their good-byes and offered me condolences. "If you ever need anything, call me," they would say. I didn't even know their names.

After some time, it was just my father and me. We sat in the living room, he in his chair and me on the couch. An empty space was next to me, it was mom's favorite spot.

Dad turned to me and mumbled, "I should have saved her."

"Save her? Dad," I questioned, "What do you mean, save her?"

"What good is time travel?" Dad ranted. "It can't bring back loved ones. It can't change the past. I've invented something that isn't going to help mankind at all. I should have been a doctor, a medical scientist. I could have discovered a cure for her illness. Instead I became an engineer and created time travel. They told me it was the most important discovery and invention since the printing press. They gave me a Nobel Prize, honored me at the White House. If it was so damn important, then why couldn't it cure her? She'd be sitting right there, right now, if only I could have saved her." He stormed out of the house into the garden, and fell to his knees in front of mom's rose bush. There he stayed and wept.

Dad never said much to me after that evening. The loss of my mother destroyed him and he internalized the pain. He buried himself in his work, spending weeks on end in the lab, but his scientific accomplishments waned. Other younger scientists were leading the field now, and my dad's newer discoveries seemed to be overshadowed.

I rarely saw my dad anymore. But when I did, talking about mom was off limits. Dad never asked me how I felt, what I was going through. If I tried to bring it up, he would change the subject. I was left on my own to grieve my mother's death.

I admire Paul for his protection and love for his daughter. I wish my father had done the same for me.

But one thing I did learn from my mother's death is how strong I really am. I would not go the route of my father and ignore the pain inside. Instead, I would deal with it head on. I'll never forget some of my mom's final words.

"You can always change your destiny," she told me. "You can always do something different. You can run from the hardships of life, or you can stand and fight."

For the past few years, I've been running. Running away from my life and burying my future, living 1989 over and over again. I've isolated myself from just about everyone I know and took solace in the familiarity of a year that didn't know my mom. I couldn't know the pain of losing her because in 1989, she doesn't exist.

It's time to stop running from myself. It's time to be who I am destined to be. But first, I have to figure out who that person is.

A sudden jolt wakes me from my memories. It only seems that I've been out a few minutes and there's no way we've made it to Canada in the little time I've been asleep. The truck's air breaks have engaged, but the engine continues to idle. There's shouting going on outside. The voices are incomprehensible. I can't understand what they are saying. After loud exchanges, there's gun fire. Then silence. Heavy boots climb the side of the tanker. Inside, everyone is now awake and they look up to the hatch. Someone unlocks and opens it. We can see light poking through the cracks in the special container.

"There is no gas in here, sergeant," says a man with a thick German accent.

"Nazis," I whisper to Frank. A hush comes across the inside of the tanker. No one says anything. No one moves.

"*Unerreichbar!*" someone yells from outside with the same

German accent. "Get down and I will check myself."

Boots travel quickly down the outside ladder, followed by determined steps on the rungs going up. The flash light shines through the cracks again, but this time there is more searching. He takes longer. We all wait in the tanker. After a moment, a coin plops on the special container. Whoever is looking into the tanker is smarter than your average soldier.

"This is a false bottom," he yells. "The gas is below." The soldier starts shifting the container left, then right. Finally he rotates it clockwise and pops it out. "See," he yells down to his colleague, "There is gas in here after all."

We all brace for the inevitable. The soldier shines his flashlight down and looks into the tanker. He realizes that he's looking at about 50 Chinese-Americans and begins to laugh. "Well, hello in there," he yells down. "Where do you think you're going tonight? Why don't you come out and we can all visit for a while?"

One by one, all of us climb up the inside ladder then out of the tanker. My head clears the tanker and I look around quickly to assess the situation. The other tanker is nowhere in sight, only ours has been stopped. On the side of the road is a large German Truck pulling a huge cannon on wheels. Both look like a German version of an American Humvee and howitzer. It seems as if they ran out of gas.

There are six Nazis monitoring us as we get out of the tanker. Each one has a machine gun pointed in our general direction. One of our drivers is on his knees with his hands tied behind his back, being guarded by a Nazi. The other driver lies lifeless next to him with a bullet wound in his head.

We all gather around the base of the tanker. There are men and women of all ages. Frank and I are the only two that aren't Chinese. Even the drivers, including the dead one, are Chinese. We stand in the back and hope we're not found. Hopefully, they'll drain the gas from the tanker's cab, be off, and leave us be. Worst case scenario, they kill us all.

"We have to get out of here," I whisper to Frank in his ear. "Let's see if we can hide under the trailer."

Frank looks at me and adamantly shakes his head "No." He motions behind him. That's when I see a very frightened Lynn shaking feverishly in Paul's arms.

"I'm not going to leave them behind," whispers Frank.

How heroic. I step to my left to stand by his side and help hide Lynn. But I forget to look first and my foot finds a branch that snaps as I push down on my heel. All the Nazi guards look at me.

"What do we have here?" says the Nazi Sergeant. "I don't see any slanty eyes on you." All the men laugh. I really hate the Nazis. They take bigotry to a whole different level. "Come closer, Fräulein, and bring your friend with you, too."

The Chinese part like the Red Sea and leave Frank and me standing by ourselves. We are frozen. Retreat is not an option. Suddenly, the sergeant pulls out his side arm and fires it at the dirt in front of us.

"I said come closer, *Amis!*" he shouted. We moved closer to him. I catch a glance of Frank out of the corner of my eye. He's as clueless as I am for what to do now.

"Klaus!" yelled the sergeant.

"Yes, sir." He stood to attention.

"Siphon the gas from the trailer into our truck," he commands. "I want to get out of this armpit within the hour."

"Sir. Yes, sir." Responds Klaus as he runs off to gather tubing and gas cans.

The Sergeant turns to Frank and me. "Lucky for us that we've found you here tonight. Unlucky for you," he grins. He's missing teeth and I grimace from his breathe. "What? I am not good enough for you, Fräulein?"

The Sergeant gets closer to me. "If you are lucky, I will decide to kill you quickly. But I may have my way with you first."

In all my training, I've learned to continually wait and assess my options. While instinct may say attack, my logic prevails and I don't do anything. But Frank can't suppress his emotions. His chivalry kicks in.

"You'll leave her alone," commands Frank.

"I'm not sure you're in a position to give orders," the sergeant smiles. "See, we have superior German weapons. You have, well... nothing." He laughs again. This guy finds everything about himself extremely amusing.

"Klaus," the sergeant yells over his shoulder. "Let's go. How much time is left?"

Klaus has managed to rig some tubing into the cab's tank and diesel fuel is steadily pouring out. He's portioning it into several large metal gas cans. A few other Nazis are then transferring the fuel into their truck.

"Our truck is almost full. I'm going to get three more cans of gas out of here and then we can leave," responds Klaus.

"I don't care what you have left to do. How much time until we're ready to go?" he yells back.

Klaus stands up and looks at his watch. He begins to respond, but suddenly BAM! A rocket comes flying down from the hill, hits the cab, and explodes in a huge fireball, lighting the night sky. The trailer is now an inferno. The tubing whips around freely shooting fiery gas everywhere, leaving little pools of fire dotted on the ground. Klaus is enveloped in flames, burning faster than a dead tree in a forest fire.

"We are under attack," yells the Sergeant.

Nazis always state the obvious.

His troops ignore the plight of Klaus and turn to the hillside, aimlessly firing where they think the rocket came from. Return gunfire rains from a different direction – from behind the fiery cab, nailing all the Nazi troops in their backs. They fall to the ground dead. I look around to find all the Chinese have scattered, leaving just Frank, me, and the Nazi sergeant. This is our chance to flee, and we should have taken it already. I motion to Frank to get out of here, but the sergeant grabs me around the chest, pulls out his side arm, and holds it to my head. I'm his prisoner.

"If you don't show yourselves," the sergeant yells, "I will shoot her dead. You have 30 seconds to comply."

Frank stands there staring at me as if to say, "What do you want me to do?" We both know these insurgents aren't going to show themselves. They don't know me, and probably don't care if my blood is spilled tonight.

"Twenty seconds," the sergeant yells in all directions.

Fortunately, I've been trained in Internationally Integrated Meridian Manipulation and Control. For decades, there had been a growing interest in alternative medicines. As doctors and researchers began to understand we were treating symptoms instead of the real causes of disease, they realized what modern medicine was doing was just as barbaric as the bleeding that medieval doctors did. A deeper insight of alternative and Eastern medicine opened the door to ideas that were previously scoffed at. Research at the Michigan State University School of Biomedical Engineering discovered that the human body works more like a machine then we originally thought. Electric energy flows through our systems and our nerves are the conduits carrying messages. When you stop the conduits from moving electric current to different parts of the body, it causes negative reactions. Some are minor, like tingling or lack of touch, some are major, like instant brain damage. This is why acupuncture works, it's the manipulation of the meridians, or electric currents, and improves their flow throughout the body.

What MSU researchers also discovered is that there are pressure points throughout the body that when activated, can instantaneously cause certain reactions. For example, pinching the neck in a specific way causes someone to sit. Twisting the arm causes someone to stand on their toes. I studied these pressure points and their reactions for a full quarter during Inspector School.

A difficult, but effective, pressure point to manipulate is one called The Wizard's Lighting Bolt. It's located deep inside the tissue of the inner left thigh. When activated, it sends a shock through the victim's whole body and turns them into Jell-O for a full 60 seconds. I'm rather good at it.

"10 seconds!" nervously yells the sergeant, fully knowing he'll have to follow through on his threat and once he does, he'll have nothing to bargain with.

With my left hand, I reach down to his left thigh and quickly dig my thumb deep into his flesh with my nail tip, piercing through his pants and skin. His whole body stiffens, he gasps, and goes limp, falling to the ground like a rotten tree branch that finally cracked off its trunk. His hand hits a rock and the gun goes flying, landing at Frank's feet.

Frank instantly picks up the gun, walks up close to the sergeant, points it at his skull, and fires the weapon. Brains splatter across the gravel road.

"That's for Mojmir," he whispers.

"Freeze," commands a deep American voice. "Drop your weapon. Hands in the air!"

Several men step out of the shadows of the trailer. They are dressed in black from head to toe and their faces are covered with ski masks. They are not wearing formal uniforms; instead, it's a hodge-podge of black clothing that doesn't match. They are pointing rifles at us, and while I'm sure they are happy we took out one of the Nazis, I don't think they are that comfortable about Frank having a gun right now.

"DROP YOUR WEAPON," the leader commands. It's an older gentleman, about in his 50s. There's a little bit of gray hair peeking out from underneath his ski mask.

I'm guessing Frank believes these guys means business because he lowers the gun in his hand, lets it hang from his fingers, and tosses it on the dirt path in front of the men dressed in black.

"Hands on your head. On your knees," he directs. We oblige and are surrounded by the men, all guns pointed at us.

"I'm going to ask you a few questions," the man says, "And you're going to answer them truthfully. Do you understand?"

"Yes," I reply. Frank nods his head.

"First you, woman," says the man. "Who was the 16th President of the United States?"

Crap. This is an American history quiz to test our patriotism. It's gonna be easy for me. "President Lincoln," I respond. Frank, on the other hand is totally screwed.

"Alright, you know your presidents," the man smiles. "Let's

see if you know other things. Who holds the record for most home runs?"

I'm clueless on this one. If they are going to ask me sports questions, they might as well just shoot me now.

"The Sultan of Swat himself, the great Babe Ruth," smiles Frank. "Seven hundred and fourteen career home runs. Last one was in 1936 against the Pittsburgh Pirates." Sweet. I forgot that Frank knows about more than just hockey.

"Very good," responds the man. "But you appear too confident, as if you memorized your answers from a text book." The man pulls off his mask. He looks like an Irishman with his thick black-gray hair, square cheek bones and bushy eyebrows. He stares at me, dead in the face, as to read my every thought. "One final question, and here's something you can't memorize," he pauses for dramatic effect. "What does it mean to be American?"

Really? This one is easy for me.

"It means waking up each morning knowing you have the power to make today better than it was yesterday," I respond. "It means that if you work hard enough, your life can be better than your parents', and your children can have a chance to do better than you. It means holding yourself to a higher standard, to do the right thing, to live by the American ideals of helping your fellow man. Americans believe that freedom is a gift for not just themselves, but for everyone. Doesn't matter what your nationality is, or what your skin color is. America isn't contained by borders, it's not a land, and it's not a common ancestry. America is a shared belief in the hope of a better tomorrow."

I look around and the guns have been lowered.

"If she's not an American, then I want to be where she's from," laughs one of the other burly men.

"Shut up, Roach," the bushy eyebrow leader playfully scoffs at him. "You ain't even American. You're Canadian."

"Hey, this Canuck has saved your Yankee ass at least a dozen times," jokes Roach.

"Sure. And I'm the President of the United States of

America," jests the leader. He turns to us and offers his hand. "You two can stand up, now," he says. "Welcome to hope and freedom – or at least what's left of it."

SEVENTEEN

The rebels gather Frank and me along with the Chinese and split us into two different groups. I look at our surroundings and figure we are somewhere in upstate New York, about halfway between Manhattan and Buffalo. The moon reflects onto a large lake to the south and farmland stretches over hills to the north, east, and west. There's about twenty rebels, all dressed in mismatched black clothing, and each carrying a rifle of some sort. A few men stand on the hillside as watch-outs in case more Nazis show up. Another group piles all the dead Nazis into the back of the truck, then get into the cab. The engine starts up and the truck takes off down the gravel road, towing the howitzer.

The General is talking to his second in command, the man he called Roach. He's shorter with beautiful black hair, broad shoulders and a strong build, but when he turns you see a different person. The whole left side of his head, face, and arms are badly scarred, as if he was picked up and dropped sideways on a bed of hot coals.

I look around in my group – we're all women and men, some older, some younger, but not one of us is younger than 14 or older than 50. The other group is older men and women, children, babies, and families. It's obvious what's going on here. This is some type of army and they need recruits. I look at Frank for some sign of what we should do.

"We need to get to Canada," he whispers. "The first chance we get, we're making a break for it. I don't care if we have to swim across the Niagara River. We're making it to Canada tonight."

"But Frank," I say, "This is a rebel army."

"An army of twenty men isn't really big," he argues, "And I have to get to Canada to see what's become of my family."

The General and Roach have finished their discussion. Roach begins walking toward the tanker and directs a few men to follow him. He gets into cab and after a moment pokes his head out the window.

"Alright, it's in neutral," he yells.

Several of the men get behind the cab and start pushing the trailer. At first nothing happens, but after a few moments it miraculously starts to move. Roach turns the wheel a bit and it starts moving down a hillside. It picks up speed and the men step away. It's traveling fast, about twenty miles an hour. Roach jumps out of the cab and rolls away on the ground just as it goes barreling into the lake. In several seconds the trailer is gone, submerged under the water.

Cheers go up among the men.

"Silence!" the General yells. "Do you want every Nazi within sixty miles to converge on us?" He turns to address us and the Chinese, "Good evening, everyone, I'm General McCafferty, leader of the Central New York Rebel Alliance. Our mission is to eradicate the Nazi army from the Empire State, and return the governance of the Great State of New York to its people. You might think: how are a handful of rebels running around in the night going to defeat the Nazi army?"

Yes. That's exactly what I am thinking.

"Passion. Love of freedom. Love of democracy. Love of the Red, White, and Blue."

They're going to need a lot more than that. These are Chinese. They could care less about democracy and freedom. They are not American - all they want is to get to Canada.

"We are all Americans. It doesn't matter if you're European, African, Mexican, or Chinese. Freedom still runs through each of our veins. We all want this great land of ours to once again be the land of opportunity, where we are in charge of our destiny." The General tosses his cigar to the ground and takes a few steps down from the hill.

"Decades ago, when I was a young boy," his voice gets a bit softer, "My mother and I were walking through town. She was taking me to church. It was just her and I back then. My old man had died in the war. As we were on the sidewalk, a truckload of Nazis drove into the square. They got out with rifles in their hands. The town was at a standstill. They announced in broken English they were taking women to work in the textile factories to make uniforms for the Nazi army. One by one they took young girls and older women and loaded them up on the back of the truck. A Nazi walked up to us. Without even looking at me, he grabbed my mom and dragged her to the truck. Her hand was ripped from mine. I didn't even get to say good-bye."

I look over to Frank. "This may be our chance to fight, to make change," I say under my breath. "Maybe Canada isn't the right choice."

"Tonight, I am asking for volunteers to join our army to defeat the Nazis. There are hundreds of us camped out here, and there are many more troops just like us stationed across this great state. There's a change a comin'. We can defeat these Nazis and return this land to the greatness it once was. A new dawn is rising here in the good ol' U.S.A., and I'm asking you to be a part of it."

"Stick with the plan," Frank whispers in my ear. "We're going to Canada. I need to fine my family. They can help us."

I'm not so sure Canada's the right choice anymore.

"Let's at least check this out," I say.

"I want to go home," retorts Frank.

"I'm not going to take any of you unwillingly. The first oil tanker is about 3 klicks up this road. My men are holding it there in case you don't accept my invitation. If all of you want to squeeze into the other oil tanker and make it over the border tonight, I wish you luck. But if any of you want to step forward and join our army, then do so now. Not for the sake of yourself, but to serve the United States of America."

I've always had a sense of duty towards my country, that's why I became an Inspector in the first place. It feels good to serve, and to help those who can't help themselves. I represent America and all the good it stands for. We use our might for right. And in that instant, I realize that I am still on the job. I'm still a member of the Department of Homeland Security. I took an oath to support and defend the Constitution of the United States against all enemies. I have to stay and fight. It's my duty.

"I'm in," I shout and step forward. I have to be. I'm first and foremost a solider.

Frank looks at me furiously. He knows that I expect him to never leave my side. Frank reluctantly steps forward as well.

"So am I," says Frank. After a few moments, a few other Chinese men and women join us. We are a group of eight now.

"Thank you, my fellow Americans," says the General, "I can't promise that we'll destroy the Nazis. But I can promise that we'll make their lives hell."

We say our good-byes to Paul and Lynn as the rest of the Chinese get back into the tankers.

"You take care of yourself," he says to us.

"You take care of that little girl of yours," I say. "Good luck with finding your parents."

"It is you that need all the luck in the world," he smiles. "You are brave people, fighting for this land."

"It is not land that we are fighting for," I say, "But freedom for all people everywhere."

"Alright, folks," yells the General. "We don't have all night. A few of my men will escort you up the road to the other tanker and help you get back on your journey. After that, you're on your own. Move out."

We wave good-bye to Paul and Lynn, her little hand shaking back and forth as they fade into the distance. I fully expect Frank to go running after them, to join them and head back to his homeland. I'd understand. Instead, he turns to me to say something, but never gets the chance. He's interrupted by the General's second in command.

"Come on, rebels," says the Captain, "Let's head back to base."

"Where is that?" asks one of the Chinese.

"On the other side of Lake Skaneateles," says the Captain, "We're taking boats."

We're led to a small inlet at the head of the lake where we find several boats tied to trees. We all gather into them, Frank and I get into the same boat as the Captain. As we skim across the lake, we get a closer look at the Captain's burn marks under the moonlight sky. His arm and face are a mishmash of scars and pigmentation changes. Splotches of red scar tissue mixed with dead skin pepper his body along with small patches of tan skin, normal skin, and skin as white as the bright light of a nuclear explosion. Random spots of blood vessels dot his arm, much like broken blood vessels on a blood shot eye.

"I'm Captain Jimmy Falcone," he says, "But they nicknamed me the Cockroach here. So most people call me Roach." He extends his hand, the scarred one, to Frank and he shakes. I extend my hand, and he shakes it as well.

"Alex Eviston," I say, throwing caution to the wind and giving him my real name.

"Frank Bouchard," adds Frank.

"I know that she's an American, but I'm not convinced you are. I gather you're a Canuck just like myself," says Roach to Frank.

"Maple syrup runs through my veins," smiles Frank. Roach chuckles to himself.

I consider myself an astute observer of people. I can instantly tell if someone is lying by looking at their mannerisms and listening to timbre of their speech. Once in the Academy, I was able to discover a thief among 20 other possible suspects by just simply engaging them in a conversation about that year's college football season. People are like a book to me, where most people see a blink of an eye, a head nod, or a shift in stance, I see avoidance, displacement, and distraction. I can read someone's emotion or intent with 99.9% accuracy. With that said, I can never tell a Canadian from an American. Frank says it's my natural born arrogance of believing that America is the epicenter of the world. It clouds my vision. Maybe that's true, but I still can't understand it.

"So how did the two of you meet?" asks Roach. He's assuming we're a couple.

Frank grabs my hand and squeezes. He must be choosing this as our cover so we can stick together. "We fell in love when we met in D.C."

"Spoken like a true Rebel," laughs Roach, "New Berlin hasn't been referred to as D.C. in decades."

The boat comes to a sudden stop as we hit shore and the jolt sends me flying into Frank's arms. This makes Roach laugh even harder.

"Hopefully, you won't get caught that off guard when we go into battle," chuckles Roach.

We all get up out of the boats. A few men stay behind to tie them off and Roach leads us up an embankment. Once at the top, we can see a swampland below with small cottages dotted throughout the land.

"This used to be a vacation resort back in the '20s," explains Roach, "It's now our main base. It's desolate, wet and swampy, and inhabited by snakes, coyotes and wolves. Nobody on earth wants to be here. Perfect cover. The only way to get here is by the lake." Roach points at a tree house way up in the highest tree on the embankment. "It's guarded by a post there, and one across the lake on the east side."

After some quick calculation, I see about fifty cottages, some small, some big. There are probably about 150-200 people in this army. This group would get decimated by all the Nazis we saw in Manhattan. I'm also curious to discover where they get their weapons from. Maybe joining the rebels was a bad idea.

"Come on," says Roach, "It's late. I'll show you where your quarters are."

Roach leads us down the embankment to a canoe and that's when we get to see our new neighborhood up close. It's a swampland in the middle of Upstate New York. Imagine a huge bowl of flooded cereal where mounds are poking up through the milk. Rundown cottages are barely standing upright on small islands scattered around the swamp. Some are large enough with a small field to house a few animals, some look so dilapidated that they are probably uninhabitable. Then again, I saw families living in the concrete rubble in New York City, so who knows what the people are doing here.

"Hop in the green canoe," directs Roach. "I'll give you a lift to your cottage."

"You guys travel a lot by water," mentions Frank.

"Another month or so this place will completely freeze over," explains Roach. "We'll have to switch from canoes to ice boots. Makes transportation a little more difficult."

Roach takes us past several other cottages to a small one in the middle of the swamp. It's overgrown with ivy and moss and a plastic tarp covers half of the roof. Obviously, no one's been in this one for some time.

"This is your new home," says Roach, "Let's hope it brings you better luck that the last couple that lived here."

"What happened to them?" Frank asked.

"Dead," says Roach solemnly and makes the sign of the cross, "May they rest in peace."

Roach gets back into the canoe, "I'll come back and get you in the morning. We start assessment soon after sunrise." Roach rows away to the next island over. A woman in a rocking chair gets up to hug him as he steps up on the porch. She's been waiting for him to come home. They embrace and go inside.

As soon as Roach is inside his cottage, Frank turns to me with a disappointed and frustrated look, "What were you thinking? We were almost to Canada. I was almost home!"

Frank's unhappy with me, and I don't blame him. But he's letting his longing to go home get the best of him.

"Did you hear what Paul was saying? Canada is a wasteland," I decide to give it to him straight. "How do you think your Maple Leaf friend got his burn scars? Those are not the kind of burns you get rescuing a kid from a burning house, those are radioactive fallout burns. Beside, this may be our chance to fight. To do something. To change everything! I have to do this."

"What about what I need to do?" he protests. "What about my need? My family is up there in Canada. Who knows what my great-grandfather is going through right now? All I know is I can help him. I can do my part to save my country, bring honor to our family name again."

"What country?" I snap back. "Did you hear Roach? It's

this time shift's Hiroshima. I'm not going up there. I have to stay here."

"You think it's all gone?" he pleads. "How do you know unless we go up there and find out? If there's a chance my family is alive, I have to find out."

"We have a chance here to change this war," I argue. "We have to take it. I can't do this without you."

"Listen," states Frank, "I was with you when we ran from D.C., I stood by you as we escaped from the Nazis in Manhattan, and I crawled into an oil tanker because that's what you thought was best. But I am not going to protect you anymore, because 200 people against a full Nazi army is suicide." Frank storms into the cottage and the screen door slams behind him, possibly waking up everyone in the swamp. I follow him in.

"I don't need any protection from you," I scoff. "When I found you days ago, you were a bumbling idiot and didn't even know what year it was. I saved you. You owe me."

Frank is halfway up the stairs, "You don't need me, Daughter of Time Travel. Princess," he mocks. "The first chance I get, I'm going home." He continues up the stairs, "This place is a hellhole."

I look around the cottage and he's right. The kitchen is littered with dirty pots and plates. The dining room table leans into the wall, and two wooden chairs are each held together by twine. The couch is ripped, torn open at several places, and has stuffing protruding throughout. The carpet looks like it hasn't been replaced for decades. A few paintings of nightlife in New York City during the Roaring 20s hang lopsided on the wall.

I sit down on the couch and wonder if I made the right decision. We'd be close to the border by now and who knows what we'd find on the Canadian side. On the other hand, I chose to stay here and I don't know what that will bring us either. I've spent the past five years of my life knowing exactly what each day would bring, what each decision I made would lead to. But now, I'm clueless as to what tomorrow will bring, and even worse, what will happen the day after.

I go upstairs to find one bed that looks about as lumpy and comfortable as a plastic ball pit. Frank's oily clothes are already on the floor, and he's crawled in it fast asleep, or at least is pretending to be. There's no way I'm joining him and no way I'm going to sleep feeling like I've been slimed by a sperm whale.

I rummage through a dresser and find some plaid pajamas from the former owner. Through another door are a bathroom and a shower complete with running hot water and soap. I shed my clothes, turn on the shower, and begin to wash off the grime from the past several days. I scrub myself clean as I think about the week's events. A few days ago, I was sipping coffee at my favorite breakfast place chatting with Frank about 80s music videos. Now I'm in some God awful swamp cottage in the middle of New York State.

I get out of the shower and begin to towel off. I come to the realization that I need Frank, and although he may not admit it, he needs me. We're each other's only connection to the future. If Frank and I are going to get through this, and make any positive change, we have to have a plan of action. When he wakes tomorrow, I have to convince him to stay. And after I convince him to stay, I need him to help me overthrow the Nazis. He's the only one that knows it's even possible.

But persuading Frank not to leave is going to be even harder than beating the Nazis. I've been with Frank when he's determined and right now he's hell-bent on getting back home to Canada. The only reason he's here right now is because of his loyalty to me, and it looks like that is on thin ice.

Nothing seems to be going my way, tonight. I'm swimming in the pajamas I found. Either I lost some weight or the women of this age are built bigger. Well, at least they aren't decorated with pictures of cartoon duckies. Instead, they are as plain gray as all the other clothes I've seen. I come out of the bathroom and look at Frank on the lumpy bed. While I'd like to fall asleep in his comforting arms tonight, I'm not sure he'll be as inviting as he has been in the past. I head back downstairs. I find a blanket in the closet and curl up on the couch. I make sure the window curtains are open so the sun can wake me up. Assessment starts soon after sun rise, and I can't miss whatever that is. As I doze off to sleep, I feel more alone than I ever have in my life.

EIGHTEEN

When people have a loved one pass away, they try to recall happy memories of that special someone. During college, when I was feeling down and lonely, I'd dream of a special moment with my mother and me. It was usually when I was young and we'd go to the zoo. She'd get year-round passes to the Columbus Zoo and we'd spend many a summer day laughing at the polar bears swim in their big ocean habitat, staring as the flamingos stood on one foot, or watching the lions bask in the hot midday sun. There was a Siberian tiger exhibit with a large, thick, glass display. We'd see the big huge cat pace back and forth, back and forth, looking for a way out. The zoo even boasted the world's largest snake. Mom would take me to see it and I'd just squeal. One particular day we did it all, we managed to see every animal in every part of the zoo. We had to start when it first opened and stay until it closed.

Dad was working on his research that summer, but on this day Dad meet us for dinner at the zoo. We ate at our favorite hamburger place, the one that serves the square hamburgers and a shake so thick I had to eat it with a spoon. Dad explained I graduated that summer. I was allowed to get a regular hamburger instead of the junior. I was a big girl now.

I loaded up with a hamburger, fries, Coke, and the shake. Mom and Dad laughed all dinner long as I scarfed it down and finished it all. They always said I was the fastest eater in the world. Afterwards, we still needed to visit the primates so we all headed to see the Orangutans. They were Mom's favorite. She used to say that many believed Chimpanzees were more related to humans than other great apes like Orangutans or Gorillas. If you look at pure genetics, that's true. But she theorized that you can't just look at the science, you need to look at behaviors as well. If you see the bond that the Orangutan mother has to her offspring, it is more related to the human bond than the one between Chimps and Gorillas and their offspring.

As we headed over to the farthest part of the park, I

grabbed my mom's hand and held on tight. Out of the corner of my eye, I saw my dad grab her other hand. They smiled at each other and then at me. This was truly a unique moment with our family. We were rarely together. Either my dad was off doing research, or my mom was. Our worlds just didn't intersect.

As we stood and watched the Orangutans swing from tree to tree, we saw a mother ape coddling a new born in her arms. It was the cutest thing ever, with these big black eyes and furry red hair. The hand holding between my mom, my dad, and me turned into embraces. The three of us had never been that close, nor would we ever be again. That day we were a normal family.

It was different to feel normal. Dad wasn't your typical Dad and was always a bit distant to me. He was involved in his work and research and was obviously his priority. But in this moment we were just your average loving family visiting the zoo that day, and the memory is forever burned into my brain.

Once I joined the academy, and had access to Dad's particle accelerator, I would frequently time travel to this moment and watch us. Why think of the memory when I could see it first hand? I'd sit on the park bench across from the orangutans so I could watch Dad, Mom, and young me, but not be seen. While I didn't have a view of the smiles on our faces, I could still see the warm embraces and just feel the love. It was one of those picture perfect moments, the kind that you see in movies.

Whenever I was at the darkest moments in my life, like I am now, I'd travel to this spot and relive the happiest moment in my childhood. It was almost like traveling to heaven to see my mom all over again. I missed her terribly and wanted to talk to her, but knew I couldn't.

And then one day the most amazing thing happened. One time, after a particular trying semester, I sat on that park bench watching my father hold my mother and me close to him. He had my mom in one arm, and me wrapped in his other.

But this time I saw something new that I've never seen

before. I looked across the clearing at a different park bench and saw my dad there, hiding, and watching himself, my mom and me hugging in front of the orangutans. He had traveled back in time to see the same memory.

Dad never noticed me on my park bench; he was too engaged in watching the three of us. I returned to current time without him knowing I traveled there but dumbfounded my special favorite moment, my memory of a loving family, was his memory as well. Maybe he wishes we had more of those, or maybe he just missed Mom as much as I did. I don't know. I never asked him. I just didn't have the time.

NINETEEN

I wake up to the smell of bacon. Even though the cushioning in the couch is about 20 years old, I'm not that sore. I stand up from the couch, stretch and walk into the kitchen. Frank has cleaned himself up from the night before, having found the shower as well. Wearing fresh clothes that are a bit too small for him, his tight shirt accentuates his broad shoulders, one of his attractive traits. The kitchen has also been cleaned up, dishes were drying in the sink and he had some pots and pans out making breakfast.

"Bacon will be ready in a few minutes," he said matter-of-factly. "There are no fresh eggs or fruit. But I'm cooking some oatmeal. Better find some clothes to put on, you don't want to have your assessment in those pajamas."

"Thanks," I try to say warmly and head upstairs to find some clothes. Wow. Frank is still very upset with me. I can understand he wants to get back to his homeland and find out what's become of it. But I'm sure he's torn between going home and being with me. There's always been some kind of connection between Frank and me; we've just never acted on it. At this point, who knows what will happen. I remind myself that we're a couple here. We'll have to figure out a backstory at some point. Depending on how long he stays, it might just be me making it up.

I open up the dresser drawers and discover some clothes that will fit me. Turns out the pajamas I grabbed weren't the wife's, but the husband's. Her clothes actually fit me quite well. I find a clean bra and underwear and put them on. Yeah, I know it sounds gross to wear someone else's underwear, but I've been running around in the same pair for almost five days and I need something clean. I find work jeans, a flannel, and boots. I pull back my hair and look at myself in the mirror. I'd pass for a Midwest Farmer's Daughter any day of the week and twice on Sundays.

I come back down and Frank has set a table of bacon, oatmeal, and water. Not very exciting, but it will have to do. I sit down and join him.

"Breakfast smells great," I say with a smile. "Thanks for cooking."

"This doesn't mean I'm staying," replies Frank as he slowly eats his food. He won't look me in the eye.

"Well," I say, "In the meantime, we have to come up with a background story. Remember, we're a couple."

"We met in D.C. a few years back, got married last year," Frank says coldly, "We decided to escape up to Canada for a better life. I don't think we can have any more details than that since we don't know that much about our world now. I figure when I leave, you can say there was trouble in paradise and that I really didn't love you."

"Okay," I say. Great, the one person that knows me in this time now wants to be as far away from me as possible.

"I'm sorry we didn't talk about it more before I stepped forward," I say. "Our chance was slipping through our fingers and I felt I had to act upon it."

Frank looks up with disgust and is about to answer me when there's a knock on the door.

"It's Roach," yells the captain as he looks through the window. "Time to head off for assessment. I hope you're dressed and ready."

"We'll finish this later," says Frank as he grabs a few slices of bacon. "By the way, you're cooking dinner tonight. Better talk to Roach about our food situation. Or it's bacon and oatmeal in the evening, too."

I answer the door and there's Roach with a small sack of food.

"The misses made me bring this over," smiles Roach. "It's some eggs, bread, and goat's milk. It should last you a few days. You don't need to worry about lunch and dinner around here. We eat those as a group."

I smile at Frank, "Looks like I don't need to worry about dinner tonight."

"Eventually, we'll need to find you a canoe of your own and probably sooner than later 'cause I'm gonna get tired of carting you around," Roach laughs. "Once you know you're way everywhere, we'll get you one. For now, I'll be your guide."

Frank finishes putting away the food and turns to Roach. "How long have you guys been here?"

"Too long," sighs Roach, "The wife and I got here about 10 years ago, came down from Canada for a better life. There was about fifty rebels back then. There's two hundred now. Almost enough for a solid Company of infantry. We gotta go now. The General will give me hell if we don't get there on time."

Frank and I climb into Roach's canoe, he pushes us off and hops in. "Before the war, this swamp land was drained into the lower part of the lake and dammed off," Roach explains, "But after the Nazis took over, resources were scarce and people focused on staying alive rather than worrying about whether vacation spots like this one were flooded or not. This place has no value at all. Since it's flooded, you can't grow anything here. There's no coal or oil in the ground, either, so the Nazis don't want anything to do with it. It makes a great hiding place for an army."

Roach guides us through twists and turns in the swamp. Before long, we're joined by other canoes heading in the same direction we are. "All of these people are going to some type of training. That's what we do here, train. We're waiting for Central Command to give us orders to move forward, where ever that might be."

"Central Command?" I ask. Sounds like their Central Command isn't that different from my Central Command.

"General McCafferty is in contact with Central Command, which governs the rebel alliance in the Northeast. He tells us there are troops in Massachusetts, New Hampshire, Maine, Vermont and some in Delaware. We've yet to hear from Connecticut."

Good, I think. There's more, a lot more. Maybe Frank will stay after all.

"What cities seem like the next target?" ask Frank.

"That's hard to guess," says Roach. "The Nazis have a strong hold on the coastal cities: Boston, New York City, Providence, and Portland. Those are definite no-no's, we're not ready for those. They also have a presence inland all the way up to Bangor, Maine. They may send us to Syracuse or to Albany to regain the state capital. Whatever the orders, we'll take them."

"What about Buffalo?" I ask.

"They'd never send us towards the Great Lakes. Conquering Buffalo or Niagara would give us a huge disadvantage. We don't want our backs up against a wall," explains Roach.

"But Buffalo could be a great start," brightens Frank, "And it's right across the river from Canada."

"Sure, it's right across the river and easy to get over if you know how to climb a twenty-five foot wall," says Roach.

"Wall?" I say.

"Yes," says Roach shockingly, "As in THE Wall – The Niagara Wall. You know, the one that runs from Buffalo to Niagara Falls. It's impenetrable."

Temporal change sometimes produces many strange aberrations. Since the front line isn't in Germany anymore, it looks like the Berlin Wall doesn't exist in this time shift. At least not in Berlin. It seems the Wall now exists in between the U.S. and Canada.

"Here's our destination," announces Roach. Up ahead several canoes have landed. The Chinese men from last night are already on the shore and others are waiting for us.

"And it looks like we're the last to arrive," says Roach. "That's strike one against the both of you. You'll have to really prove yourselves now."

"Honestly, Roach," I say, "I'm not sure you guys can be too picky about who joins your army. I mean, we're talking about thousands and thousands of Nazis on American soil. If you can point a gun and pull a trigger, than that's enough."

Roach is taken aback a bit by my rash comments. Frankly, though, I don't care because I'm never one to be put in my place or told what to do. If I want to join this army, I'm going to do it. Nobody is going to tell me no. I look over and this gets a small smirk out of Frank and a little shake of his head. I know what he's thinking, "The real Alex is coming out." He's right.

"Well," says Roach, "The General will determine your position in the company."

We come ashore and the eight of us newcomers are gathered in a group. I look around and find a few rickety pavilions and a dirt field they use as some type of rifle range. There's an obstacle course with ropes, a wooden wall, and tires.

We're surrounded by Roach, the General, and a few other members of the company from last night. Most of them are older guys in their fifties. Maybe they saw some war time a few decades ago, but to describe them as military men is a stretch. They look more like a bunch of guys who hunt during the weekend. But they do have a great start here, they just need some direction. They step a few feet away and discuss something out of earshot. Still feeling bold from the canoe trip, I turn to Frank.

"These guys need us," I whisper.

"Us?" he jeers back. "Who said I'm staying?"

"Look around here," I counter. "They have something here. All they need is a leader to take them to the next level."

"This is a back water shack and mountain men rebel base," he argues. "It's going to fail."

"It's not going to fail with the right leader," I say.

"There's no way these men are going to listen to you right now," he scoffs. "I mean, I know you and how talented you are. But here in the wilderness, you're just another redheaded woman. You should be back home doing my laundry."

"It's not me that I'm talking about," I say. "It's you. You can be their leader. You can be the one they follow."

"I'm no leader," dismisses Frank, "And I'm making my way to Canada."

I want to say more, but the General and his men return.

"Alright folks," announces the General, "Let's see what you can do. Who's ever shot a rifle?"

I raise my hand along with Frank and two of the Chinese guys.

"We got a regular Annie Oakley here guys," chuckles the General. The rest of the men join in laughter, except for Roach. He stands there and smiles. After our recent conversation in the boat, he probably knows I'm more than meets the eye. The General walks over to me and looks me in the eye. "You want to show us what you can do?"

"Sure," I say. "What'd you got?"

"M1 Garand," says the General, "You've ever shot one of these?"

"No," I say, "But there's always a first." The M1 Garand was standard issue during World War II. I've never fired one because the ten or so that still exist in 2085 are kept in military museums. But the good news is there is one at Wright-Patterson and I was once shown how it works. This will be easy for me.

"Roach," smirked the General, "You want to show this little lady how to fire this thing?"

"Give me the rifle, Roach," I say, "I can take it from there."

The men chuckle a little bit, but Roach isn't thrown off. Roach loads the rifle and hands it to me. "You see that pumpkin on the stump?"

"Yep," I say.

"It's about 200 yards away. Hit it."

I put the stock to my shoulder and take aim. The pumpkin is about two football fields away. I can hit that with both eyes closed and one hand tied behind my back. Just then, a deer steps into the field much farther out, about twice as far. I take aim on it, just to the center of the rear of its shoulder.

"Roach, do you like Venison?" I ask.

"Yep," he responds.

I fire away and the deer falls immediately.

"Good," I respond, "Because we're having it for dinner tonight."

There's a hush. Not a sound from anyone, not even Frank. Finally one of the other men speaks.

"General, that was 400 yards away," he says, "I haven't ever even seen Roach hit with that kind of accuracy."

"Girl," says the General, "Where did you learn to hit like that?"

When you time travel, you learn quickly that if you start to spin a story it's best to always base it in truth because then it's easier to remember. It's best not to completely lie because then you have to remember all the lies, and then you keep on spinning them and have to remember more lies. So that's my policy, tell the truth whenever you can. That's what I do here.

"In the Ohio Valley," I say, "My Grandfather Tommy taught me."

Another hush. The men look down at their feet, even the General. They are suddenly uncomfortable. Finally it's Roach that speaks.

"I should have known it when you introduced yourself last night, but I thought Eviston was a just a common name. The guys tried to convince me otherwise, but now we know. Boys, you're looking at the granddaughter of the late great General Tommy Eviston." Roach makes the sign of the cross, "May his soul, and the soul of his men, rest in peace."

The rest of the men make a sign of the cross. The General steps up to me and salutes. "Ma'am, it's a privilege and an honor to serve next to the daughter of the man who led the first rebellion army and died valiantly on the Ohio battlefield. You must be proud."

While it's my policy to always tell the truth, the plan sometimes has its faults. It's not fool proof. When time is trying to constantly reset itself, it uses the same people but in different ways. Here is case in point, my grandfather's name is Thomas Eviston, but he was named after his great-grandfather who led a company of troops in the Korean War. Major Eviston was a great leader and died on the battlefield trying to defeat the Commies. But it looks like in this temporal shift, he fought the Nazis in the Ohio Valley instead.

So now all the men in the troop think I'm the granddaughter of my great-great-great-great-grandfather who killed some Nazis. While it all of a sudden gave me a place of honor with these guys, the attention it gave me is going to make it harder and harder for me to keep my cover.

While I shined at the shooting range, the rest of the morning was Frank's. He shot just as well as I did, hitting not only stationary targets at plus 300 yards, but rabbits and squirrels as well. More importantly he smoked everyone in the obstacle course and did the 40 yard dash in 4.4 seconds.

In hand-to-hand combat, he dominated - winning every battle almost instantly. Better yet, he showed all the new Chinese volunteers his moves. Before you could say, "The Great Wall of China" Frank had created a fighting force that bested all the rebel captains.

Roach smiled with pride teasing the rest of the captains. "Never cross a Canuck," he joked. "Give me 50 more Canadians and we'll do some real damage to the Nazis." Then Roach went head to head with Frank. It was a tough battle that went on for a while. Frank knocked him down three times and instantly Roach got up for more. I finally had to call the fight and declare both of them the victors. Frank and Roach were quickly developing a close bond. Two Canadian men lost in someone else's country, someone else's world.

Throughout the morning, everyone asked me about my grandfather, what it was like to know him, and if I had any stories about the Ohio Rebellion. I'm pretty good at faking any conversation with someone. I nod my head, smile, don't say anything with any details, and don't raise any red flags. People want to think you agree with them, that you think just like them. So therefore, they just assume you know what they're talking about. I see Frank doing the same thing. They're all asking us questions, trying to grasp onto the memory of my grandfather. This is the inspiration these guys desperately needed. They want to believe that they too will have the courage to go toe to toe with the Nazis just like Grandpa

Tommy did. At lunch, Frank and I sneak away to get a little bit of alone time and we're able to fit together bits and pieces of my family's new history.

My grandfather (or great-great-great-great grandfather) grew up in the Ohio Valley and was one of the largest corn growers in the area. Corn was a huge crop for Ohio and my grandfather's was famous as the sweetest around. Eviston Irish Gold they called it. One Fall, the Nazi Army that held the Columbus area drove into town with several of their trucks. They took all of the county's corn, bushel by bushel, to feed the large amount of troops that guard Columbus and the Dayton area.

Everyone questioned why there was such a huge army in Central Ohio. They didn't see it as a strategic stronghold like Cleveland, Chicago, or an industrial center like Pittsburgh. But this made total sense to us. Columbus is where my father discovered Time Travel and in Dayton at Wright-Patterson Air Force Base is where the High Powered Particle Accelerator is housed. The Nazis know this, and they are protecting it.

Grandpa Tommy was not happy about the Nazis taking all their corn. The farmers of the area had almost nothing left to eat for the rest of the winter and no means to get more. He gathered over 100 local farmers, all with shotguns, and planned a heist to get back the corn. They snuck into South Columbus, found their warehouse, and opened fire. Although the farmers were outnumbered 3 to 1, they totally caught the Nazis by surprise and quickly killed off 250 of the guards. The rest deserted their posts. The farmers dropped their weapons and started loading up the corn in trucks to take back home.

That's when a second wave of Nazis showed up. A full battalion of 2,500 troops engulfed the place and unleashed a storm of hell on every American in the place. Every single farmer was killed within minutes. Rumor has it that my grandfather was the last to go down, praising God and the Red, White, and Blue as he was peppered with machine guns.

But it didn't end there. The Nazis went town to town throughout the Ohio Valley, burning down any crops that still stood and randomly killing men, women, and children. They sent a clear message they were in command and quelled any future rebellions.

The battle is a deep wound in the memory of every American. It was the first time we stood tall against the Nazis and shed their blood on our land. General McCafferty said the Ohio Valley Corn Rebellion was the beginning of the end for the Nazis. Our battle cry for the rest of the day became "Remember Columbus!" and chants of "250 more!" Frank and I knew that it would take more than 250 dead men to push the Nazi army back to Germany.

TWENTY

In the late afternoon Roach gathered us around and gave out our troop assignments. Most of the Chinese were put in the 2nd Infantry unit, with a few placed into the 3rd. Frank is in the 1st Calvary and I am a member of Forward Command. Roach claims my presence there would bring us good luck. He also congratulated Frank for his quick rise in position. Frank and I were invited to dine at the General's island that evening so we all headed back to our cabins to wash up before dinner.

When we got to the shore, Roach had a smile on his face. "I got sick and tired of carting you guys around so I got you your own canoe." It was old and dented, and the paddles were worn, but we were lucky to have one. The Chinese looked at us in envy because they were still being driven around.

Frank and I followed Roach back to the cabins and planned to meet again in an hour to head to the General's for dinner. We got to our cabin, tied off the boat to the dock and went inside.

"Looks like the Daughter of Time Travel is still the star of the show," chuckles Frank.

"Well it's a good thing they respect us," I say. "They've put us in some great positions so we can really affect the change of battle."

"Alex, I'm not staying," says Frank sadly. "I have to get to Toronto and help my own people. It's been 10 years since the bomb was dropped there. I'm sure there's rebuilding that has to be done and my family is at the center of it. I can help them." His animosity towards me is gone. I look into his eyes and see the pain behind his decision. It hurts him to leave me behind.

"You do what you need to do," I say. "I'd want to go back if the shoe was on the other foot." Frank comes over to me and hugs me, in a submissive way. I hold him tight to comfort him. The reality is I'm staying here for the same reasons he's leaving, our ties to country and honor are stronger than the bond between us. We're just two inspectors that ended up at the same place at the same time. At the end of the day, I'm an American and my country needs me here. He's a Canadian and needs him to bring them back to greatness. "It will be alright," I whisper to Frank. "You can make things better."

After several moments Frank lets go of me. "Thanks. I'll probably leave in the middle of the night. You better hop in the shower and get ready for dinner. I'm going to pack a few things for my long trip."

I slowly step away from his embrace and make my way to the stairs. Frank grabs my hand and stops me. "Alex," he says while looking into my eyes. There's one of those long awkward pauses, as if one of us is supposed to do something, but neither of us has the courage to do it. After several moments, he still doesn't let go of my arm. Just as I'm about to move closer to him, he lets go of my arm and says, "You'll be in good hands here. Roach, the General, they are good people. This rebellion will happen, and you'll be a success. These men need you." He turns and goes into the kitchen to pack some food for his trip. I leave him there and head upstairs. I look around the bedroom and couldn't help but wonder what would have happened to us if he chose to stay.

While I wash away the day's grime, I think about how much Frank has become a part of my life. Everything about the past five years of being an inspector has been fake to me. I've been living in someone else's reality, some other time. The art, the music, the movies, the clothing, all of it isn't mine. And what I've known from my time, I've isolated myself from. I've been away from the future for over five years. That's not mine anymore either. But Frank has been my constant, he belongs to me. I find strength and comfort in being around him. I understand he needs to be with his countrymen, but I need him, too.

I get dressed for dinner and go downstairs. He's there sitting on the couch with his head in his hands and he looks up at me.

"I washed up in the sink down here while you were getting ready," he says. "I wanted you to have your privacy."

I pause. There is so much I want to say to him, but don't quite know how to say it. "We should head to dinner," is all I manage to get out.

We get into the canoe, meet up with Roach and his wife, and head over to the General's cottage. Frank doesn't say a word to me the whole time. I know he's torn between going to his homeland and staying here with me. I desperately want him to stay. I want to tell him not to go, to stay and fight. Remind him that these men can use his leadership, that the battle is here and not in Canada. But I don't want him to stay because the rebellion needs him. I want him to stay because I want him near me, and that's just something I'm not yet ready to speak aloud. So we sit in silence, with only the rhythmic sound of the paddle in the water. Frank just looks ahead, focused on following Roach and his wife in their canoe.

We've built a quick friendship with Roach and I found it odd that he hasn't yet introduced us to his wife. As we follow his boat, I start to see her scars and understand why.

In the night sky we see a gorgeous silhouette of a woman, flowing long black hair, high cheek bones, narrow shoulders, and slender arms. As we paddle next to them and get a bit closer, the moonlight starts to peaks through the trees. It shines a light on her body and we see a different story. Her scars from the nuclear fallout are much worse than Roach's. They run up her right side from her long feminine fingers all the way to her high forehead. It looks as if someone took melted Swiss cheese and stretched it all over the right side of her body. The scars are darker than her normal skin on the left side, but with patches of depigmentation throughout. Deeper white scars spread in all directions like scattered tree roots popping up from the ground. It's a horrifying scar that's made worse by the contrasting beauty of her untouched, undamaged left side.

I'm examining her body, trying to understand what's happened to her, what she's gone through, when she turns to us to see where we are. I look away and hope she didn't realize I was staring. I'm embarrassed that I was most likely caught gawking at her, but even more embarrassed by quickly averting my gaze instead of smiling at her warmly. We all continue to paddle in silence.

The General's island is in the middle of the swamp, and it's the biggest one. At the top of a small hill sits a large cottage that appears to be his residence. On the lower lands, close to the docks, is a large fire pit with tables and benches off to the side. Many of the women are already here preparing the side dishes along with a large burly man who is butchering the Buck that I killed earlier that morning. The rest of the men are tending the fire, describing that morning's kill and laughing amongst themselves.

"Thank God, she's a great shot," I hear one of them say. "Otherwise we'd just be eating pumpkin pie again tonight!" The men erupt in laughter.

We bank our canoes and once we're on the shore Roach introduces us to his wife. "Alex, Frank, this is Ella." Ella sheepishly gives us a slight bow of her head and averts her eyes. I extend my hand.

"Ella. That's a lovely name," I say. "It's a pleasure to meet you. Roach has been very kind to us. I'm sure you've taught him well."

Ella blushes under her scars and looks at me and smiles. "Thank you," she whispers. Out of the corner of my eyes I can see Roach is touched by our warmth.

"Yes," says Frank, "a pleasure to meet you." He shakes her hand as well. Up close we get a full view of her body that's shrouded in deep scars from head to toe. It's no wonder we haven't met her, yet. She must be a recluse here. The nuclear blast was not kind to her at all.

"Come," says Roach, "Let's head to the fire. They'll be putting venison steaks on soon and we'll need to help with the cooking."

As we tend to the fire and cook the steaks it's obvious that Ella and I are not part of the norm. There is a clear separation of the sexes, with the women preparing the meal and the men tending the fire and cooking the steaks. But Ella never leaves

Roach's side and I've been brought into the fold of the men.

Many of them continue to ask me about my Grandfather and I don't have much more to tell. I explain that I only spent a week or two every summer on the farm and didn't really know him that well. The good news is they all took in my white lies and embellished the stories with their own knowledge of my grandfather.

After some time the steaks are done, the sides are finished, and the food is served. One of the Captains goes to the General's cottage to let him know dinner is ready and the rest of us sit down on a few benches. I looked around and only see a handful of families.

"Roach," I ask. "Is this the whole army?"

"No," he explains. "The General only eats with his Captains most nights. You and Frank are special guests."

The General and his wife come down from their cottage and stand at the head of the table. Everybody stands up as well and hold hands. Ella reaches out for my hand and bows her head. Frank and I join in.

"Dear Lord," speaks the General. "Tonight we have so much to thank You for. We thank You for this wonderful meal that You provided and for the hands that so skillfully prepared it. We thank You for each other, for the warmth and comfort we give each other every day. We thank You for Alex and Frank, that You have led them to us and that they have strengthened and renewed our passion for justice. Lord, please shine Your light upon us. Help us bring better days to this great land of ours. Give us the power to save our people from this villainy and evil doings, and recapture our homelands. Show us the way, O Lord, and help us heal Your people. In the name of Jesus Christ, Amen."

The rest at the table respond with "Amen," and we all sit down for a wonderful meal. An amazing amount of food is passed our way: thick Venison steaks with a pepper garlic rub, mashed Sweet Potatoes with cinnamon butter, fresh broccoli, zucchini, red peppers, corn on the cob, and apple pie. Frank and I fill our plates and gratefully take seconds when they are offered. After all the Chinese food in New York City, we needed a good ol' American Midwest meal. It's the best dinner we've had in over a week.

At the end of the meal, not much food is left over. These people had learned to cook only what they need and never waste anything. The fat is put aside for making soap and the remaining pieces of venison are carried to the smoke house and hung for jerky. Any other scraps are fed to the animals that happily eat it up.

After the tables, plates, and silverware are cleaned, we gather the benches around the fire. Since the November nights get cold in upstate New York, the fire is stoked with more wood. Couples snuggle together under blankets that are passed around. Frank and I get one as well, which I promptly wrap around us. Frank snuggles close to me. It may be so he could continue our cover as husband and wife, but it may mean something more.

Roach and Ella sit next to us around the fire, wrapped in their own blanket. She places her head on his chest and he pulls her in tight, as if he was protecting her from the pain of a life long gone.

We are all quiet, resting after a full meal. You can hear the nighttime crickets, owls, and birds talking to each other. Out in the far distance a coyote is howling. The fire crackles loudly in front of us.

"Well my fellow Canuck," says Roach to Frank, "What brought you down here to the states?"

"My parents died when I was young," Frank lies. "I was sent down here to be raised by a distant relative."

"You must have had no family whatsoever in the Great White North," laughs Roach, "Because before the bomb I wouldn't have sent my worst enemy down here."

"It was a while ago," Frank explains. "Way before the bomb." After a long pause Frank asks, "What happened up in the homeland after the bomb?"

Ella twitches a little with the mention of the bomb and Roach pulls her tight. She takes a deep breath. "Canada was the last bastion of freedom in North America," she says. There's a hush across the fire camp. It's obvious that Ella rarely speaks, and when she does it's of dark memories like this one.

"Toronto was the great leader of the freedom movement. Most of the war was fought out of it. Fighter planes ran nightly runs, dropping bombs on Manhattan, D.C., and Philadelphia. We knew we were killing Americans, but we were trying to drive out the Nazis and free us all from their grip of our Continent. We lived outside of Toronto, on the Eastern end of Lake Ontario in Hamilton. Jimmy and I worked in a secret shipyard, building the smaller ships that we're used for transporting troops from the Canadian shore to the American shore. The first bomb was dropped on Toronto, August 6th at 8:15am. It was a Monday morning. Factories and offices were full of civilians just starting their work week. The army bases had just changed duty, with the night crew heading to bed and the day crew starting maintenance of the planes. Because so many adults had to work in the factories, they established school all year around. I can see images in my mind of all the kids sitting at their desk learning their ABCs, never knowing what was about to come."

Ella pauses for a moment, sucking back a tear as Roach holds her close.

"They never knew it was coming," she continues. "The Nazis flew in one B-29 bomber. The Canadian army figured it was a reconnaissance mission and they had nothing to hide in Toronto. The bomb landed on Sunnybrook Hospital, and instantly destroyed everything in a five mile radius. From the Lake to Bayview, and from Highland Creek to the Airport was all gone, a burning lake of dirt. The blast was so strong it leveled everything. Imagine one moment you're looking at a 50 story building and the next moment it's disappeared," Ella pauses again to wipe a tear from her eye. Roach just stares into the fire.

"My cousin was at Sunnybrook that day," says Roach somberly. "She had just given birth to a boy two days earlier.

Her husband, she and the baby were supposed to check out that afternoon and come home to Hamilton. They never even had a chance to survive, the bomb killed them all." Roach pauses to hold back tears.

"They instantly shut down the factories in Hamilton and we all went home that day," continues Ella. "We were glued to the television, watching reports trying to get any visual of what had happened. Frequently, the Canadian broadcast was hijacked by the Nazis who promised more atrocities if we did not surrender. In the evening, our President came on and told us to go back to work. That the factories were opening back up and we must double our efforts against the Nazis for the sake of freedom."

"We thought of leaving that night, and making a break for the New York border," Ella says embarrassingly. "While we were strong patriots of our homeland, we didn't want to meet the same fate of our cousin. We one day," Ella touches her womb, "we one day wanted a family of our own." Ella falls silent for a long while, but none of the others at the fire speak. While they had heard her story before, they stay quiet out of respect.

It is Roach who breaks the silence. "So we went back to work. Our country needed us. During the day, the factory routine made things seem normal even though our pace was quickened. At night things were different. Images of the devastation were finally coming in and broadcasted from six to midnight. Interruptions from the Nazis Propaganda Machine were dotted throughout the evening, claiming they had more targets if we did not surrender."

"We were good citizens," Ella says, "Going to work bright and early and working hard for the good of the country. That Thursday we were hard at work at the factory and the sirens started around 10:45am and we thought we were under attack. The sirens stopped and we were relieved. Jimmy came running to me and hugged me. He whispered in my ear that we'd make a run for it that night. Right then and there we heard the explosion and knew the sirens should have never stopped.

Jimmy grabbed my hand and dragged me to the edge of the nearest dock where he knew there was a finished boat." I guess Ella is never able to use Jimmy's nickname of Roach.

"I had a plan figured out, just in case," Roach explains. "The day before, one of the other guys and I were talking and figured if a bomb hit, the target would be 5 miles inland. The Nazis wouldn't drop the bomb near the lake and waste nuclear damage on the water. They'd let it go farther into the city for maximum effect. We knew when we heard the explosion we had a few moments to survive. We could run to a finished boat and try and get out on the lake as soon as possible. I jumped in a boat with Ella and started it up. It was all gassed up and ready for delivery. Moments later, my buddy Greg and his wife, who also worked at the factory, hopped in and we took off into the middle of Lake Ontario as far away from the blast center as we could. But we weren't fast enough. Radioactive fallout hit us like a Canadian snow storm in January. It covered us and the boat, burning our bodies. Once we were out on the lake we jumped in the water and were able to wash some of it off. But it had already done its damage and the water made the pain even more unbearable. We climbed back into the boat and drifted in the middle of the lake undetected. After nightfall, we slowly made our way to the New York shore by paddling under the moonlight sky. We made it there unnoticed by the Nazis. We left the boat, completely washed our bodies of the radioactive fallout and hid out in a cottage by the lake. We found clean clothing and food, slept there and tried to heal our bodies. After a few days we were well enough to walk and knew we couldn't stay there. The Nazis frequently patrol the shoreline. They'd find the boat, then they'd find us. The next night we started walking South and eventually ended up here."

"What happened to Greg and his wife?" asks Frank.

"Funny thing about radioactive fallout," says Roach. "It's a gift that keeps on giving. You see, it just doesn't burn your skin, it gets inside your body and starts eating you from inside out." Roach places his hand on Ella's head as she snuggles tightly. "You see, Ella and I, we'll never know the pleasure of being a family," he pauses.

"And Greg and his wife," adds Ella, "Well, they're the former tenants of your cottage. Both of them have been fighting cancer for the past five years. They lost the battle earlier this summer."

Frank holds my hand tightly and I pull him close. We've been sleeping in Greg and his wife's bed, eating at their table. I'm wearing her clothes.

"My Canadian countrymen never surrendered," says Roach with pride and sadness. "The Nazis kept on bombing their cities over and over again, but they never surrendered. It's a nuclear wasteland up there now. Millions are dead. The Government is dissolved. No way to get food, water, or anything. Survival is near impossible. Be glad you're here."

"What about Burlington? How has that fared?" Frank wonders.

"The Nazis destroyed everything on the shoreline from Hamilton all the way up to the Prince Edward Peninsula," explains Roach. "Nothing stands there anymore, including Burlington."

I hold Frank tight to me and he starts to quiver a little. Destruction of the whole lakeshore means the death of his family. His father is Minister of Defense. I'm sure he was targeted.

"One day we'll eliminate the Nazis from this world," commits Roach. "We'll bring peace once again. Then we'll all gather side by side and rebuild this world into the greatness it once was because the people deserve to be happy."

General McCafferty stands up and places his hand on Roach's shoulder. "One day, Roach. One day soon."

"We'll get those bastards," Frank adds. "If it's the last thing I do."

I look deep into Frank's eyes. There is anger, pain, and determination. Will he stay here and fight? Or still escape to Canada tonight? Before I have a chance to ask him, two younger men suddenly appear from the darkness escorting a third even younger man.

"Lieutenant Kelley, Lieutenant DeGroff, why aren't you at your posts?" asks the General.

"General, sorry to disturb you this evening, but we've found this boy on the shores of our lake," says one of the men. "He claims he's from Central Command and has a message for you."

"Well, boy, speak up," commands the General.

"Identify yourself," says the boy boldly.

"What is the secret code?" responds the General.

"All tyranny needs to gain a foothold is for people of good conscience to remain silent," the boy announces.

"The secret to happiness is freedom. The secret to freedom is courage," the General responds.

"Private Courier Steve Nepa," salutes the boy.

"General McCafferty of the Central New York Army. At ease," responds the General.

"General, I'm here to deliver these orders from Central Command." The boy reaches into his backpack and hands a small leather satchel to the General. The General begins to unwind the twine around it.

"Men return to your post," he commands to the young guards. "Someone get this Private Nepa a plate of food. He must be famished."

"Yes, sir," one of the captains responds, and takes the boy to get a meal.

The General begins to read the papers included in the satchel and his face turns ashen. He slowly folds the papers together and places them back into the satchel. He looks us all in the eyes and announces, "Men, go home to your families tonight. Kiss your wives, hug your kids, say your prayers and make peace with God. Tomorrow morning we head north to the Niagara outpost. Tomorrow, we go to war."

TWENTY-ONE

When we get inside our cottage, Frank falls into my arms and weeps. If a strong grown man like Frank cries on your shoulder, then you know he's gone to an emotional place of no return. We stand there for a long time, while Frank cries for his country and countrymen, but mostly for his family.

"It's all gone," laments Frank. "The cities, the people, my family... gone. Canada has been decimated."

I hold him. It's all I can do. I've never seen this side of Frank. He's always been the strong one, the confident one. But then again, he's never lost everything he's ever known.

"I'm going with you to war," he resolves. "Not just to inflict pain on those Nazi bastards, but because you're all that I have left." We sit down on the couch in silence, with me holding Frank in my arms. It seems like time stops for us; that we're the only thing that exists at that moment. We fall asleep there, hoping we can return this place to the world we know.

TWENTY-TWO

"1999 to 1989. 1999 to 1989, is there anyone there?" I am woken up by Frank's communicator on the coffee table. It hasn't been much help to us since we can't talk to Central Command, so we've been using it for its real purpose: as a music player. It's ironic how the music from 1989 which I find annoying has actually now become comforting.

But this wasn't music; it was someone trying to contact us.

"1989? Is there anyone out there?" says the male voice on the other side.

I pick up the radio, hit the right sequence of buttons and speak into the headset. "This is 1989, can you read me?" I say.

"1989? Thank GOD there is someone out there," responds the voice. "But wait a minute, your voice is female. Where's Frank?"

I shake Frank and try to wake him up. "Frank is sleeping – out cold. Who are you?"

"I'm Canadian Inspector Collin Kaffe," he says, "I oversee 1999. I've been trying to contact Central Command and have had no luck. A few days ago I realized this communicator can contact directly from year to year, I've been looking for a field counterpart ever since. You're the first person I've been able to reach and I started with 1875."

Wow. This guy's been going at it for a long time.

"Who are you?" he asks. "I don't recall any Canadian females assigned to 1989."

"I'm not Canadian. I'm American," I say. There's silence on the other end. I've definitely thrown Collin for a loop. To him, I may be a Nazi spy. That's when Frank finally wakes from his deep sleep.

"What's going on?" he asks.

"We have your Canadian counterpart from 1999 on the line," I say.

Frank brightens up instantly, "Crazy Collin? I went through the academy with him!" Frank grabs the communicator from me.

"Collin, my man," Frank yells into the communicator, "What's uppppppppp!"

"Frank!" screams back Collin in excitement. "It's awesome to hear your voice. I've been stuck here in Vancouver with no one to talk to. I thought everyone was dead. Thank God you're alive."

"We're okay. We're fine." says Frank. "I'm glad you're okay. I feared the worst, too. After finding out about all the nuclear bombing raids on Canada, I just assumed everyone was dead."

"The radiation blasts never got this far West," Collin explains. "But Vancouver is overrun by refugees from the East. A lot of people have gone up to Yukon Territory and Alaska to live in the wilderness."

"Well, we Canadians are resourceful like that," Frank smiles. It's the first bright smile I've seen on his face in days.

"Who's the American you're with?" asks Collin. "I figured they were all Nazis now."

"I couldn't be any safer," Frank proudly announces. "If I had to pick anyone to get stuck with in a Level Five Temporal Shift it would be Alex Eviston."

"The Daughter of Time Travel???" Collin shouts out. "THE Alex Eviston? Didn't you write your final thesis on her?"

Frank blushes. He turns bright red in embarrassment. "Yep," he says. "That one."

"My God," says Collin. "You were always one to get the ladies during school. Left me to pick up the scraps and get the bimbos."

Frank looks at me and turns even deeper red.

"Final thesis?" I whisper and smile slyly.

Somehow, Frank manages to get even redder. He's majorly embarrassed. For his sake, I decide to switch the conversation.

"Collin," I say. "Do you have access to the Internet?" As an inspector the Internet is our best research tool. When you're stuck in 1989, you can easily call Central Command and discover anything you need to. But since Central Command is run by the Nazis now, they obviously wouldn't be that helpful to me.

"Yes," says Collin. "It's been set up by the Soviets instead of Americans, so the dominant language is Russian."

"Do you know Russian?" I ask Frank.

"No," he smiles, "but Collin speaks it fluently. He dated a girl in college who was a Russian History major."

Collin lets out a huge belly laugh. "What do you want to know?"

"We're going to war tomorrow," Frank explains. "We're being sent to the Niagara New York border to defeat a Nazi outpost."

"Can you research and find out what happens?" I ask.

"Sure, I'll look it up." says Collin as he starts typing away. "I've been able to hack into a KGB database and learn a lot about what's happened over the past century. Basically the Nazis manipulated every major event since the unification of Germany back in 1871. Whenever you'd think time would shift back to normalcy, the Nazis do something to keep tearing it apart."

"I hope they don't create a temporal fissure," says Frank.

"There's no scientific data to support that," I counter trying to calm fears. But I'm lying. The VanVliet Theory has been stirring in the back of my mind ever since we left Mao Tai Jui. If the Nazis continuously created divergent events in the gravitational pull of time, they may have produced such a rift that splits time into two separate flows. If the divergence is long enough there could be a time fissure all the way back to the beginning of time.

VanVliet's Theory concluded a long enough divergence would cause an explosion bigger than the Big Bang. He never tested his theory, nor did anyone else in fear of destroying the world. Looks like the Nazis are running that experiment right now.

"I found it," says Collin. "The Battle of Niagara Falls, November 9th, 1989."

"How's it end?" asks Frank.

"Bad news my friend," says Collin. "According to this research, there are 2,000 Nazis stationed there."

"Frank," I grimace. "There are only 200 of us."

"You get slaughtered," reveals Collin. "The Army of Central New York led by General McCafferty gets completely wiped out. The U.S. Rebellion sent them there to get a quick win and inspire others to take up arms. Instead, the troops get obliterated and the rebellion gets squashed."

There's silence between us all as the sun starts peeking through the window. Our day is about to start. We need to meet our fellow troops at the training center.

"You can't go, guys," says Collin. "You're going to get killed."

"Well," I say, "looks like we're going to have to change history. I bet the Nazis weren't counting on a few inspectors to be at the battle."

"Collin, you have to help us out," adds Frank. "Keep on searching the KGB database. See if you can figure out how they lost. Maybe we can change the battle plan."

"Sure," says Collin apprehensively. "If I can figure out a way for you to take out 2,000 Nazis soldiers you'll be the first to know."

"Don't write us off so soon," I say. "We've got one thing the Nazis don't have."

"What's that?" asks Collin.

"Time is on our side," I smile confidently.

TWENTY-THREE

In the early morning dawn there are four large Semi-trucks parked on the dirt road along the field where we had target practice yesterday. About 200 men are checking and rechecking their gear waiting for the General to give the word to move out. Roughly 10% of us are women. It is great to see us represented among the rebel army. We have as much right to freedom as anyone else, and we are also willing to lay down our lives for it.

Roach approaches Frank and me. "The General wants to see you."

We follow Roach to the pavilion where the men from last night's meal are gathered around a large table looking at maps. The General looks up as we enter and smiles.

"I didn't have time to explain the good news last night," he says feverishly. There's a sinister look of excitement on their General's face, as if he's been waiting years for this moment and it's finally come to fruition.

"Both of you have been promoted to Captain," the General explains and reaches out to shake our hands. "Captain Bouchard, you'll be leading our 1st Calvary unit. Your mission is critical. You'll be our initial charge and will get to the Nazis before anyone else, attacking the Niagara outpost head-on before they even know it. We'll bring up the rear and supply additional troops when needed. The element of surprise is of utmost importance."

"Yes, General," Frank shoots me a glance of concern. Anyone with military training would realize that a frontal attack against a tower of 2,000 armed Nazis is a recipe for failure. I'm beginning to understand why this battalion was wiped out.

"Captain Eviston," says the General, "You'll be by my side helping me redirect troops if necessary. You'll take my commands and communicate it down to the field."

I'm shocked. All I am is a gopher. A flag bearer. Shouldn't I be leading a troop of men? The second infantry unit? A group of snipers? I'm confused about my lack of responsibility, and apparently, so is Roach.

"But General," interrupts Roach. "She's our best shot! We have dozens of privates that can relay messages."

"Roach, I am the General and my word is final. Captain Eviston will carry out her orders as directed, as will you. Everyone will carry out their orders as directed, is that clear?"

A unified "Yes" fills the pavilion.

"Men, our target is the Niagara outpost," says the General. "It's a 250 foot tower at the edge of Niagara Falls on Goat Island and it serves as a lookout and battle station for the Northern Front of the Nazi Army. No Allied army has been able to cross the Niagara River under its guard. When we take it out, it can open up the battle lines on the Northern Front and allow troops to easily come over the border. Our mission is to secure it and take possession."

"Why don't we just blow it to smithereens?" asks Roach. "We have the howitzer we captured from the Nazis."

That's right, the large gun we got when they ran out of gas and the rebels exploded the oil tanker. It's basically like a gun that sits atop of a tank and provides a hell of a lot of fire power. That's definitely a plus for us. We can make some real damage with it, and maybe win this battle.

"No, leave the howitzer here" said the General firmly. "We are not to destroy the tower. The Rebellion sees the building as a strategic tool in our ability to secure the area."

"I'm bringing it just in case," says Roach. "It can wallop hundreds of Nazis and I'm not leaving it behind."

"You can bring it, but only fire it on my command," says the General and then points to the map on the table. "Now, we'll be approaching the Outpost from the Northeast. It's highly fortified. Captain Bouchard and his men will have the element of surprise and should successfully take out the first few waves of Nazis. We'll send the 1st and 2nd infantry out after them to back up their troops. I'll be here on this hill and will be able to see the whole battle. Captain Eviston will be with me here and relay any messages down to the field. Any questions?"

"Yes," says Roach. "When do we leave?"

"Now," says the General with an evil grin.

We all disperse to get our troops ready for battle. The four Semi-trucks that are parked in the field had been refurbished as transports for our small army. Each truck sits 50 people, 25 on each side. On the walls hang weapons, artillery, rocket launchers, ammunition, and other gear. Most of the Captains are to ride in the cabs in case of an ambush from the enemy. Frank was assigned to ride in the trailer with his troops so he could get to know his men and rally them for battle.

"The General is clueless. This plan will fail," says Frank before leaving my side. "None of us will survive this. We're taking on a Nazi outpost of 2,000 men head-on and they will flatten us."

"We'll find a way," I say trying to comfort Frank.

"I'm leading a bunch of boys," he counters. "They are kids, and their fate is in my hands. Sure, I've done theoretical military computer simulations in Inspector school, but this is REAL. People are going to die if I do something wrong."

"Frank," I smile at him. "There is no one else I'd rather have leading these kids than you. You'll make the right decisions and we'll have a victory by the end of the day. Remember, this is not how the future is supposed to be. Temporal gravity is on our side."

"Well, let's hope for the best. Collin better figure out a way to turn this around somehow. You take the communicator," he says handing me his Walkman. "You're in Forward Command. It's better for you to have it."

"Thanks," I say and not knowing what else to do, I lean forward and kiss him on the cheek. "You'll be an awesome leader," I whisper in his ear and hug him tight. "I'll see you when it's all over." I turn and walk away without looking back, so he can't see the tear running down my cheek.

I pull myself together and hop in the front of the Nazi heavy truck. The General wanted me to ride middle seat in his cab, but I decided to ride shotgun with Roach instead. He's got to drive the howitzer onto the battle field and is taking up the caravan's rear. A couple of his men get into the truck's flatbed.

"Some of the boys and I played with the howitzer yesterday afternoon," Roach explains. "We had to test it so we fired off a few rounds. I'm pretty sure we have the hang of it. I can't wait to take out some Nazis with it."

"But what about the General's orders," I ask. "Didn't he say use it only on his command?"

"Sure," smiles Roach. "And he says those commands are coming from you. All you got to do is say the words and BAM – we'll have a whole handful of Nazis blown across the river to Canada."

I smile back at Roach. I hope he gets his chance. After some thought, I know he's going to get his chance. This is our ticket to winning this battle, and eventually I'm going to start giving the orders.

The sun has completely risen as we head out West. It's about 9am and we should get there a little before noon. I find it odd that we're attacking in broad daylight, but the nights have been getting colder around here and may not be that conducive to battle. Roach doesn't say much as he drives. He's focused on the road ahead of him and the job we must all do.

I lean up against the window and try to get some rest to calm my fears. I've been in a few intense situations before with gunfire, but nothing like I'm about to face today. This is war. Not just one person will be out to kill me, but thousands. They won't want to capture me, they'll want me dead. I don't have much protection, either, just a handgun and a rifle. I can't time travel myself out of this one.

As I drift off to sleep I find myself thinking about my Temporal Newtonian Physics Professor, Bruce Davis. Professor Davis was this unique character. He was laid back, cool, hip, and jazzy. He brought a perspective to Temporal Newtonian Physics that was a little avant-garde for his field. Everyone in the program flocked to take his course, which he never taught the same way twice. When alumni would get together they'd trade stories about his class, and inevitably you'd learn something new. He was the most memorable professor in the school.

Temporal Newtonian Physics was the study of how objects and events can affect temporal gravitational pull. It was widely accepted that time had a flow and each of us were pulled in that direction. When we time travel, we're taken out of temporal gravitation and into a new environment. But the thing is we don't belong there. Any force we apply against any object that's moving toward the gravitational pull will be temporarily pushed off course, but will eventually return back to its original destiny. Professor Davis would give an example of a huge rock falling down a dried up granite channel of a mountain stream. It doesn't matter what you do to that rock or what direction you push it in, it's going to roll back into the main part of the channel and continue down the mountain until it reaches the base.

One of the things that Professor Davis argued is that this sounded a lot like predestination. That everyone was pulled in a certain direction and we couldn't do anything about it. But Davis didn't believe in Predestination. He imagined there were greater forces at work that none of us could ever understand.

For example, if someone were to destroy the rock completely as it was traveling down the channel, then it would never reach the bottom in its original form. But students didn't buy this argument. They were so entrenched in the basic theories of temporal gravity that they couldn't believe in anything other than predestination.

One experiment he conducted to disprove this was a challenge to all students. He said we had the option to break the path we were on with our coursework and never attend his class. But he reminded us that the syllabus stated if we miss a class, we would fail. Since it was a core class, we needed it to complete our degree. So there was the dilemma: miss his class, prove that predestination didn't exist, but fail. Or, continue to attend class, agree with Temporal Newtonian Physics, and pass the course. Almost all of his students picked the second option because his class was exciting to attend and the option of not attending and failing didn't exactly seem like the best option.

On the other hand, Temporal Newtonian Physics was something I understood since the eighth grade. I could have taught the class in my sleep. But it was a prerequisite for my degree and I couldn't graduate from the school without it. After my first lecture, I went up to Professor Davis and explained this. I also asked him if in lieu of attending his class, I could write a paper supporting his position that Predestination of Temporal Newtonian Physics didn't exist. He obliged and I became the first person in the history of his course to not attend his class and still pass.

I explained in my paper that objects have independency within the gravitational pull. They have inherent energy and they may, at times, exert opposable energy against an object that's exerting energy against it. Let's take the classic pool table example. If the cue ball hits a stationary eight ball on a pool table it transfers its energy to the eight ball which continues the trajectory predetermined by the cue ball. That's an example of predestination. On the other hand, if that eight ball was replaced with a land mine which has considerable inherent energy, the land mine would react differently. Instead of energy being transferred to it and rolling across the table, the land mine would explode, conferring its energy to the cue ball, pool table, and other pool balls as well as the person who hit the cue ball to begin with. You could say that I blew the Predestination Theory out of the water. That semester I learned you can control your destiny and determine your own course of action.

We all have inherent energy within us. It's up to us to figure out how to use it. I plan to use mine today to kill Nazis. Lots of them.

Roach throws the car in park which jolts me out of my sleep. "We're here," he says solemnly.

I open my eyes and discover that we're out in the open on top of a hill. If the Nazis haven't realized we're attacking them today, then they are dumb. And normally, Nazis aren't stupid, they are really smart. The General's not doing a very good job of hiding us. The good news is we can clearly see the observation deck of the outpost. The bad news is they can clearly see us.

We've arranged the Semi-trucks around the edge of the hill to provide a makeshift wall to defend our base of operations. Unfortunately, they've left no room for Roach to drive the howitzer truck through. In fact, there's barely enough room to get any troops through.

Roach parks the truck in the center of the clearing. I hop out and look around to see if I can find Frank. Dozens of troops are milling about, getting their gear ready to head off to battle. Little do they know it's to their deaths. I can't find Frank anywhere, but I know he's out there somewhere. The General has set up Central Command on the top of the foremost Semi-Truck. I climb up a ladder to the roof of the Semi to join him. That's when I really get an understanding of what we're facing.

The Outpost rises high into the sky on top of Goat Island. It sits right at the edge of the falls and looks menacing as hell. Bright white concrete rings the lower level of the tower. The upper levels have several balconies or turrets giving the Nazis the ability to shoot in all directions. At the highest level is a glass observation deck from which the Nazis have a perfect 360 degree view of everything in the area. In a way, it kind of looks like a huge Air Traffic Control Tower.

A twenty-five foot tall wall protrudes from the side of the tower and runs the length of the Niagara River on the American side for as far as the eye can see. Traditionally, Goat Island splits the Niagara River. Most of the river goes over the Canadian side on the Horseshoe Falls. The rest of the river gets sent over the American and Bridal Falls on the South side of the island.

But in this temporal shift, the Nazis have dammed up the river on the American side as it approaches the falls. The flow of water has stopped on this side of Goat Island shutting off the American Falls. It makes the rushing waters on the Canadian side run even faster.

This is a huge strategic advantage for the Nazis. First, no one can attack them from the Canadian side. Anyone attempting to reach the tower from the foreign side will be instantly washed over the falls. On the American side, it creates a valley of rocks, boulders, and slippery stones which our troops must cross before reaching the tower. This slows down our attack and allows the Nazis to pick us off one by one.

Looking at the size of the tower and its height, it is safe to assume there are some 2,000 troops in there, most of which never even have to step out of the tower to fight our troops. They just need to stand out on the turrets and from their vantage point, shoot, and kill us. Our troops will never even get half way across the river bed. Frank will be leading the charge. He'll most likely be the first to be picked off.

I turn around and look at our troops. They've gathered into groups of four: the First Cavalry, the First and Second Infantry, and the Last Wave. There's about fifty in each group and they look like four football teams waiting to take the field. They are pumped up and ready to fight for their freedom. I spot Frank among his troops, shouting at them, patting them on the back, and doing his best to inspire them. This might be the last image I have of Frank, and I do my best to fight back the emotion. While he looks like a fierce leader, his men look more like boys. Most of them seem about sixteen, but there are several as young as twelve. He's like the coach of Junior Varsity football team. Our First Cavalry is a group of kids!

The First and Second Infantry are filled with all the soldiers that I've practiced with on the training fields. Average shots at best. Oddly, Roach leads our last wave. They are the older, tenured troops. Some bested me with their target ability.

This is ludicrous. I turn to the General who is now deep in thought looking at battle plans on a TV tray that's being used as a temporary map station. I look up at the Nazi Outpost. They have a clear line of sight to us. They must be looking down and laughing at us.

"General," I say, "Point of order." I have no idea what protocol is for interrupting him. He doesn't look up.

"Yes, Captain Eviston," he replies stoically.

"Why do we have our younger, less proficient troops in the First Cavalry, and better, stronger men with the last wave?"

The General pauses, but never looks up from the map.

"Have you ever been to war, Alex?" he asks.

"No."

"Ever led men on the battlefield?"

"No."

"Ever shot something other than a deer?"

I have, but I'm guessing a 'Yes' is not going to be welcomingly received. "No," I say.

The General looks me dead in the eye, "I am in command here and I will call the shots, not some daughter of a rebel that led an army to its death."

There's a hush among all the men on the roof of the Semi. I've been put in my place and knocked down several pegs. Yesterday, they honored me as the granddaughter of the man who led the infamous rebellion in Columbus. Today, I'm now just a woman in a man's world and I've never taken kindly to that. There's something strange going on here, but it's best to bide my time until I figure it out.

"General," one of the men asks, "How soon to battle?"

"We're going to do this Old West style," smiles the General. "We attack at high noon."

That gives me about thirty minutes to figure out my plan. I climb off the Semi and down with the troops awaiting battle. I find Frank and pull him aside.

"Something is definitely wrong here," I tell him. "There's no element of surprise. The Nazis can see us from their observation deck. They have to know we're here. Worse, yet, we're going to wait another 30 minutes before attacking."

"These kids are scared shitless," Frank tells me. "Some of them have never even fired a weapon. They're not cavalry. They should be back home in school."

"The General has Roach with all the experienced men in the last wave," I explain.

"No wonder these men were decimated," Frank says, "They are being led by a lunatic. We got the reincarnation of

General Custer up there. All ego and no brains."

"I'm going to go talk to Roach," I resolve. "He's itching to kill some Nazis, maybe he knows what's going on."

"All right," says Frank. He grabs my arm as I start walking away and pulls me back. "Alex, if I don't see you again, I..."

I cut him off, "But you will see me again. Trust me. And yourself."

I head over to the back of the area and find Roach with his men. They are checking and rechecking their guns, ready to start charging at a moment's notice. Roach already has the howitzer ready to go with plenty of ammo stacked in the truck. They all see me running up to them and start to get into a formation. They think I'm coming to give them an order. Roach figures otherwise.

"What's going on here, Alex?" Roach says to me immediately. "Has the General gone batty? All the best men are taking up the rear. Frank's not leading a company of men; he's leading a company of boys."

Roach can see how messed up this plan is, and I'm guessing that so can all the others. I look around, there's not much confidence in anyone's eyes. The troops are all assembled and ready to go, but no one knows where they are going. The Semis are arranged in such a way that we won't be able to get many troops through them quickly.

"Is there any way you can drive the howitzer between these trailers?" I ask.

"Even if I greased her down, there's no way I'd be able to squeeze through them," Roach said emphatically. "I'll have to swing way around them and approach the tower from the side."

That gives me an idea. "What kind of reconnaissance gear do you have in the truck?"

"What do you mean?" asks Roach.

"Binoculars. Do you have any?"

A private that's been listening to our conversation opens his backpack and tosses me a pair. "Thanks," I say. "I'll give them back after the battle."

"What are you thinking?" smiles Roach.

"I don't know. I've got to go talk to the General. After that, I'll have to come back down and deliver his orders." I smile ear to ear with a devilish grin. Roach nods his head in approval.

"We may not win this battle," says Roach. "But we're going to kill a shitload of Nazis."

"Oh, we're going to win this," I shout to him as I head back to the Semis. "And today is only the beginning."

I have no intention whatsoever of involving the General in my plans. Call it an outright coupe or whatever you want, but if General Custer's men had the guts to do what I'm doing right now, they might have survived the Battle of Little Bighorn. On my way back, Frank's Walkman buzzes in. I put the headphones on.

"Frank? Alex?" Collin is calling, "I have some more information. I found a KGB analysis of the battle. The overview gives some information on how they thought the Americans could have won."

"Let me guess," I say. "A full out frontal assault was a bad idea. We should have trapped them in their tower and picked them off one by one as they tried to get out."

"Wow," says Collin. "Right on. How'd you know?"

"American ingenuity." I respond.

"Well, how do you think your American impatience is going to factor into that?" Collin laughs.

"Not easily," I joke back. "But this time a woman is going to be giving the orders. Over." I reach Central Command and climb up to the roof of the Semi. It's close to high noon so I don't have too much time to finish my plan. I pull out the binoculars and survey the land. The river bed where the Niagara River once rushed through on its way to the falls is now dry. It's about as wide as the length of a football field and the banks are rather steep, dropping about fifteen feet deep. Crossing over it will be difficult. The Nazis have cut down all the trees and bushes between the Outpost and the river bank to give them a clear view. They could easily come out on the embankment and fire away until we're all dead. On our side, the trees go to the edge of the bank with some having grown their roots into the river bed itself. The trees can hide several of our troops and provide adequate protection. There's a clearing about halfway down the shoreline on our side between the Niagara Wall and the base of the Tower. It's a perfect spot for the howitzer.

I now turn my focus to the tower itself. Where is its Achilles' heel? The base is made of fortified concrete and steel. There's no way the howitzer can quickly blow through that. Layers of concrete continue for the next 150 feet until it gives way to three rings of battlements spaced 20 feet apart. These are the turrets they'll be attacking us from if they choose not to meet us on the battlefield. A great offensive move would be to target these battlements, but the interior would still be impenetrable and any blast would not cause much damage to the tower itself. Above the three rings, near the top of the tower, is a ring of glass windows. I can see uniformed Nazis milling around and observing the surrounding area. In fact, a few men are looking straight at us and reporting back to their superiors that are stationed at desks in the center of the observation floor. They shout back at them. One pulls out a simple mirror and using the light from the sun, reflects light back right at us in a fast repeating pattern.

I turn to the General whose arrogance is oozing out of him as he tells stories to his men. "Today, the Nazis will remember the name General McCafferty. It is a day that will live in infamy. It's a day when a strong, resolute General from the Great State of New York crushed the Nazi army with his bare hands and choked its last breathe from its shocked and surprised face."

The General looks over the battle field and up at the tower. Does he notice the reflecting light? I don't have enough time to figure it out. He turns to me, "Captain Eviston. Give the men the command. My finest hour has begun. CHARGE!"

I climb down the ladder and head over to Frank and his troops. "Change of plans," I say.

"The General's plans or your plans?" Frank asks.

"Mine," I smile. "Here's what you're going to do. About 100 feet from here is the edge of the river bank. The Nazis have damned up the Niagara River so it's a 15 foot deep dry river bed between here and Goat Island. I want you and your men to line the river bank and hide in the trees. Wait for the Nazis to march out. Wait to see the whites of their eyes, then open fire."

"You're going to send 2000 Nazis my way? How are you going to get them out?" Frank asks.

"You worry about hiding in the trees," I yell as I run away. "I'll worry about getting them out. It's time for you to lead these men to a victory, Frank. Now, CHARGE!"

Frank and his men begin shuffling through the spaces between the Semis and head towards the river bank. I take off and find Roach in the clearing. He and his men are gathered around the howitzer watching the young men run off, shaking their heads.

"Those boys are going to get killed, and their blood is on our hands. That should be us," yells Roach to me as I approach. "You, me, and all these guys should be the first wave!"

"Stop your complaining and get your ass in the truck," I grin as I climb in the passenger seat. I motion to a few of the other men standing around. "Get in the back or follow us on foot."

Roach leaps into the driver's seat, starts up the engine, and throws the truck into gear. "Where are we heading to Captain?"

"Pull around to the left of the last Semi," I direct him. "There's a dirt road that goes down to a clearing along the river bank. I think the Outpost will still be in range."

"Why do I think these aren't the General's orders?" smiles Roach as he hits the accelerator.

"Why do I think you really don't care?" I wink at Roach.

Roach smiles at me and opens the back window of the cab. "Get ready to load that baby up, boys! We're killing us some Nazis today and gonna make the world a little brighter! Woohoo!!!"

Roach puts the truck into high gear and takes it around the left side of the Semis. I look in my side mirror and see dozens of troops following us, waving their guns in the air and hollering like they've just won the lotto. These are the guys that have been training for months, some years, looking for a chance to bring freedom back to America. Today, they'll get it.

As we head down to the embankment, I share my plan with Roach. "Do you have any ammunition that will travel 200 feet high and about 1000 feet far? It's got to bust through glass."

"Glass is not a problem – even if it's pretty thick. What's the target?"

"There's a control center at the top of the outpost. About 200 feet up. There's a full ring of glass around it, my guess is it's pretty thick. There's about 30 Nazis up there and they seem to be using it as a command center. If we take it out, they'll probably lose all the communication to Headquarters and the Outpost will lose their leadership."

"I got several M107s back there. They'll do the trick. Plus if we aim them right, they'll take out a few floors above and below," smiles Roach.

"Awesome. Because that's the second part of the plan, we need so much commotion that the Nazis abandon their posts and evacuate the tower in panic."

"Are you nuts?" Roach shouts. "There's got to be a thousand plus troops in that thing. Do you want all them coming at us at once?"

"There's a dry river bed at the base of the tower, about fifteen feet deeper than the shoreline. Frank's boys are going to line the embankment and hide in the trees. The Nazis come running out of the tower in confusion and we pick them off one-by-one like panicked deer running from a burning bush."

At that point we hit the clearing and I get ready to jump out, "Position the howitzer so it's aiming right at the tower, I'll grab a few men to help with the firing and send the remaining men along the tree line."

"Go! Go! Go!" yells Roach.

I jump out of the truck and Roach starts to reposition it. There's just enough space for him to turn the truck around and operate the howitzer. We're right at the bank and have a clear shot of the Outpost from the side. Our moment of truth is approaching, it's time to return this country to the Americans.

Five burly guys jump out of the truck and I turn to one of the guys who was at the fire pit with me last night. I'll have to trust him, "Captain!" I yell.

"Yes, Captain Eviston," he responds with attention.

"Do you believe in freedom?" I ask him.

"Yes, Ma'am!" he says beaming with pride.

"Do you believe we can have it today?" I yell.

"Yes, Ma'am!" he says even louder.

"Then take the rest of these men and line the river bank from here until you meet Captain Bouchard's men. Wait for his signal to fire, for his signal only! Do you understand me, Captain?"

"Yes, Ma'am!" he proclaims. The excitement is beaming from his face.

"Captain, today the Nazis will pay. They'll pay for every American soul they've ever taken - every father that's died on the battle field, and every mother that's been ripped from her daughter's arms," I say staring him right in the eyes. "And your hands and the hands of your men will extract that payment. Today is retribution day."

I turn my attention to the dozens of men who have gathered around me. "Now go, I say. Go in the name of the United States of America!"

A huge cheer goes up and the men take off running towards the tree line and preparing themselves for battle. As Roach gets the howitzer in place, I check the tower with the binoculars. The Nazis are watching us, but it looks like they haven't quite figured out our plan and how they are going to react. Somehow, we're catching them off guard. The Nazis on the battlements are trying to take aim at the trees, but seem to have a hard time finding a target. Plus, no one has given the command to fire. They haven't spotted us with the howitzer, yet, either. Nor do I see any heavy artillery moving to take us out. It's as if they are waiting for us to make the first move.

"Captain Eviston!" a soldier yells as he makes it down the path. It's one of the men from the 2nd Infantry. "The General sends word to call off the attack and retreat. They are loading up the rest of the men on the hill into the Semis and getting ready to pull out. You're to gather up the men down below and start a hard retreat immediately."

"Retreat?" I question. This doesn't make sense at all. There's no glory in retreat. Why does the egotistical General want to back off? That's when the static on my Walkman chimes in and I hear a familiar voice.

"Alex," says Collin. "I have some more information and this time you're not going to like it."

Roach and the private look at me strangely. They've never seen a Walkman, nor heard one talk. I have no time for secrecy, but I throw on the headphones so they can't hear Collin. "Go ahead, Collin."

"Well, it appears there was one survivor from the Battle of Niagara Falls. KGB found your General McCafferty living the highlife in Buenos Aires in Argentina," Collin pauses. "Alex, he's a Nazi spy."

That explains it. The attack in broad daylight. Putting the inexperienced kids in the first wave. The suicide mission. The flashes with the mirror in the control tower. The General was planning for us to be defeated. Since his plan has gone astray, he's pulling out so the Nazis can track us back to our camp and kill every last resistance. But I'm not going to let him do that. Now I have the element of surprise with the General. I know he's a spy.

"Roach," I yell. "When you get that howitzer in position, you fire at will."

"Yes, Captain!" he yells back. "We're about five minutes until firing."

"Make it two," I say and I hightail it up the hill back to the base to stop the General.

TWENTY-FOUR

At the top of the hill two of the Semi-trucks are getting ready to head off. I jump onto the runner of the lead cab as it pulls out of first gear. "Stop!" I yell.

The driver looks deeply confused.

"Stop immediately," I yell with more affirmation, "That's an order!"

He slams on the brakes and I almost fall of the cab.

"Captain," the driver says as he steps out of the truck, "The General gave us a direct order to retreat and head back to camp. He said we underestimated how many Nazis were stationed here and there's no back-up. We're to meet up with other troops from the rebellion and regroup."

"Change of plans," I say. "We're to move forward. We're attacking immediately. Get the troops out of the trailer and prepare for battle."

"No can do," says the driver. "The General said he relieved you of your command. I can only take orders from him."

Damn. The General knows I've gone rogue.

"Well, where is the General?" I ask. "Let's go to him to resolve this."

"He's in the other cab," says the driver.

As we approach the other cab, I take out my side arm. Somehow I've got to take out the General, convince these two drivers to let out the infantry, and then convince everyone to go to war. This is not going to be easy.

The other driver pops out of the cab. "Henry, what's going on? I thought we were moving out."

"Captain Eviston says there's a change," says the first driver, "She needs to talk to the General."

"The General's in your cab, not mine," says the second driver.

"No, he's not," says the first driver, "he's in your cab." Looks like the General fooled each driver into thinking he was in the other's cab and has taken off.

"The General has deserted us," I say. "I'm in command

now and we're going to war."

"You're not second in command," the driver argues. "Roach is."

Just then a loud explosion comes from the battlefield. I look up at the Outpost to see fire and black smoke pouring out of the windows of their command floor. The howitzer hit its mark. Flames are flickering out of the shattered windows and scorching the brick outside. Nazis are leaping out of the broken windows and to their death below so they can avoid being burned alive. On the turret floors, the men have abandoned their stations at the battlements and disappeared inside. The place is going up in flames and smoke. Nazis will be pouring out any moment.

I turned to the driver who questioned me and yell, "Who do you think just fired the howitzer? Santa Claus?"

The drivers stare off at the Outpost in amazement.

"Men, get those trailers open now," I command. "Roach has fired the first shot. The battle has begun. To war!"

Both drivers run to their perspective trailers and open the bay doors. Men begin jumping out of the back with guns in hand. "This is not a drill!" I yell. "This is war. Can you smell freedom in the air? Victory will be ours!" I grab the Captains of both infantries and explain the plan.

"General McCafferty has abandoned us. I'm giving the orders now. You'll take your men down to the tree line at the riverbank immediately and meet up with the 1st Calvary. The Nazis are going to be pouring out of that tower any minute. Don't shoot any of them until they are inches from our shore. Wait until you see the whites of their eyes. Am I clear?"

"Yes, ma'am!" they shout.

"Godspeed, men. And God bless the United States of America," I follow the troops down to the riverbank and find Frank at the central point right across from the Outpost entrance. Smoke is flowing out from every hole in the tower. About 200 Nazis have stumbled out of the building and are making their way towards the river bank.

"Roach's first hit was dead on," cheers Frank. "The

observation deck erupted in flames and smoke instantly. Their command floor is gone. No one is giving them orders and their army seems disoriented."

"They'll gather their wits eventually," I counter. "A leader is coming their way." I point across to the far end of the river at end of that gives way to the falls below. Among the rocks secretly crawls General McCafferty making his way to the Outpost.

"What's he doing?" asks Franks. "Does he think he can take out the whole army single handedly?"

"No," I explain. "He's a traitor, Frank. He's one of theirs. He cooked this whole plan up so we'd come here to die. Collin was the one who discovered it."

"That explains why the General didn't want you out on the battlefield, and why he sent me with all these kids. The plan was for us to be decimated all along."

"Precisely," I add, "except he had no idea that we could read his battle plan from the future."

"What do we do now?" asks Frank.

"My guess is 2,000 Nazis are going to pour out of that tower. When they get to our shoreline, you're going to lead your men to kill them."

Frank and I, along with the other 200 men on the shoreline, wait patiently for the Nazis to cross the riverbed. After about 30 minutes, a total of 2,000 Nazis stumble out of the Outpost and gather on the lawn right in front of it. General McCafferty is among them and shouting at them in German. Our men can clearly see the General giving the Nazis orders and they become enraged. The men begin murmuring that the General is a traitor.

"Hold your fire!" I whisper and the message spreads all the way down the embankment. The General gets the Nazis into formation and they begin marching across the river bed. They are a whole 100 yards away and it will take some time to reach us, especially with the rocky and slippery riverbed. We motion to our men to stay calm, stand their ground and hold their fire. It is tough. A huge army is slowly making their way towards us.

Everyone is itching to take them out, but we have to wait. If we fire too early, they'd retreat. Our only hope is to wait until they can't return. We can win, but the odds don't look good. We know we are 10% of their forces and we may not be able to stop them. We need extra firepower.

"Frank, you give the command to fire," I say. "I'm going to talk to Roach. We're going to need him to help blow away some of these Nazis if we're going to win this battle."

"Will do," says Frank.

I start sprinting along the tree line to the clearing where the howitzer is. I hear some static and someone calling my name. I almost forgot I had the Walkman.

"Alex, come in. Come in, Alex. It's Collin."

"Go ahead, Collin," I answer.

"Alex, things are changing right before my eyes. Words are shifting on the documents I've found and it's almost happening too quickly for me to read."

"Great, we're making some change," I say confidentially.

"Unfortunately, not enough to win," Collin says. "The Nazis are monitoring the battle, too. They know it can make a difference." Collin pauses. "Alex, they are bringing planes. They're going to take you out from the air."

We're sitting ducks on the tree line and the Nazis won't think twice about risking their own men's lives to take ours. "I'll figure something out," I say and quicken my pace to Roach, "Call me back when you have good news." This is now an ever changing chess game, with each move affecting the outcome of the future. I have to think five moves ahead of the Nazis if I'm going to win this battle.

As I reach the clearing I hear the distinctive sound of gunfire echoing through the afternoon air. I turn around and see the battle has begun. Over two thousand troops stretch across the riverbed and the first few lines have almost reached the tree line. Our men are picking them off one by one, but the Nazis are returning fire and some of our men have fallen dead into the riverbed.

"Roach," I yell out. "Did you come here to fire that thing

once and be done with it?""

"Hell no!" he yells back.

"Then point that thing at those Nazis and take out a couple hundred."

I know deep down inside that that one howitzer isn't going to be enough. Even if we manage to kill off all the Nazis at this outpost, we're going to get bombed by whatever warplanes are headed our way.

"Boys, aim that howitzer at the riverbed and let's go bowling for Nazis," Roach commands. "Let's make sure that November 9th, 1989 is a day the Germans will remember forever."

I stop in my tracks. Today is November 9th and it definitely is one the Germans will remember forever. In fact, it's one of the most historic days in Germany. Today is the day they begin tearing down the Berlin Wall. But there's no Berlin Wall in this temporal shift. Instead, it's the Niagara Wall that's right in front of us.

"Roach," I start waving my hands at him. "Point that thing in the other direction!"

"Are you crazy woman?" he asks. "There are no Nazis in that direction, only a wall."

"Right," I explain, "And there's a river on the other side of that wall that wants to run through here and over the cliff."

Roach smiles at me ear to ear. I add, "And there's a whole bunch of Nazi vermin in of the middle of the two who will just happen to get washed over that cliff if we unleash the river." Roach quickly understands my plan.

"Boys, it's time to turn on the American Falls again," Roach yells. "TEAR DOWN THAT WALL!"

The howitzer gets shifted and they aim it pointing directly at the part of the wall that damns up the river. Roach's men load a huge payload in the howitzer.

"Fire!" he yells. The bomb hits the top of the wall, taking out the upper half, but not a trickle of water comes out. I turn around to see that the first line of the Nazi army has reached the shoreline. They are so involved in their skirmish that they didn't notice the blast from the howitzer. I look up at the tower and see that General McCafferty has reached the battlements. He's now directing men to place a howitzer at the top of the tower and aim it towards us. I have to somehow stop him.

"Roach, no matter what happens, keep on firing at that wall as quickly as you can," I tell him. "I'm going to kick some Nazi ass."

I start sprinting across the riverbed before Roach can ask me any questions, hoping he follows my orders. A moment later there's a big explosion and a large chunk in the middle of the wall has been taken out. It's not that low, but this time water is starting to trickle out. At the other end of the riverbed some of the Nazis have noticed what's going on. They are trying to scramble back to Goat Island or quicken their pace to our shoreline. I'm about half way across the riverbed when I hear another explosion. I look and this one hit dead center at the foot of the wall. It starts to crumble and the river comes pouring out of it. With about another 100 feet to go, I run full steam towards the shore. The river is rising quickly and picking up speed. If I don't quicken my pace I'll be knocked down and swept over the falls with all the Nazis.

That's when I hear another explosion. But this time it's on the bank I just left. Up in the tower on one of the battlements, the General got his howitzer and team together and managed to shoot a round off at Roach. But I don't have the time to turn around and look if Roach is okay. The water is up to my waist and I have another 20 feet to go.

Suddenly another explosion hits the Niagara Wall and an eruption of raging water and rumbling stone fills the air as my hands reach up to the bank and I rapidly claw at dirt and stones. Pulling with all my might, I manage to flip myself up on the shore. I turn around and look across the river. There's Roach and his men shouting for joy as they reposition the howitzer and aim for the tower. The river in front of me has become a violently rapid jet stream of water, 15 feet deep. It's like someone turned on a giant water faucet that's been shut off for decades. I look downstream and see the Nazi army with their arms flailing above the rapids. They are struggling to swim in water that's traveling over 25 miles per hour. They've lost their footing, having nothing to grab onto. Every now and then I see a head bob underwater and not come back up.

Further downstream there's nothing on the horizon. The river falls over the edge, disappears, and become the American Falls. The large and mighty Nazis army looks like black carpenter ants that have been swept away by a garden hose.

One by one, they are pushed over the edge by the thundering waters, screaming to their deaths. After a moment, the army is gone. All that is left is a dozen or so men that have reached the opposite shoreline and are holding on to tree roots for dear life. That's when I see Frank peer out from the trees and approach one of the Nazis gripping at a tree root. He removes his side arm from his holster and pounds the butt of it on the man's fingers. First his pinky lets go, then the ring finger. Frank pounds on the remaining fingers relentlessly until the Nazi's instinctual reactions get the best of him and he finally lets go from the searing pain. The rushing river quickly pulls him farther out, sends him downstream, and pushes him over the falls. Frank yells to the rest of his men to do the same. Directing them like a true field commander. Along the tree line are young boys from the 1st Calvary pounding their side arms, rifle butts, and the heels of their shoe at the Nazi soldiers who are hanging on to avoid their eventual fate. None of the Nazis are strong enough to endure the pain, and they have to let go. Each one gets flushed down the falls. After a few moments all the Nazis have fallen over the edge of the American Falls.

We just defeated 2,000 Nazis soldiers, but there's no time to celebrate. I'm shaken from my joy by a mortar that hits the river right in front of me. The explosion kicks me in the air a few feet towards the tower and I fall flat on the ground. Up at the turrets is the General pointing me out to his men. They want me dead. I get up uninjured, knowing that the next time I won't be as lucky. My work here is not done. There are still things I need to fix and I still need to make some correction so time can change back. I rush towards the tower as another mortar strikes the shoreline. This time, I'm out of range.

Suddenly, the roar of jet engines fills the air and five fighter jets with swastikas on their tails buzz across the sky. The Germans have sent a few warplanes to finish this battle and in moments they'll be making a second run that will certainly be fatal. I look across the shore to see Roach aiming the howitzer towards the sky. Only pure luck would help him hit a moving target like that, but it is our only hope and he is going to try. As he is repositioning, a bomb hits about 100 feet away from him on the other shore. Up on the battlements the General and his team are cheering for joy. They quickly reload their howitzer and aim it for a more accurate shot. I have to get to the General before he hits his target and takes out our only hope.

I run into the burning outpost. Smoke is pouring down the stairwells. Not only would it be impossible to make it up to the battlements that way, climbing the 15 flights of stairs would take way too long for me to reach the General. I decide to take my chances and head to the elevators which are probably located in the center of the tower. The doors are bent open and I can see the crushed metal from the cars peeking through. The original blast that took out the observation floor must have busted the cables and sent the cars crashing down to the main floor.

The only other option seems to be to take the stairs. But if I do, all of our soldiers might be dead by the time I make it up there. The General had gotten up there pretty quickly, so there's got to be a better way up than the stairs. I look around some more, opening doors and looking for a way up. I find bathrooms, storage closets, and sleeping quarters. Rounding the corner, I discover my last hope, a freight elevator. I press the up button and it lights up as cables start moving the car towards my floor.

Anyone educated in any type of attack and defense training will tell you to never use the elevator and always take the stairs. But I have no time for stairs so I throw caution to the wind. The doors open and I hop into the elevator. I guess the battlements probably start on the fifteenth floor but I decide to get off at thirteen, that way I can sneak up a few floors and try to catch the General by surprise. The doors close and my metal cage starts flying up. I watch the floors tick off. When it stops at thirteen, the doors open and black smoke drifts into the car. I step into the cloudy hallway and the noxious scent of burning drywall hits me. There's definitely a fire somewhere on the floor, but it's hard to tell where. I get down on my hands and knees and crawl to the stairwells. They are smoke filled, too, but it's more of a haze. Climbing on all fours, I make my way to the fifteenth floor and find it ablaze.

Fire shoots around walls and thick pillars of smoke as sweat and soot mix together on my brow. The General is screaming off in the distance for the soldiers to get more ammunition so I know I've made it to the right floor. I slowly step out, but retreat when an explosion erupts somewhere on the floor. It's followed by the ricochet of bullets bouncing off steel girders. Ammunition is being stored on fifteen, and any future explosions can send more bullets in any direction. No soldier would risk his life walking through this floor so it's highly unlikely I'll encounter any opposition. Likewise, I'm a sitting duck if I stand here any longer. I get back on my hands and knees and start looking for an exit to the outside battlements.

After a few twists and turns in a hallway, I head for an open archway and discover sunlight. I take a peek out and see the Canadian country side. At least I'm assuming that's what it is. For miles it is nothing but a desolate wasteland. Hotels, buildings, roadways and trees have been leveled flat. It's like an infinite desert landscape covered in metal and rubble. Here and there are traces of a street, or a corner of a building, but there's nothing alive. No trees, bushes, or animals. It's the effect from the damage of nuclear war.

For the moment, I'm safe. The General and his men are on the other side of the tower focusing on fighting the Americans below. I stand up, gather my thoughts, and assess the situation. There's the General and probably four or five men, maybe more. I have a side arm with six rounds in the gun and another full clip for back-up. Not much, but thank goodness I'm a good shot. Up in the sky, I notice four jet planes heading right towards the tower. They look much different than the German jets, but vaguely familiar. The four jet planes suddenly slow down a bit and point their noses to the sky, showing me the belly of their planes. It's a maneuver that can only be done by one type of jet plane: Soviet MiGs. And it's often done while they are being pursued by enemy planes. They can slow down just enough for them to be passed by the enemy, and then can suddenly attack from behind. Just as I suspected, the German warplanes fly over the Soviet MiGs at a higher altitude and pass them up, approaching the tower at high speed. The Soviet MiGs right themselves and each one fires multiple rockets at their German targets. The rockets hit their marks and each of the five German planes start spewing out smoke. They lose altitude and dive through the sky, still aiming in my direction. One-by-one the planes hit ground, making their way towards the tower. The first two bash into the Canadian countryside, erupting in a cloud of dirt, metal and fire. The third hits right on the shoreline of the river and explodes, sending flames high into the sky. The fourth lands at the edge of the falls, bursting in black smoke as it teeters over the edge and disappears. The last one makes it to the Niagara wall and busts through it, right into the base of the Outpost. A huge blast shudders up through the tower and knocks me off my feet. I stumble and fall, banging my head against the concrete. Everything goes dark.

TWENTY-FIVE

I wake up from unconsciousness and hope I was only out for a few moments. At first, I think I'm in my apartment in Washington, D.C., rising to inspect another day in 1989. Then I look around and realize that's not the case.

My memory comes flooding back. Nazis. Niagara. Battle. MiGs. Explosion. Traitor. Need to make wrong right.

I get to my feet and look around. I don't see the MiGs anywhere in sight, but I do hear our troops down at the tree line hollering that we've won. Instinctively, I realize I have to get out of this tower. That plane probably caused considerable damage at the base and this tower is completely unstable. It's going to come crashing down any minute. But if the General and his team are still alive on the other side, they'll try and take out as many of our soldiers as they can. My troops have to survive this battle, but I don't. They'll have Frank as a strong leader and he can take them to freedom. I have to kill the General and his men even if it means I die with them. I shake off my fogginess, hug the wall, and sneak my way to the other side of the tower.

As I come around the corner, I see Nazis. The first has fallen back against a wooden box and has a splintered wooden board sticking through his neck. He's dead and not my worry anymore. But he's gripping a piece of paper and something catches my eye. I ever so cautiously bend down and try to gently pry it from his dead finger tips.

Yes. I confirm my fears. I see fragments of a picture on the paper, and it's clearly my curly red hair. I manage to remove the paper intact and slowly unfold it. There on the right is a picture of me, a la historical 1989 with my big curly red hair. At the top of the paper is the headline, "WANTED DEAD OR ALIVE," written in both German and English.

But there are three other pictures on the paper. Next to mine is Frank. It seems both his picture and mine are from early last week when we were at the coffee shop the day he handed me the VHS tape of the Madonna video. Christ, we were under surveillance! The picture next to Frank is a muscular broad-shouldered dark skinned African-American man in this late 20s. The guy is cut with short dreads hanging down. It's a photo from a police line-up and he looks pissed. I've never seen the guy before and from the looks of him I don't want to run into him. Maybe he's an inspector, maybe he's not. I have no idea.

But I'm shocked to see the next face. It's Ella, Roach's wife. The photo is from pre-nuclear fallout, and my goodness, she's more gorgeous than I ever even imagined. Not only is she stunningly beautiful, she has that little girl smile that exudes happiness. The kind that makes you naturally smile right back, even if you're looking at a photo.

How do the Nazis know who Ella is? Why would they want her? I don't have time to figure this out now so I fold up the paper and shove it in my pocket. I've got to get off this tower and warn Frank that he's marked for murder. Somehow, I have to explain to Roach about Ella. I'll figure that out later, too. Right now I have more Nazis to kill and survive.

I keep inching against the wall and find two more Nazis also on the ground, maybe unconscious, maybe dead. I'll worry about them later. A fourth one is slowly standing up and shaking off his fogginess. He sees me and grabs for his side arm, but he's slow for a Nazi. I send a bullet smack damn in the middle of his forehead. Blood starts flowing out and he falls to the ground. The gun shot stirs the two unconscious Nazis and I take them out as well, bullets to the head.

My position has probably been revealed by firing my gun so I keep sneaking around the wall even slower than before. I must keep on moving to discover who else is out there other than the General. I'm like an inch worm crawling along the wall, stepping forward ever so slowly with my gun pointed out and my eyes darting back and forth, scanning the battlement for a hint of the General or another Nazi.

"There's no escape, Alex," shouts the General. He's close. "There are another hundred Nazis in this tower below us. Even if you manage to get off this floor, you'll never get out of the tower."

Escape has never been part of my plan. Kill the General and as many Nazis as I can and give the Rebels a victory. Fix the course of time. That's been my plan. But things have changed since I discovered Frank and I are marked for murder. Now I've got to do all that, and warn Frank.

"I can offer you a truce," claims the General. "The Nazis gave me a great vacation home down in South America and endless gold. I can get you the same if you just walk away right now."

He's lying and trying to distract me. It's an old technique, something they teach you in the first day of hand-to-hand combat class. I don't buy it, nor do I respond to it. I know I'm close and keep inching forward looking for the General.

One of the other things they teach you in Hand-to-Hand Combat 101 is to never let down your rear guard. I haven't checked behind me for some time now so I turn around and find a Nazi charging after me rapidly. I try to step aside and avoid him, but he's too close and tackles me to the ground. My gun gets knocked out of my hand and goes flying over the side of the tower. The guy is huge and must have 70-100 pounds on me. I do what they taught me to do when fighting people bigger than me and use our momentum to keep on rolling. The Nazi starts squeezing me tighter to him, but my hands and legs are still free to give me leverage to keep rolling. Eventually we're going to hit something and stop, and then I'll have to really fight for my life.

The sound of gunfire quickly catches my attention and a bullet grazes my shoulder. It sends a stinging pain down my arm, but I've been shot before and this wound is mild. I keep on rolling as more bullets keep whizzing by my head and body. While this huge guy can certainly manhandle me once we stop, he's also a great human shield. I take my chances and wait for the next gunshot before rolling. The hammer explodes in the gun so I shift my weight away from the direction of the gun shots, and move my assailant between me and the shooter – which I can only assume is the General.

I can feel the Nazi take a fatal hit in his back and his grip on me goes limp along with the rest of his body. This guy makes a great human shield so I keep my position as I peek my head over his body to take in the situation. I'm on the New York side of the tower now, with the Horseshoe Falls to my back. In front of me, the General quickly races behind a howitzer, ducking for cover. He must not realize I've lost my gun.

The dead Nazi provides a bit of cover for me, lying between me and the General. I check his body, looking for a weapon, and discover a side arm sticking out between his body and the ground, buried underneath his hip. Dead weight is always so much heavier and it takes most of my strength to roll him forward to pry the gun from his belt. I have to grind my bleeding shoulder into the man's chest to get extra leverage, biting my lip as pain shoots down my left side. But it works, and I free the gun from his belt. I check the magazine and find three bullets. That should be enough.

Suddenly a huge explosion rocks through the tower. The whole place begins to shift weight a little bit, but settles back into position.

"That was the fuel tanks on the first floor," shouts the General. "The fire from the plane colliding into the tower finally set off that blast. The only thing that's holding up this tower is the steel beams at the base. When those melt away from the heat, this thing is going to collapse. Neither of us is going to get out of here alive."

I look over my shoulder at the Horseshoe Falls and figure out how I'm going to survive. "Speak for yourself, General," I shout back. "I'm gonna live." I've got to get off this tower and warn Frank he's being targeted. I have to save him. I also need to figure out why they want Ella.

I see the General crouching behind the howitzer and find a perfect hole that will leave his body defenseless. It's just a matter of getting his body to shift there. He pokes his head up over the top and I fire off a bullet, missing him. But his body gets closer to the hole. Two bullets left, either the next one hits him, or it moves him towards the hole.

"If you let me go, we can get out of here now. We still have a chance to make it out alive." There's desperation in the General's voice.

"Are you scared of dying?" I yell back. "Dying as a patriot is the greatest sacrifice you can make for your countrymen. But I guess you can't accomplish that anymore. Instead, you'll die as a traitor, and a Nazi."

"Alex," the General says with hesitation. "You know how this turns out. I'm sure you talked to someone in the future. I survive this battle and end up in Argentina. But you," the General pauses, "You don't."

I have to live. I need to warn Frank.

"Your friend never mentioned your future, did he?" yells the General. "Your name isn't in the history books. It's not there because you die today, an insignificant death when this tower goes down. I, on the other hand, escape. The future can't change, Alex. My destiny is in Argentina."

Destiny. What does the future hold for each of us? If we're all being pulled in some temporal gravity, where am I going? The General is right. Collin never mentioned my name in this battle. I don't survive this battle. My fate is to die. Collin said no one survives but the General.

Then again, much has changed since that conversation. How much can I manipulate things so my future changes? All I know right now is I have to warn Frank that he's being hunted by the Nazis. I have to save Frank. For my plan to work, I need the General's dead body. I can fix this. I am the master of my own fate. Temporal gravity ain't gonna win this time.

I peer over to the howitzer and I can see the General poking his head up on the other side. I take aim at the top of his head and have him in my sight. I pull the trigger just as he moves up his head and bam! It finds its target, shattering the top of the General's skull. His body slumps down and falls to the ground.

Never needed the last bullet.

I tuck the gun into my holster at my waist and slowly stand up. I step over to the General and find the top of his head gone. He's dead.

"Alex." My Walkman goes off; it's Collin. "If you're still in the tower you have to get off. That thing is going down."

"I got a plan," I say.

Anyone who doesn't understand simple physics would be totally screwed in my situation. The fuel has been burning down on the first floor for some time now and heating up all the steel girders that support this tower and all its concrete. In a few seconds the girders will start to soften from the heat and bend, the weight of the concrete will increase the pressure exponentially. At first the tower will lean slowly, then it will pick up speed and quickly come tumbling down. Because of this inevitable destruction, running down and out of the tower is not a viable escape route. It will take me a good 15 minutes to reach the bottom, and if I did, the inferno will be so hot I'll never be able to negotiate past it. Even if I got through all that, the rubble will come crushing down on me killing me in an instant. There's only one way off this tower – jumping into the Niagara River, but I'll need some help from the General.

I reach down, bending at the knees, and throw the dead General over my shoulder. He's about 180 pounds, but I once squatted 200 and when your adrenaline is pumping it gives you a little extra strength. I stand up and start walking toward the edge of the battlement. I reach the wall and look for a way to climb up it. It's near impossible for me to get up on the wall with the General over my shoulder in a fireman's carry. I'm going to have to toss him on the wall, climb up, and lift him over my arms. A feat that's near impossible.

Just then, the creaking of metal becomes so loud it drowns out the pounding sound of water from the falls. I feel the tower tilting in the direction of the Canadian side. Perfect. If it tilts over far enough, I can dive off and into the river. I press my body up against the wall waiting for the perfect moment. Concrete starts crumbling, too. I hope that it will lean just enough so I can jump off before gravity takes over and the whole tower comes crumbling straight down.

Finally, the tower leans enough so that the wall is out over the river. This is all I need. I stand up, throw the General over my shoulder and I raise a bended knee against the wall. In front of me is only air. I can see the Canadian wasteland and the falls below. The logic in my brain is telling me not to jump, that I'm safer with my feet on solid ground. Exerting all my mental and physical strength to counter my instincts, I push forward, jump off away from the tower with the General on my shoulder, and leap into the sky.

I'm 200 feet high and I have only six seconds before I hit the water. I quickly drop the General from my shoulder and stand on him, tucking my feet under his belt. This will slow my descent and velocity. Next, I calm myself, tuck my legs together, cross my arms down over my chest, and place my hands over my groin. Impact comes way too soon.

A couple of things help me from instantly dying. First, the Niagara River is traveling at about fifteen miles per hour. Jumping into standing water is like jumping into concrete. Moving water helps the fluidity and resistance in breaking the surface of the water. Second, I'm standing on the General who helps with the water displacement. His dead body is very buoyant. It's like landing on the ground with a huge air bag strapped to your legs.

Third, when we hit the surface I bend my legs to give me a little extra flexibility and absorb any shock to my body. And once I hit the water, I immediately extend my arms to slow my body down as I fall through the water. Although the bottom is only 15 feet below the surface, the buoyancy of the General, my extended arms, and the rushing waters, all keep me from slamming into the ground under the river. Almost instantly, I bob back up.

Breaking the surface, I unhook my feet from the General's belt and he pops out of the water. I grab onto his body and hold on for dear life. I'm safe, for only a short time. One hundred feet in front of me the river gives away. I'm heading straight towards the middle of the Horseshoe Falls. I survived one drop, and now I must survive another.

The rushing waters of the Niagara River surround me. The pounding of over 200,000 cubic feet of water per second fills my ear drums and embeds every thought of my mind. I'm twenty feet away and approaching quickly. I can see the water cresting over the outer tips of the Horseshoe Falls. Panic sets in. My body wants to swim away, to let go of the General and make a feeble attempt to get to the shore. I force myself to hold on. Ten feet away, I can start to see the river below. I'm traveling even faster now, totally out of control. My body tenses up and prepares for the doom ahead. I try to clear my mind and focus on what logic tells me to do, instead of responding to my emotions. I wrap my hand around the General's belt and start to feel the water give away.

I plunge one hundred and seventy-five feet down. Doing some quick calculations, I estimate it's going to take five seconds for me to hit the water below. I count in my head, one one thousand…, two one thousand…, three one thousand…, four one thousand…, FIVE.

BAM! I go under the water for a few moments, but the General's buoyant body brings me back up to the surface. I'm instantly greeted by the thrashing waters of the Horseshoe Falls hammering at me from above. Kicking out my legs, I try moving forward to pick up one of the currents in the rapids. It's chaotic. I can't see what's forward, what's behind and can barely comprehend what's up or down. I pray that I'll catch the right current, but everything is white water rapids.

I realize I've been going in circles stuck at the base of the falls and don't have the energy to do this much longer. I can't kick both me and the General forward. He's served his purpose as my life raft long enough and I take my chances without him. I let him go and he immediately gets caught in the middle of a whirlpool rapid. There's no time to watch and see what happens to him. I don't care. I kick out my feet and start swimming away from the whirlpool to what I hope is the lower Niagara River.

I thrust as hard as I can with my feet and scoop my hands

over my shoulder with all my might, forcing the water behind me. I say a quick thank you to my mother for making me take swimming lessons every summer, even when I argued with her that I knew everything there was to know about swimming.

After a few strokes, I realize I'm going in the right direction. Swimming is getting a bit easier and I'm able to increase my efforts. I fight the circling waters and swim with all my strength. I've forgotten about the pain in my shoulder. I've forgotten about the shock my body has taken from the fall from the tower. I've forgotten that I'm stuck in 1989. I just swim. I clear the rapids, but the water is still quickly pushing me down river. I'll be washed away and stuck for miles along the sheer cliffs that hug the river as it travels to Lake Ontario. Exhaustion is setting in and I fear I'll never survive. To my left is a rock shelf along the Canadian shoreline. It's my only chance at survival. I make my way there. I need to warn Frank that the Nazis want him dead. I need to warn Roach about Ella. I need to tell them about the pictures in my pocket.

Fight against the river, I swim as hard as I can. I kick with every ounce of energy I have left. The current still keeps pushing me down stream. In several moments I'll be past the rocks and all hope will be lost. I hear my mother's voice in my head, "Swim Alex," she's yelling. "You can do it! I have faith in you." I double my efforts and keep swimming, never stopping. I'm not going to let my mother down. I want to make her proud. "You can do it," she says over and over again in my head.

I'm within inches of the mossy rocks. I reach out my right hand and dig into the shore, with all my might try to pull myself up. The current still is kicking me downstream, and the river splashes up over my face. I don't let go. I spit the water out and with my left hand reach up for more rocks. I get leverage and yank myself up on the shore. My legs are still in the current, but my body is safely and securely on the shore. I roll over on my back and look to the sky. The sun is shining. I'm alive.

"Thank you, mom," I whisper and I pass out.

TWENTY-SIX

When I was nine years old I had a nasty bicycle accident. We lived in one of those suburban areas where the people didn't believe in sidewalks. They preferred nice plush, lavish flowing front lawns that went from the house to the curb. This meant that anyone who wanted to walk, bike, or skateboard had to use the street along with all the cars. This was not a great situation for a nine year old girl who wasn't that proficient on a bike.

One Saturday morning, I was riding my bike to my friend Margaret's house. We loved pretending we were a singing group and that Saturday we planned to work on our dance routine. I never saw the car that turned onto my street. Nor did he see me. His vision was impaired due to the six beers he had at the bar after third shift at his job. His reaction time was pretty bad, too, because after he hit me head on it still took a while for him to engage the brakes. Luckily, I rolled over the car and off the hood instead of under it.

I don't remember much after that, because the impact knocked me out. I was rushed to Children's Hospital and apparently things didn't look that good. I had a broken right arm, a dislocated shoulder, and a cracked skull. My mom explained years later that I had some swelling in my brain and they were really worried about permanent brain damage.

It took days for me to finally come to. I never told anyone, but I remember waking for a few moments before they wheeled me to get an MRI. I had heard my parents' voices.

"She's going to be fine," my dad said calmly.

"Look at her, James," my mom squeaked out as she choked back tears, "Some drunk driver hit her going 30 miles an hour. She's not going to be the same."

"She's going to be fine," my dad repeated sternly. "I know this. She's going to be okay."

"I'm not worried about her arm or her shoulder," mom said. "It's the swelling in her brain. I have medical training. I know what this means."

"And there are things I know," responded my dad, sternly, but as gently as he could be. "She's special. She's going to be fine. She'll make it through this."

That was the last thing I remembered in the E.R. It wasn't until three days later that I woke up in the hospital room surrounded by my smiling and very much relieved parents. Three months later, I was back on that bike heading to Margaret's house again. We finished the dance routine and it was awesome.

———————————

As I come to from my blackout this time, I'm not as fortunate to be surrounded by my parents. Instead two Russian soldiers are talking over me. A Halo Soviet helicopter is a few feet away, idling. A pilot and co-pilot sit in the cockpit, silently and patiently waiting for the two Russian soldiers. I have no idea what they are saying, but they seem to be arguing about what to do next. I've never learned Russian and when I listen to someone talking the language they always seem passionately angry about something.

The older Russian soldier is pointing at me, and motioning to pick me up and carry me into the helicopter. The younger one is vehemently arguing with him. He points to his neck, then moves his two hands together as if he was breaking a stick with his hands. There's no way I'm going with these guys. They want to either kidnap me or snap my neck and kill me. I haven't gone this far to be killed by Commies.

I slowly rise to my feet and try to take a few steps away before they notice me. I figured I can try and climb the cliffs on the Canadian side and escape that way. It's not much of a plan, but I have to try something.

I reach into my pocket to make sure I have the paper with the Nazis' notice to kill me and the others. All I find is a waterlogged wad of paper pulp. The trip over the falls destroyed it. Now I must get back to camp and warn the others. Warn Frank that he's marked for death.

I take a step forward and a wave of exhaustion hits me. My legs get wobbly. Things get a little blurry and my head starts to feel dizzy. I promptly throw up on some boulders. I look over at the Russians who start laughing at me. The older one smacks the younger one on the back, makes a neck cracking motion, and they both start laughing even harder.

These guys are going to kill me. I'm going to die puking my brains out in Canada. I didn't survive the falls to be murdered by the enemy. I need to get to Frank.

"At least take me back to my homeland and kill me there so I can die on American soil," I shout.

"Kill you?" says the older soldier in English, with a thick Russian accent. "There's no way I'd harm the Daughter of Time Travel. You're the savior of the world today!"

Confusion fills my head and the dizziness starts again. The Russians lunge forward and catch me before I fall into my own vomit. The younger one picks me up, smiles at me, and carries me gently into the Russian helicopter. Out of the corner of my eye, I see the older Russian soldier pull out a Sony Walkman and talk into it.

"It's Chief Inspector Vazlymov," he says. "We have Mother Goose and are returning her to her nest. Over."

Great. I have a nursery rhyme code name. Couldn't they have picked something bolder like Joan of Arc, or sexier like Jessica Rabbit? She's a redhead! No, I got Mother Goose. The rotors whirl and the helicopter takes off. I pass out. Again.

TWENTY-SEVEN

I wake up on a cot in what must be the medical tent. There are a few men with me, most have bandages around their shoulders or head. I recognize them as members of our New York Rebellion. They are playing poker, laughing, and seem to be recovering from their injuries well. Laughing the loudest are the men I left behind with Roach at the howitzer, but I see Roach nowhere in sight. Did he survive?

Sitting up in bed, I wince. Everything aches. I rub my shoulder and seem to be floating in my hospital scrubs. The life of a short, skinny woman – I'm always destined to be in clothes too big for me. Anyway, I hope one of the Chinese women that went to battle with us dressed me and not one of the burly men that are here playing poker. I stand up and a silence comes across the tent. I turn to see all the men looking at me in awe.

"Are you alright to stand, Captain?" one asks. "Shall we get you a wheelchair?"

"No, I'm fine." I'm lying. The pain is shooting through my shoulders and legs. I start walking slowly towards the exit of the tent.

"Captain," says one of the guys who's not bandaged up. "We're under strict orders from the General not to let you out of our sight."

"The General? He's a traitor," I explain. "I killed him at the top of the tower and used his body to survive the falls. He's somewhere out on Lake Ontario by now."

"That's not the General they're talking about," says Roach as he walks into the tent. "They're talking about me, and I'm very much alive." All the able bodied men stand and salute when he enters.

I'm relieved to see Roach and tears fill my eyes. He extends his arm since he's glad to see me, too. I say to hell with protocol and I wrap my arms around him and hug him deeply.

"Thank God you're alive, Roach." I say.

"Are you kidding me? All I did was survive a blast from a

howitzer," he argues. "You just jumped off a tower and went over the falls. You're the one with nine lives!"

"How long have I been out?"

"Three days. Since the tower tumbled, we've been clearing the area of Nazis. The Russians showed up and have been bombing the Niagara Wall. It's now a pile of rubble from here to Lake Erie. Frank and Sergeant Vazlymov have become good buddies. They took a division of our guys, met up with some more of the New York Rebel Alliance, and marched towards Buffalo. Vazlymov also brought in two dozen Soviet Halo helicopters and a couple of MiG jet planes for air cover. Word has it your husband Frank is a real leader. He's been directing troops and developing strategic battle plans. Without him, we'd still be wondering what to do. Right now he's in Buffalo with Vazlymov. Early word has it we've slaughtered the Nazis there, but we're waiting to hear the official announcement that we've taken the city. Frank's plan after that is to move down to Erie, then to Cleveland. Maybe after that, Youngstown, Pittsburgh, and down the Ohio River. We're looking for waterways to the Mississippi to split the country in half."

"Sounds like a great plan," I say.

"How are you feeling?"

"Good," I lie. Whenever I move I wince from the pain in my shoulder. I didn't know it at the time, but the bullet lodged in my upper clavicle. They weren't able to get all of it out and I still have bullet fragments stuck in my bones.

"Nurse!" yells Roach.

"Yes, General," a man turns and salutes.

"Get the Captain here some aspirin or other pain medication. But not the heavy stuff, we need her coherent. And get her some camos to put on."

"Yes, sir, whatever Captain Eviston needs. It would be my honor to serve her," responds the nurse and heads off to get some medical supplies and clothes.

"Alex, you're kind of a hero around here."

"Hero?" I say sheepishly, "I'm not a hero."

"You led us when no one else was willing," says Roach.

"You got us here today. There's a war that's started and it's because of you. Things may still be bad today, but now we have a chance at freedom."

The nurse returns and hands me some aspirin and a glass of water. I take the pills and gulp down the water. Hero? I'm just a woman stuck in 1989. I don't want to be in the history books. Stepping behind a screen, I change out of my scrubs and into pants and shirt that fit much better.

"Can you walk?" asks Roach.

"Sure," I say flinching a little bit as I walk back out. "But we have to go slow."

Roach offers his arm and I take it. He leads me out of the tent. We're still in the same clearing that we arrived at days ago. The four Semi-trucks have been turned into buildings for our base. About two hundred tents line the clearing. That's much more than we had to begin with, so more soldiers must have arrived since I've been out. On top of one of the Semi's they've built an observation deck that they are using as Central Command. On the far end of the clearing are a few Russian Halo choppers.

But in the middle of the clearing I see the strangest thing I've ever seen. Soviet military in full camouflage are training American Rebel soldiers how to use AK-47s. There are boxes of them piled against the trailers marked with the Soviet Hammer and Sickle. They are laughing together, patting each other on the back and speaking broken English and broken Russian to each other. They are friends. I wish I could share this moment with Mojmir.

"It's been over a half a century since we've joined forces with the Soviets against the Nazis," says Roach. "It's good to have them back on our side."

"Well, it's better to have them instead of the Chinese," I say.

"Why's that?"

"The Soviets will better handle this New York Winter we're about to get."

Roach and I laugh loudly, enough to get the attention of

some troops around us. A hush falls over them and they stop what they're doing, frozen in awe. More soldiers recognize what's going on, and they turn to see us as well. After several moments, every soldier has stopped what they are doing and are standing at attention towards me. I recognize one of the Russian soldiers from the helicopter that rescued me. He yells a command and the troops salute en masse. Out of the corner of my eye I see that Roach has stepped back and joined the troops. He is at full attention as well. This honor is mine.

The Russian soldier from the helicopter ceremoniously steps forward. He looks me in the eye and speaks in a thick accent. "Captain Eviston. On behalf of the Soviet Army, we thank you for your valor, courage, and drive to destroy the overreaching arm of the Nazis." He salutes me once again.

I return the salute. "And thank you and your men for rescuing me. Without them, and their support on the attack of the tower, I would not be alive. And we wouldn't be standing on American soil today."

The sound of helicopters fills the air and a dozen Russian Halos come into view. They head toward the far end of the field and gently land on the clearing. The rotors slow down and the men pop out of the cabs yelling and shouting happily. This is the confirmation we've been waiting for. We've taken Buffalo. We are at war.

In the distance, Sergeant Vazlymov and Frank are walking together towards the clearing. Frank looks up, sees me, and instantly comes running in my direction. I start walking towards him as quickly as I can without hurting. Frank double times it to me and wraps his arms around me. I squeeze him tightly, stronger than I've ever held anyone in my life - even my mother.

"I'm so glad you're alive," Frank whispers in my ear. "I thought you were dead." He doesn't let me go.

"I'm okay."

"Promise me you'll never do that again," he says.

"Well it's not like I'm interested in going over the falls a dozen times," I laugh. "Once is enough for me."

"I don't want to lose you," says Frank. "Ever."

"Well, you're stuck with me," I smile at him. "In 1989."

Sergeant Vazlymov reaches us and it's all business again. "Captain Eviston," he says, "Can Captain Bouchard and I have a word with you privately?"

"Sure," I say.

"Let's walk over to my quarters," says the Sergeant, and leads us to a tent off to the side. We step into his quarters and it's just him, Frank, and me. He motions for us to sit down.

"Frank knows all of what I'm about to tell you. Now that you've awoken, this is the first chance I can explain things to you," says the Sergeant. "I'm Chief Inspector Victor Vazlymov. I'm in charge of all the Russian Inspectors monitoring decade 1980. My personal post is 1989. Three days ago, during the Battle of Niagara, one of my men was monitoring all the radio channels looking for any signs of any inspectors from friendly nations. That's when we came across Collin's communications with you. Our Russian inspector in Vancouver made contact with him and discovered your situation. Understanding our countries haven't been on the best of terms for the past several decades, we were hesitant to help. But smarter minds prevailed, for we have a common enemy in the Nazis and it's better to fight together than apart. We dispatched four Russian MiGs to assist. They took out the German aircraft to give you coverage to crush the Nazis. We then arrived 20 minutes later in our helicopters and pulled you from the shoreline bringing you to safety here."

"It was a huge shock for us to see the Soviets," said Frank. "Especially for the Americans. These guys have never fought with the Soviets and it's been decades since they've heard about them battling the Nazis. But as you can see now, we've welcomed them with open arms."

"When it comes down to it, we have a common interest," smiles Vazlymov. "Neither of us wants to see the Nazis succeed. As long as they have the power, we'll fight side-by-side to defeat them."

"The good news is there are about 2,000 Allied troops in

Buffalo right now holding the city. These are members of the Soviet Army, New York Rebels, and even some Canadian troops that crossed the river yesterday. We now control the river area from here to the Pennsylvania border," says Frank. "Word has spread throughout the Northeast and rumor has it that there's an Appalachian Rebel Alliance in Pennsylvania that is making their way to Buffalo. We're going to wait a few days to see if they arrive and then move along the Lake Erie shoreline until we reach Cleveland."

I'm still in shock that we're teaming up with the Russians. "Times have changed," I say. "One week ago I'd never trust a Russian. Today, I'm trusting you with my life."

Vazlymov laughs, "A few days ago, when we found you we thought you were dead. Then when we realized you were alive, we were worried that the fall had damaged you so much that we could injure your back or neck when we moved you. We're all glad that you're okay."

First Mojmir sacrificed his life for me. Now I've been rescued by the Chief Inspector of 1980. That's when I realize this guy is Mojmir's boss.

"Mojmir," I stumble out. "He died saving us in New York. He was shot by Nazis. I'm forever in debt…"

"We understand," interrupts Vazlymov. "Frank told us the whole story. Mojmir's been given the Order of Glory medal posthumously. It's one of the highest honors we can give a soldier. He will not die in vain."

I'm now massively in debt to the Soviets. But then again, they are in debt to me for starting the war. Maybe this is not about who owes what to whom. Maybe this is about all of us working together.

"What's Collin say about the future?" I ask.

"Our communicator was destroyed during the collapse of the tower," Frank explains. "It must have fallen off your body."

"The good news is we've been able to keep in touch with Collin through our Soviet connections," smiles Vazlymov. "The future seems to be moving back to the way it was, like a magnet slowly pulling itself to its polar opposite. But there's no word from U.S. Central Command. As far as we know, the Nazis are still in charge of the future."

That's when I remember the Nazi's notice.

"Frank," I caution. "You're marked for death by the Nazis."

"Of course they want me dead," he laughs. "What are you talking about?"

"When I was on the roof of the tower I found a paper in one of the Nazi soldier's hands," I explain. "It was a notice to kill us on sight. There was a picture of you on it, along with me. We were at the coffee shop in D.C."

"They shared a picture from a different timeline," asks Vazlymov. "That's a huge violation of international laws."

"The Nazis have broken more laws than that," counters Frank. "It's okay, Alex. Of course they want us dead. Look what we've done to their plans already!"

"But Frank, there's more," I add, "There was a picture of an African-American prisoner I've never met. And a picture of Ella before the nuclear blast."

"Ella?" Frank is taken aback. But before I can respond there's a knock on the wood outside the tent. Roach walks in.

"The Halos are refueled," explains Roach. "We're ready to take off when you are."

"It's time to head out," commands Vazlymov. "We can finish this conversation later."

"Where are we going?" I ask.

"To do something we've been waiting days to do," says Frank. "We didn't want to do it without you."

I follow all three men across the clearing to the nearest helicopter with its rotors spinning. I'm helped in and take a seat among several soldiers. One of the men is tightly gripping a wrapped package in a satin bag against his chest.

We take off and for the first time I can assess everything from the air. Our base is rather big. Not only are there a dozen Halos at our camp, but there are six Russian MiGs parked at a make shift airstrip. Two of them take off back to back and provide us with an air escort. Whatever we're about to do, this is an important mission.

The rest of the base is much bigger than the clearing. There are tents strewn across the country side, with both Americans and Canadians being trained by Soviet Military. New ammunitions and artillery have been flown in and dot the base.

The war has been renewed. These are men and women fighting for their freedom. It may be 1989, but it feels like 1942. And to think this was all started by a simple attack on a tower at Niagara Falls. One person's actions can change time forever, or at least change it back.

As we clear the trees I can see Niagara Falls. Both the Horseshoe Falls and American Falls are flowing strong. Even the Bridal Falls are shooting over the side of the cliff. A huge pile of rubble and steel rises above Goat Island, remains of the Nazi outpost. There is a smaller line of rubble that follows the Niagara River upstream as far and I can see. The Niagara Wall looks more like a break wall than an ominous division that separated the Nazis from the rest of the world.

At the tip of Goat Island, close to the falls, is a tall flag pole, 50 feet in the air and towering over the falls. A large Nazi flag still flies from it, the Swastika piercing through the sky. Our helicopter heads straight towards it.

As we get close to landing, two of the soldiers pull out film cameras from bags on the floor. One of them checks the magazine, engages the battery, focuses it on me and turns it on. We land on a clearing, and we all jump out, except the camera guy pointed at me. The helicopter takes back off with the camera guys still filming us. The second soldier with a film camera adjusts his on Vazlymov who begins to speak ceremoniously in Russian. He points to the flag pole, the Nazi flag, and then to me.

After he finishes, Vazlymov motions to us, "Come, we have an important job to do."

We all walk up to the flag pole. Vazlymov unhinges the rope and slowly starts to pull down the Nazi flag, with the camera man filming him the whole time. The flag reaches us and Vazlymov treats it with complete disrespect. He allows it to touch the ground. He grabs it, rips it from its hooks, looks for the Swastika and spits on it. Balling it up recklessly, he throws it towards the river.

The wind catches it and takes it high. It hovers for a moment, unfurling a bit and gently lands atop of the American Falls. It gets wet and is pulled beneath the waters somewhat, but still floats on the surface. Before long, it slips over the edge and falls to the rapids below, and is seen no more.

"Soldier!" commands Roach. "The flag!"

The rest of the men, Americans, Canadians, and Russians, snap to attention. Two men, one Russian, the other American, gently remove an American flag from the satin bag he was clutching on the helicopter. Vazlymov leads in a salute and we all follow. The soldiers slowly unfurl the flag. It is tattered and worn.

"This flag was once flown over the White House before the Nazis occupied D.C.," Vazlymov explains. "A former White House housekeeper Lillian Rodgers Parks saved it. It came into our hands through a Russian inspector monitoring D.C. and then through a KBG agent. The Soviets had the foresight to keep it for an occasion just this. Today, Alex Eviston, we'd like you to honor us and your country by raising it up the flag pole."

I'm taken aback. This is a historic moment and a symbolic gesture to the free world, and I, a short little redheaded girl who's been a stone in her country's shoe for the past five years, has been chosen for this honor. I wish my mom was here to see this. My emotions well up inside me. My eyes get misty and tears start moving down my checks. At first, I'm self-conscious, thinking since I'm the only woman on this island and it's stereotypical that I can't control my emotions.

Frank winks and smiles at me. All the other soldiers are getting misty eyed, too. Everyone knows the meaning of what we are doing here today. The United States of America has been controlled by the Nazis for over fifty years and they have dominated the entire world during that period. The Russians understand that while they've had their differences with us, they'd prefer our sense of humanity over the Nazi's disregard for non-German life.

I step up and take the hooks from the rope on the flag pole. Gently, I attach the hook to the first eyelet and then affix the second one. I grab the rope and pull, ignoring the pain that shoots up my shoulder. The soldiers carefully hold onto the flag so it doesn't touch the ground, but step back as it starts to unfold. The flag is huge, at least twice the height of Frank, if not more. After a few more pulls, the flag is above ground and the soldiers let go. It completely unfurls triumphantly. All the men salute as it flaps in the wind. I keep on pulling it up, hand over hand, yanking on the rope until the flag reaches the top. I flatten the rope and tie it off on the pole. Stepping back, I'm in awe of this beautiful sight, a large American flag waving in the wind atop of Niagara Falls, over the land of the free and the home of the brave. I raise my hand up to salute and ceremoniously lower my hand. The rest of the soldiers around me lower theirs as well. Suddenly, one of them is moved to sing "America the Beautiful" and we all join in. In the distance, the helicopter is filming the whole event.

I am proud to be an American today, and even prouder to be among all the soldiers that joined us. At this moment, we aren't Americans, Russians, and Canadians. We are all humans trying to create a better future for our families and friends. Vazlymov calls back the Halo and we gather in the clearing.

Out of the corner of my eye, I see something shiny in the rubble catching the sun and reflecting back to me. I run over to it and discover my Sony Walkman poking through the rubble. I uncover some rocks and pull it from the wreckage. Voices are coming from the headset. I check the receiver to discover it's still set to the channel we've been using to talk to Collin and that it's miraculously still working. Putting on the headphones, I speak into the microphone.

"Collin? Are you there?" I say, but hear different voices respond.

"Inspector Jamie Grove, 2008, American, reporting in."

"Agent Sara Rose Munger, 1913, Ireland."

"Inspector Abasi el Masri, 1971, Egypt."

"Agent Paco Moreno, 1985, Venezuela."

"Captain Antonio DeNunzio, 1954, Italia."

"Sergeant Tom Talbott, 1935, Her Majesty's Service."

"Agent Mei Deng, 1965, China."

The voices keep on going. The Inspectors around the world and from every time have suddenly discovered an open channel for all of us to communicate. I listen for a while and hear inspectors from every time imaginable, and from dozens of countries.

Unexpectedly, the voices are interrupted.

"Attention all Inspectors, Agents, and other members of the Allied Rebellion: This is General Stefan Kaiser, head of the Gestapo and second in command of the Third Reich. I know many of you must feel emboldened by what has happened in a small town on the remote country side of New York State in 1989. But these are a handful of lucky rebels and are no match for the power of the Third Reich. Remember what we had done to Canada when they tried to stand against us. Their country is now a nuclear wasteland. Nothing grows there, nothing can live there. It's desolate. If you want your country to encounter the same fate, by all means continue your fight against the Nazi Machine. We will decimate all of you one-by-one and make you our slaves. None of you are a match for the brilliance of the Third Reich. We have ruled North America for over fifty years; this minor battle is just a blemish, a stone in our shoe, which we will crush. Don't suffer the same fate as these rebels who will soon die at our hands. We are the Third Reich, we are the superior race. There is no running from us. We are one step ahead of you. You will die. You can't win."

Silence, no more inspectors are chiming in, but I gather they are all still listening. I hear laughter coming from the General Kaiser and a few other Germans in the background. I turn on my microphone.

"This is Inspector Alex Eviston, 1989, from the United States of America. For those of you that may not recognize my

family name understand that I am the Daughter of Time
Travel. Three days ago, my battalion of two hundred men and
women attacked the Niagara Outpost and defeated a huge
Nazi Army of over two thousand men. Most of the Nazis were
swept over the American Falls, the others were shot and killed
by our troops. At the end of the battle, Russian MiGs arrived
and destroyed Nazi warplanes that were coming to attack us. I
killed all remaining troops in the tower. None remain alive."

"When my task was done, I stood at the top of the Niagara
Outpost Tower and jumped off into the Niagara River before
it crumbled to the ground. I then tumbled over the Horseshoe
Falls and survived that as well. Afterwards, our troops united
with more members of the Russian army, along with Canadians
and other American Rebels and now we hold the city of
Buffalo as well. It wasn't luck that won these wars. It was
American ingenuity, Russian perseverance, and Canadian
strength."

"I didn't survive those battles to be bullied by some Mr.
Heini Kraut. And no one, especially some asshole Nazi, can tell
me what to do. Now, I want to be clear about something, and
I'll speak slowly so you pea-brain Rhine Monkey can
understand what I'm saying. There's no stopping freedom.
And all of us will make sure it lives. We may be from different
countries, have different backgrounds, speak different
languages, and worship different gods. We may even have
different forms of governments. But we all have one common
belief: that our future is in our own hands."

By now the rest of the troops, include Vazlymov and Frank
have gathered around me.

"So we will fight you and we will not stop. We'll drive you
back to your country, back to your doorstep, drive you back to
the rat hole that you came from. And when we get there, we
will burn down your house and stomp on your grave. You've
done more than mess with Americans, you've messed with
freedom that this world holds dear. And General Kaiser, I pray
to God that when I get to Berlin, I'll be able to stand up to you
face-to-face and blow out your brains just like I did to your

Nazi pawn General McCafferty. I'll take your lifeless body and cast it into the trash to rot and be devoured by rats and other vermin. Because that's what you are: food for rats." I pause. There's no more laughter coming from the Nazis and the line is silent. Everyone is hanging on my every word. The Inspectors throughout time, the Nazis, and the men in front of me - they are all listening to what I have to say.

"The world is coming for you Third Reich," I command. "We're not going to stop until every one of you is dead and we ensure that freedom will live forever. Be scared. Be ever so scared. You're darkest nightmare is now reality. We're coming to get you. Your future is over."

END OF BOOK ONE

ABOUT THE AUTHOR

Wal Ozello (1971 - TBD) is a child of the 80s. He was born in Cleveland, Ohio and attended film school at The Ohio State University, where he was a founding member of the Columbus hairband, Armada. After graduating, Wal moved to New York City's Upper West Side, worked in broadcast television, and sang for the prestigious Saint Patrick's Cathedral Choir. Assignment 1989: The Daughter of Time Travel is Wal's first full length novel in a series of three. He currently resides in Upper Arlington, Ohio with his wife, two young boys, and the world's most amazing dog, Vito. He favorite writing place is Colin's Coffee where if he isn't working on a novel, he's blogging for the website, Pencilstorm. Wal wishes he could time travel to San Francisco in July of 1983 to see his favorite band, Journey.

FOR UPDATES ON THE DAUGHTER OF TIME TRAVEL SERIES:

Like: www.facebook.com/assignment1989
or
Follow: www.twitter.com/wozello

BOOK TWO
Revolution 1990

BOOK THREE
Sacrifice 2086
(Summer 2015)

ACKNOWLEDGMENTS

I'd like to thank the following people for their support in writing this novel.

First and foremost, my ever-awesome wife Kate. You are my sweetie-pie. Thanks for never questioning my need to go write. I could never have done this without you. My love for you is timeless. Another thanks of support to my young sons, James and Sam, who have enjoyed watching me write this and have learned about fighting Nazis. My only wish in life is that I inspire them to follow their dreams.

A special thank you to Vito Ozello. Without our long walks I would have never came up with half the stuff I wrote. You're the world's most amazing dog.

To the kick ass Jamie Grove, you're the man. Thanks for your enthusiasm on this project and pushing me forward. Without you this novel would have never been written.

To my sister, Aggie. Thanks for everything – your encouragement, insight, and most importantly being a great sister. Thanks also to the rest of my family, especially my mom, my dad and my father-in-law, Michael. I am immeasurably grateful for your endless support and love over the years.

To David L. Johnson, thanks for your honest feedback and inspiring me to breathe life into my characters. Without you this story would only be plot driven. To Margaret Standing, Natasha Randall, and Craig Roberts, thank you for helping me improve my work and inspiring me to do better. Your feedback has helped make this book so much better. And to Alissa Caldwell, Tim Baldwin and Jason Hency for their support as well.

To all my friends for their endless excitement for this project, I thank you. Many times when I woke up early to write and really didn't want to, all your Facebook likes on my "noveltime" status drove me to work harder. Every time I'd read through all your names and it was a true inspiration to me. It helped me realize that I wasn't just writing for myself anymore, I was writing for you, too. A special shout out to my Wendy's family – and I do mean "family". Thank you so much for all the help you've given me over the years.

Also, thank you to my teachers for "stoking the fire" in me when I was in high school and inspiring me to do something creative with my life. A special thanks to Glenn Jambor, Mike Shively, Ron Jones, and Bob Sledz (Physics Band RULES!)

Lastly, I'd like to thank Colin Gawel, Catherine, and the rest of the staff at Colin's Coffee. Most of this book was written there. Every weekend morning they served me a cup of dark roast coffee and their signature McRoy. If you're ever in Upper Arlington, Ohio, stop in and say hello for me.

www.ingramcontent.com/pod-product-compliance
Lightning Source LLC
Chambersburg PA
CBHW050926120626
46552CB00001B/68